Hannah Dennison was born and raised in Hampshire but spent more than two decades living in California. She has been an obituary reporter, antique dealer, private jet flight attendant and Hollywood story analyst.

Hannah writes the Honeychurch Hall Mystery series, the Vicky Hill Mystery series and the Island Sisters Mystery series. Hannah lives in Devon with her two high-spirited Hungarian Vizslas.

www.hannahdennison.com
www.twitter.com/HannahLDennison
www.instagram.com/hannahdennisonbooks

D0047921

Death of a Diva at Honeychurch Hall

Hannah Dennison

CONSTABLE

CONSTABLE

First published in Great Britain in 2020 by Constable

3 5 7 9 10 8 6 4

A CIP catalogue record for this book
is available from the British Library.

ISBN: 978-1-47213-379-3

Typeset in Janson Text LT Std by SX Composing DTP, Rayleigh, Essex
Printed and bound in Great Britain by Clays Ltd, Elcograf S.p.A.

Papers used by Constable are from well-managed forests
and other responsible sources.

Constable
An imprint of
Little, Brown Book Group
Carmelite House
50 Victoria Embankment
London EC4Y 0DZ

An Hachette UK Company
www.hachette.co.uk

www.littlebrown.co.uk

For my beautiful daughter Sarah a.k.a. Pose

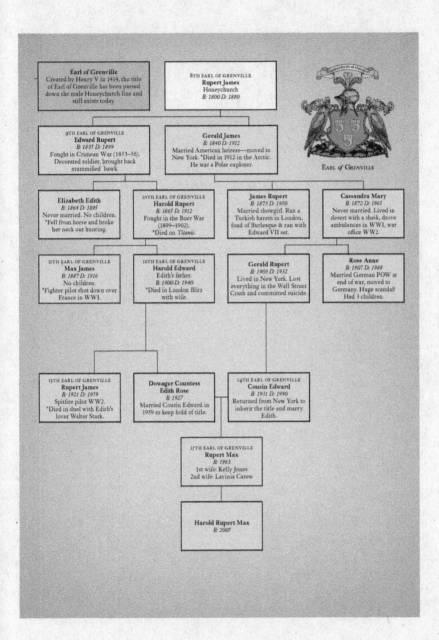

Earl of Grenville
Created by Henry V in 1414, the title of Earl of Grenville has been passed down the male Honeychurch line and still exists today.

8TH EARL OF GRENVILLE
Rupert James
Honeychurch
B: 1800 D: 1880

EARL of GRENVILLE

9TH EARL OF GRENVILLE
Edward Rupert
B: 1835 D: 1899
Fought in Crimean War (1853–56). Decorated soldier, brought back mummified hawk.

Gerald James
B: 1840 D: 1912
Married American heiress—moved to New York. *Died in 1912 in the Arctic. He was a Polar explorer.

Elizabeth Edith
B: 1864 D: 1895
Never married. No children. *Fell from horse and broke her neck out hunting.

10TH EARL OF GRENVILLE
Harold Rupert
B: 1865 D: 1912
Fought in the Boer War (1899–1902).
*Died on *Titanic*.

James Rupert
B: 1873 D: 1950
Married showgirl. Ran a Turkish harem in London, fond of Burlesque & ran with Edward VII set.

Cassandra Mary
B: 1872 D: 1965
Never married. Lived in desert with a sheik, drove ambulances in WWI, war office WW2.

11TH EARL OF GRENVILLE
Max James
B: 1887 D: 1916
No children.
*Fighter pilot shot down over France in WWI.

12TH EARL OF GRENVILLE
Harold Edward
Edith's father.
B: 1900 D: 1940
*Died in London Blitz with wife.

Gerald Rupert
B: 1903 D: 1932
Lived in New York. Lost everything in the Wall Street Crash and committed suicide.

Rose Anne
B: 1907 D: 1988
Married German POW at end of war, moved to Germany. Huge scandal! Had 3 children.

13TH EARL OF GRENVILLE
Rupert James
B: 1921 D: 1959
Spitfire pilot WW2.
*Died in duel with Edith's lover Walter Stark.

Dowager Countess Edith Rose
B: 1927
Married Cousin Edward in 1959 to keep hold of title.

14TH EARL OF GRENVILLE
Cousin Edward
B: 1931 D: 1990
Returned from New York to inherit the title and marry Edith.

15TH EARL OF GRENVILLE
Rupert Max
B: 1963
1st wife: Kelly Jones
2nd wife: Lavinia Carew

Harold Rupert Max
B: 2005

Ad perseverate est ad triumphum

EARL *of* GRENVILLE

Chapter One

'You're alive!' I finally heard the bolts draw back and the door of the Carriage House slowly opened. My mother's pale face peered out.

She did not look happy.

'You're not answering your phone,' I said. 'I've been standing in the carriageway yodelling for hours.' I expected a smile at the last comment but Mum seemed uncharacteristically out of sorts. Pointing to the arch-braced roof with a central skylight that ran the length of the carriageway, I added, 'The acoustics are really good in here— Gosh, are you okay?'

Mum produced a Kleenex and snuffled into it. As I looked more closely I noticed her nose was red and her face blotchy.

I was immediately concerned. 'I wondered why you weren't in your writing house. Are you not feeling well?'

A horrible flu bug had swept through the village of Little Dipperton. So far Mum and I had escaped it, but now I wasn't so sure.

'You haven't caught that flu bug, have you?' I demanded. 'Lavinia has been in bed for days.'

In fact, Lady Lavinia Honeychurch's illness was the reason why I was dressed in jodhpurs on a sunny Wednesday morning in early May instead of manning my antique business, Kat's Collectibles & Mobile Valuation Services.

With Lavinia out of commission, I'd volunteered to help her mother-in-law, the formidable octogenarian dowager countess, Lady Edith Honeychurch, exercise their six horses. I didn't mind: I loved riding. But the extra work meant that I hadn't seen my mother for nearly a week.

In fairness to me, I knew that she'd been working to a deadline with her latest romantic masterpiece, and would have hated to be disturbed. Even so, I felt guilty and had picked some wild daffodils as a peace offering.

'I really don't feel up to visitors,' Mum said quietly. 'I just want to be left alone.'

'I'm not a visitor,' I said. 'I'm your daughter.' I handed her the bunch of bright yellow flowers. 'For you. Aren't they cheerful?'

Mum uttered a heavy sigh and dabbed at her nose again. 'If you say so.'

'I think you should be in bed,' I said briskly. 'Let me in and I'll make you a hot toddy. Have you got a headache? Sore throat?'

Mum's reply was inaudible. She stepped aside to allow me to pass, then made a point of locking the door once I was safely inside, which was highly unusual. Something definitely wasn't right and, taking in her unkempt appearance, my concern deepened.

I followed Mum down the narrow corridor to the kitchen.

It was after eleven in the morning but my mother was still in a baby-pink hooded dressing gown from Marks & Spencer. She was make-up free and her unbrushed hair was showing the beginnings of a grey stripe at the roots. In short, she looked a mess.

Mum prided herself on her appearance, claiming that should she ever have a heart attack and end up in hospital, no one could ever accuse her of being a slattern.

Whatever was going on must be serious.

'Go and sit down.' I took the daffodils back from her and headed for the sink. 'I'll just put these in a glass of water for now. You can arrange them later. Okay?'

Mum dragged out a chair and sat down heavily at the large Victorian pine table where copies of the local weekly newspaper, the *Dipperton Deal*, lay scattered amongst used Kleenex tissues. She didn't say a word. She just sat there, staring into space.

As I waited for the kettle to boil I couldn't help but notice the state of the kitchen. The washing-up hadn't been done for days. Dirty cups, bowls, plates and a crystal tumbler sat on the countertop along with crumbs of toast and the odd cornflake. There were two empty bottles of Honeychurch Gin, with the distinctive sheep's head on a blue label – my mother's own brand – and crumpled cans of Fever Tree tonic water. Maybe she didn't have a cold.

Maybe it was a hangover. Had my mother become an alcoholic?

I touched her forehead for signs of a temperature. It didn't feel clammy. I also noted that although the used-up tissues indicated otherwise, Mum wasn't sneezing.

'Let me see,' I said as I headed for the oak dresser. 'Who will you be this morning?'

As a diehard monarchist, my mother collected royal commemorative plates and reproduction Buckingham Palace bone-china cups and mugs. Today I spotted a new addition to her collection of framed photographs of the royal family – the Duke and Duchess of Sussex.

'I see that Prince Harry and Meghan Markle have made your dresser of fame.'

'That won't last either,' said Mum gloomily. 'Nothing ever does.'

Considering Mum's mood, I selected a mug bearing a picture of the unfortunate Princess Caroline of Brunswick, whose marriage to George IV was notoriously so unhappy that she was forbidden to attend his coronation and missed being crowned Queen.

I picked Princess Margaret for myself and marvelled at the power of the subconscious. Her love life hadn't been smooth either. Just like mine was turning out to be.

I set down a pot of tea and the two mugs and joined Mum at the table. 'Princess Caroline is especially for you today.'

At last Mum gave a very small smile. 'Did you know that after Caroline was banned from her husband's coronation she fell ill that very night and died three weeks later?'

'Well, hopefully that's not going to happen to you.'

Mum regarded her cup of tea with disdain. 'I thought you were making me a hot toddy.'

'I changed my mind because there is nothing wrong with you. Physically, that is.' I reached across the table and took her hand. 'What's really going on, Mum? Did the publisher reject your manuscript?'

I knew that she had been working feverishly on another steamy *Star-Crossed Lovers* novel. Writing secretly under the pseudonym of Krystalle Storm, Mum's productivity was staggering and showed no sign of slowing down, despite the fact that she'd recently turned seventy.

'He can't reject it yet because I haven't sent it,' Mum said with a hint of defiance.

'What?' I was horrified. 'I thought the manuscript was due back last week.'

Mum shrugged. 'I don't care. It's done when it's done.'

'You must care!' I scolded. 'You've spent decades building up your writing career. You have to stick to deadlines. Isn't this book supposed to be published in October? That's less than five months away!'

'I can't please everyone,' she retorted.

And then I guessed. Dr Reynard Smeaton – he of the 'wonderful hands' – and my mother had been enjoying a torrid relationship since Christmas. At first I'd been delighted, but as time went on, I observed her ride a roller-coaster of emotions. One moment she was euphoric and madly in love, and the next she was feeling crowded and needed her own space. Of course, keeping her writing a secret didn't help. Mum had had to resort to the old excuses she'd made during my childhood, namely feigning a migraine, so she could escape to her writing house in the converted piggery.

'I hope all is well in paradise,' I said.

At this comment, my mother burst into tears.

'Oh, Mum!' I said. 'Has something happened?'

To my astonishment, she produced an iPhone from her dressing-gown pocket.

'You've got a *mobile*!' I was stunned and, to be honest, a little hurt. I'd been trying to persuade her to get one for months.

She nodded. 'And an iPad.'

I was flabbergasted. 'Since when?'

'Reynard gave them to me for Christmas so we could keep in touch around the clock.'

'Why on earth didn't you tell me?'

'Because you would gloat about me entering the twenty-first century,' said Mum. 'That's why.'

She made a good point. I would have done just that.

My mother frowned. 'I'm on WhatsApp as well. It says Reynard's online but he still hasn't responded to my text.'

'It doesn't mean he's actually looking at his phone,' I said. 'He's just available.'

'Oh, really?' She frowned again. 'I feel like a stalker. Before technology, if a man didn't call, we didn't think the worse of it – although, deep down, we knew that if he didn't call, he wasn't interested.'

'Is this what's upsetting you?' I said. 'The fact that he hasn't been in touch?'

'I keep checking his Facebook page,' said Mum. 'But he's not posting anything.'

I couldn't believe it. 'You're on *Facebook*? If you're on Facebook then why on earth don't you—'

'No! Stop right there,' Mum exclaimed. 'The answer is no. I do not want a computer. I only want to type on Dad's Olivetti. It's my lucky typewriter.'

'I'm sure that Reynard's just busy,' I said. 'He does have a job, you know. This flu thing is awful. Maybe he even has flu!'

'I hope he has.' Mum took a sip of tea and hesitated. 'He told me that he needs some space.'

'*Space*?' I was dismayed. 'Oh. Well. That's different.'

'He says he's confused.'

My heart sank. Call me a cynic, but I knew full well that when a man asked for space and said he was confused, it usually meant that another woman had caught his eye.

I didn't know what to say. Having had my fair share of heartache, I found it hard to understand that my mother's attachment to the silver fox – her nickname for him, not mine – could have developed so quickly.

Mum had been married to my father for forty-nine years and widowed for nearly two. I had been genuinely happy when she found a companion and friend, but this behaviour was alarming. She was acting like a lovesick teenager. If my mother was in this state of turmoil at the age of seventy, what hope did the rest of us have?

'I've been reading *Men Are From Mars, Women Are From Venus* by John Gray,' Mum went on. 'You should read it. It might help you.'

'I have read it and it didn't.'

'Usually Reynard calls in here every day or we meet somewhere for coffee,' Mum mused. 'And then at night—'

'Spare me the details, please.'

'I have to say it's put me horribly behind with my writing,' Mum continued. 'I think about him all the time. It's like I'm obsessed.' Tears filled her eyes. She grabbed a used tissue and angrily wiped them away. 'I know I write about yearning passion and all-consuming love, but, to be honest, I've never felt it up until now.'

'What about Dad?' I protested.

'Your father was like wearing a comfortable pair of old slippers. Don't get me wrong, I adored him, but Reynard is so exciting. And his hands—'

'No hands!' I felt nauseated at the vision of them together but made a supreme effort to be kind. 'When was the last time you spoke to Reynard?'

'Five days ago. But he's been acting very distant for the last few weeks. And then I read *that*,' she gestured to the copies of the *Dipperton Deal* and tears filled her eyes again, 'and I just knew.'

The newspaper was turned to the Dear Amanda problem page. The identity of Dear Amanda was a mystery. Her brutal advice was usually the topic of derision every Saturday morning when Mum and I would sit down over a coffee and try to guess which of the villagers in Little Dipperton had written in with a personal problem. We'd had to skip the last two Saturday mornings so this was all new to me.

'Read it,' she commanded. So I did.

I read aloud: 'Dear Amanda, Do long-distance relationships ever work?'

Signed: Hopeful.

Amanda says: No.

'Long distance?' I said. 'He only lives in Totnes.'

'Not that one,' Mum said. 'The second one down.'

'Dear Amanda,' I read aloud again. 'I have received startling news that an old flame has come back to the area. Although I have not seen her for nearly forty years, I have never forgotten her. The problem is that I am dating a real sweetie and I don't want to lose her.'

Signed: Confused.

Amanda says: Dump the sweetie.

I winced. 'Has Reynard mentioned an old flame to you?'

'No,' Mum said, 'but he calls me sweetie all the time. There's more . . .' She withdrew *another* page from under the pile of newspapers. 'From this Saturday's edition.'

I read aloud yet *again*. 'Dear Amanda, although I have not seen my old flame yet we have been in touch on Facebook and the sparks are flying. I will dump the sweetie.'

Signed: Grateful.

Amanda says: Don't burn out!

I regarded my mother's mournful expression. 'How do you know these are from Reynard?'

'I noticed a new friend pop up on his Facebook page weeks ago. Reynard keeps "liking" her comments.'

'That doesn't mean anything. And this is exactly why I don't do Facebook, Mum.'

'It's a long-distance relationship because she lives in Italy,' said Mum. 'Her name is Lucia Lombardi and she's single.'

'Ah. But remember what Amanda said? Long-distance relationships don't last.'

'They've probably been direct messaging each other,' said Mum gloomily. 'I can't tell but she must be in England by now.'

My heart sank again. 'Wait . . . *the* Lucia Lombardi? One of the greatest sopranos of all time?'

Mum blanched. 'Have you heard of her?'

'Of course I have. She's been all over the news! How can you *not* have heard of her?'

I hunted through the scattered newspaper pages on the table until I found the page I was looking for. The headline read: *Local Girl Made Good. Julie Jones is Back!* Below it was a grainy photograph of a young woman with a Vidal Sassoon wedge-style haircut holding a giant cheque for fifty thousand pounds. The small print said Julie Jones had been the Winner of the Torquay Talent Contest 1978 and that she now went by the stage name of Lucia Lombardi. The column went on to say that Lucia was one of the few singers who could actually hit the world's highest note, the elusive High G10.

Unfortunately Lucia's triumphant return to the South West had been plagued with problems that put the fate of the amateur production of *The Merry Widow*, in which she would be headlining, in jeopardy.

Last week a terrible fire had all but destroyed the iconic

Nightingales Theatre on the outskirts of Dartmouth. Worse still, Victor Mullins, our tax accountant and Lucia's co-star, had died in a car crash on the very same day.

'She's famous,' Mum said flatly.

'So are you,' I reminded her.

'But no one knows *I'm* famous. Everyone knows *she's* famous.' Mum thought for a moment. 'What on earth is a professional opera singer doing coming all this way to sing with a bunch of amateurs?'

'I have no idea,' I said. 'But these amateurs take it very seriously.'

'I mean . . . *Victor Mullins* as her co-star?' Mum said with scorn. 'He's about as exciting as a wet rag. I can't imagine him roaming around the stage in tights . . . yodelling.'

'Don't speak ill of the dead, Mum,' I said. 'Victor was all right and you've got to admit, he took everything you said at face value when he filed your taxes last year. If I recall, you even got a huge tax refund.'

'Well . . . if *Lucia* doesn't have a co-star or a venue, the show won't go on and she can go back to Italy.'

This made what I was about to tell her very awkward.

'What's wrong?' Mum said. 'Why have you got that weird look on your face?'

'I don't want you to freak out, but . . .' I took a deep breath. 'The show will go on. It's going to go on in the old ballroom at Honeychurch Hall.'

Mum's jaw dropped. 'Lucia Lombardi, one of the greatest sopranos of all time, is coming *here*?'

'I'm afraid so,' I said. 'Honeychurch Hall is going to be the new Glyndebourne.'

Chapter Two

'I just don't understand why the dowager countess would agree to something like that.' Mum sounded bewildered. I had thought the exact same thing and said so.

Mum frowned. 'Do you think she's going senile?'

Although occasional events had been held in the grounds – the re-enactment of the English Civil War to name just one – Lady Edith Honeychurch rarely opened the Hall to the public. Following the disastrous Museum Room open house last December, her decision seemed all the more out of character.

'At least it will give Delia something to do,' Mum said with a tinge of malice. Ever since Reynard had come on the scene, Mum's on-off friendship with the Hall's housekeeper had been strained. 'All those divas wandering the corridors . . . yodelling.'

'I'm glad you've recovered your sense of humour,' I said. 'But no, it's just one diva and Countess Olga Golodkin.'

'If that name should mean something to me, it doesn't,' said Mum.

'She's D.O.D.O.'s director.'

'Dodo?' Mum said with a snigger. 'Isn't that an extinct flightless bird?'

'It's the acronym for the Devon Operatic Dramatic Organisation.'

Mum burst out laughing. 'Perhaps it's an omen.'

'Well . . .' I tried to keep a straight face. 'Edith told me it's going to be Olga's swansong.'

'If Reynard's not careful it will certainly be his,' said Mum. 'What else did her ladyship tell you?'

'Apparently the Countess is a bit of a legend in operatic circles and managed to persuade Lucia to come out of retirement for this one last production. Tickets have been sold out for months. Edith told me that Olga is a distant cousin of Tsar Nicholas II. Maybe you can add her to your dresser collection.'

'I still don't understand why her ladyship would agree to it.' Mum shook her head. 'The upheaval will be enormous.'

'Olga was a family friend and it's a favour,' I said. 'Supposedly, the ballroom has perfect acoustics.'

'Ah yes, it does. I remember those days,' Mum said wistfully. 'Did I tell you that when I was a child, Bushman Travelling Fair and Boxing Emporium used to camp in the park?'

I regarded her with amazement. 'Yes you have, a gazillion times. Are you sure *you're* not going senile?'

'Wait – did you say the *ballroom*? Not the Great Hall?'

'Edith said the ballroom,' I said. 'Why? Is there a difference?'

'Of course there's a difference,' said Mum. 'It makes sense. The ballroom is in the east wing with its own entrance. That means the general public won't need to tramp through the main house.'

'It is an upheaval,' I agreed. 'The ballroom will have to be transformed into a theatre.'

'What about the sets and costumes?' Mum asked.

'Some of the sets have to be rebuilt, but luckily the costumes were saved because they were kept in a Portakabin in the Nightingales Theatre car park.'

'And who will be paying for it all?' Mum asked. 'Nothing comes for free.'

'Sir Montgomery Stubbs-Thomas,' I said. 'I really do know everything.'

'You certainly do.'

'Edith was very chatty,' I went on. 'Sir Monty and his wife Suzanne – actually, she died a couple of weeks ago – are opera buffs. They've been sponsoring D.O.D.O. for years.'

Sir Monty was also someone I occasionally bumped into on the antique circuit. In fact, I didn't like him very much, but I wasn't going to open that proverbial can of worms. My mother would want to know why.

'Wait a minute,' Mum said, 'what about the bats? Isn't their summer roost in the roof above the ballroom? They won't like all that noise.'

'Edith told me they've not been seen so far this year.'

I was well aware that the future of the endangered greater horseshoe bat was a heated topic in the village; according to Edith, there had been plenty of opposition to staging the opera at the Hall.

'It all sounds a bit of a headache to me,' said Mum.

'But it's not your problem,' I said. '*Your* problem is sending off your manuscript. Go and have a shower, put on some make-up and pull yourself together.'

'Easy for you to say,' said Mum.

I got up and took the teapot and mugs to the draining board. Perhaps I was being too hard on her. 'Do you really like Reynard, Mum?'

'Sadly, yes.'

'You're never going to win him back looking like that. Where is your fighting spirit? What would your heroines do in – what's the title of the latest *Star-Crossed Lovers* book?'

'*Desperate.*'

'Oh dear. You definitely don't want to seem desperate,' I said. 'And I don't like that title. The others were tantalising – *Gypsy Temptress, Forbidden, Ravished, Betrayed. Desperate* seems just . . . too desperate.'

'John Gray says I should give my man as much rope as he needs to hang himself,' said Mum. 'I will tell you something: if he and Lucia/Julie – or whatever she wants to call herself – ride off into the sunset together, I'll hang him myself.'

I checked my watch. 'I can't stay too long, I'm afraid; I have a meeting with that awful Douglas Jones. He wants to sell me something.'

'I can't imagine what he'd have that's worth buying,' Mum said unkindly. 'He's living in a yurt.'

'Excuse me? A yurt?'

'That's what Reynard told me,' Mum said. 'Douglas has set up camp in Honeychurch Woods. If his lordship finds out he'll burn it to the ground.'

'I'm surprised I haven't seen it,' I said. 'We ride that way all the time. Anyway, how does Reynard know? Did Douglas send up smoke signals?'

'Douglas caught the flu and Reynard made a home visit.' She rolled her eyes. 'Apparently, Douglas has a mobile phone.'

'Wait – do you think he's related to Julie Jones?'

But at that moment we both heard someone hammering on the front door. A familiar voice called out, 'Iris! Hello! Are you home?'

Mum gasped. 'It's Reynard!'

'Speak of the devil,' I said. 'Stay right there. I'll tell him you're out.'

'No,' Mum said. 'You're right. I've got to get a grip. Pretend everything is normal.'

'Be happy and busy,' I said, adding, 'That's the advice from *The Rules* – another self-help relationship book for you.'

Mum nodded. 'Happy and busy. Got it. Now go and invite him in.'

I unlocked the door to find the ruggedly handsome doctor with his mane of silver hair and full beard reeking of aftershave and holding a huge bunch of daffodils. He'd obviously had the same idea as me, only his flowers still had clumps of earth attached to their roots.

Reynard seemed surprised to see me. He also appeared jittery as he fiddled with the knot in his red and white striped tie.

'Is Iris all right?' he said. 'She doesn't usually lock the door.'

'She's just busy,' I said brightly. 'I'll see if she has a minute for you. Wait here.'

'Yes! I have a minute!' Mum trilled from the kitchen, completely defeating the object.

We trooped down the hall to find a miraculous transformation had come over my mother's countenance. She had applied lipstick and swept her hair into a red-chequered tea towel turban-style.

'You caught me coming out of the shower,' said Mum coyly. She readjusted her dressing gown to expose an eyeful of cleavage. 'Would you like some coffee or tea?'

'If you've got time, Mum,' I reminded her. 'Remember how busy you are.'

'Well, unfortunately it's me who doesn't have time today,' said Reynard. 'And you might want to wrap yourself up a little more sensibly. There is a nasty flu bug going around.'

Mum defiantly left her cleavage on view. Suddenly she spotted the problem pages of the *Dipperton Deal* spread out on the table and gave a little gasp.

I scooped them up. 'Thanks for these, Mum. I'll return them when I'm done.'

'Do you read the Dear Amanda problem page, Reynard?' Mum asked.

Reynard reddened. 'Who? No. Why?'

'It's gripping stuff,' said Mum.

'Will you excuse me?' I said. 'I've got an appointment at noon.'

'No need for you to rush off, darling,' said Mum. 'I'm never too busy for you.'

Reynard cleared his throat. 'Can we have a little talk, sweetie?'

This did not bode well. I know what those 'little talks' mean and the presence of the flowers, presumably to soften the blow, seemed ominous.

'I really must go,' I said.

'No, Kat,' said Mum. 'Stay. Please.'

'Sweetie, I'd like to talk to you in private,' Reynard said.

'Reynard, I don't want to talk to you in private. And don't call me sweetie. Kat, sit down.'

'Is it hot in here?' The doctor fiddled with his tie again. 'I really would rather this was between—'

'She's staying,' Mum declared. 'And stop fiddling with your tie.'

I sat down.

Reynard took a deep breath. 'Iris, you are a very special woman, a lovely woman, a real sweetie. You are one of the kindest and funniest people I know but—'

'You already told me you needed some space,' Mum said coldly. 'No need to labour the point. Unless, that is, you are off to outer space and never coming back.'

'Um. Well.' Reynard shot me a look of desperation. 'The thing is . . . there's a flu epidemic—'

'Hardly an epidemic,' said Mum with scorn. 'Just a few bad colds.'

'And as you know – or maybe you haven't heard yet—'

'Heard what?' Mum demanded.

'V-V-Victor Mullins—'

'Victor Mullins. Yes. He had that awful car accident,' said Mum. 'Yes. I know who he is – or was.'

'Mum!' I exclaimed. 'Let Reynard finish.'

'I've been asked to replace him as Count Danilo Danilovitsch in *The Merry Widow*.'

'Danilo who?' Mum said.

'I'll be singing opposite Lucia Lombardi,' said Reynard. 'It's a dream come true.'

The colour drained from my mother's face. She had often boasted that Reynard's wonderful hands were matched by his wonderful voice and how fond he was of serenading her. Now it looked as though he would be serenading her arch rival.

'With the flu thing and intense rehearsals,' Reynard blundered on, 'I'm too busy to have a r-r-relationship at the moment. It's not fair on you—'

'Don't give me that rubbish, you cowardly little man.' Mum's tone was icy. 'You're asking for space because you've still got feelings for Julie Jones.'

Reynard's jaw dropped. 'She likes to be called Lucia. Wait? Have you been stalking me on Facebook?'

'Believe me, I am *far* too busy for Facebook,' Mum snapped.

I will say one thing for my mother: she might have been acting like a wimp earlier but Reynard would never have guessed. Her cold fury was reducing him to jelly.

'I don't think I can g-g-give you what you want at the moment,' Reynard stammered and thrust the daffodils at her, which she refused to accept. 'But I might be able to when it's all over.'

'When *she's* gone back to Italy, you mean?' said Mum. 'And for the record, you were the one who gave *me* the iPhone so we could message each other all day. I would never stalk.'

Reynard seemed to rally now he'd got his speech out. He straightened his shoulders. 'You know how I feel about you, Iris. Julie is just a friend but if you are going to act all jealous, I don't think—'

'What I think,' Mum said quickly, 'is that yes, we should have a break. Not a *space*. A break. I'll let you know if I change my mind. *Not* if you change your mind. If I change *mine.*'

'Oh, right. Then this is your decision.' Reynard's relief was palpable. 'So *you* have decided to actually *break* up with me. Fine. I will follow your lead. Excuse me.' He scuttled out of the kitchen still clutching the daffodils that dropped clods of earth all over the floor.

'I'm sorry, Mum.' I braced myself for tears but instead she remained defiant.

'Follow my lead?' Mum fumed. 'Follow my *lead*? I don't want a man to follow my lead. I want a man to lead me!'

I was impressed. 'You handled that really well.'

'That's because you were here,' said my mother. 'No, I'm furious now. He blatantly lied to my face.'

'I think he's confused.' I reminded her that his first letter to Dear Amanda was signed Confused. 'If anything, he's being honest. He doesn't know how he feels about Lucia and thinks he is being unfair if he leads you on.'

Mum regarded me with surprise. 'You're not Dear Amanda, are you?'

'Of course not.' I laughed. 'Honestly, you're a true inspiration. I don't want a weak man either. I want a man who will come and sweep me up on his white horse.' I thought of my so-called boyfriend, Detective Inspector Shawn Cropper, and his dithering. 'Unfortunately it would appear that men like that only exist between the pages of a Krystalle Storm novel.'

'That's why my readers love them. Pure escapism.' Mum thought for a moment. 'Do you really think I should change the current title from *Desperate*?'

'What's the story about?'

'Ava Meeks is one of the Duchess of Stanhope's maids,' said Mum. 'The Duchess has the pox and is attended by a handsome physician. Ava is desperate for the doctor to notice her but fears he never will because she's low-born and he's betrothed to another.'

'How about *Delusional*?' I suggested. 'I mean, clearly, there is a class problem there.'

'Are you saying I'm delusional?'

'Mum, you are not Ava Meeks.'

'I am *all* of my characters,' she replied. 'No, the physician fancies the maid like mad.'

'How about *Dangerous*?' I suggested. 'Sounds a lot more racy.'

Mum nodded. 'I like it. *Dangerous* it is.'

I headed for the door. 'Are you sure you're going to be okay?'

'Kat, it's only been a few months with Reynard,' said Mum. 'Relationships either fizzle out after that or grow into something deeper. I admit I was upset that his behaviour suddenly changed, and with no explanation. And then he didn't have the courage to be honest. I don't need that.'

'I hear you!'

'If I do allow a man to come into my life, it's only to make it better. I'm perfectly content living alone.' She gave a mischievous grin, adding, 'And anyway, the sex was beginning to wear off.'

'Argh, too much information,' I shrieked. 'I don't want to hear about that.'

'There was a survey in *Cosmopolitan* magazine,' said Mum, warming to her theme. 'Apparently the body can't physically stand that intense level of excitement for more than three months otherwise it implodes. It's nature's way of keeping us in balance.'

'You are a mine of information,' I said. 'Are you sure *you* aren't Dear Amanda and have been keeping yet another secret from me?'

'Don't be silly. Who has the time!' Mum got to her feet.

'One more thing: are you going to the community shop today?'

'Yes. I have to go to the post office,' I said. 'Why?'

'Be a dear and take a few more bottles of Honeychurch Gin,' Mum said. 'Bethany tells me that they've run out.'

'Just be careful,' I said. 'Remember that you are not supposed to be selling it commercially.'

'Oh . . . it's just a few left-over bottles. Your policeman will never know.'

My mother seemed to have had an awful lot of 'left-over' bottles.

After the postmistress died, her niece and partner had taken over the post office and general store. Many villages had turned their local shops into community-run enterprises, which, along with the usual items included homemade wares – like my mother's gin. It had proved hugely popular.

'I'll go and get them.' Mum disappeared into the pantry for a moment and returned with three bottles. 'Thank you, darling.'

'I hope you are going to get back to your writing now,' I said.

'That's the end of Reynard,' said Mum with a sigh. 'But first I'm going to get into the shower to wash that man right out of my hair.'

Chapter Three

Twenty minutes later I was back in my car, having dashed home to shower and change before heading to my showroom in the west gatehouse.

As I approached the terrace of three cottages that bordered the Victorian walled garden on the service road, I was forced to stop while Eric Pugsley loaded a long three-section stepladder and a pair of poles wrapped in a large plastic banner onto a trailer. The service road was too narrow to pass his red Massey Ferguson tractor so I had to sit and wait for him to finish.

I admired Honeychurch Cottages, which looked very pretty with their window boxes filled with red geraniums. It was here that Delia Evans the housekeeper, Peggy Cropper the cook and Eric, who owned the 'End-of-Life' scrapyard next door to my mother's Carriage House, lived. I thought of how much Mum used to dislike the burly labourer, but as time passed his fierce loyalty to the Honeychurch family had evoked her grudging respect. She continued, however, to nickname Eric 'beetle-brows' in honour of his magnificent eyebrows, which seemed to have a life of their own on his weather-beaten face.

Eric waved a greeting and came over to my car. We exchanged a few pleasantries, one of which included a grumble about having to erect the banner over the granite pillars of the main entrance to the Hall.

'I'm surprised her ladyship is allowing Julie Jones anywhere near the place,' Eric declared.

Despite not wanting to be drawn in I had to ask: 'Why?'

'All that business from before, that's why.' Eric regarded me keenly. 'Bet Julie can't believe her luck mixing with the toffs and feeling important.' He shook his head in disgust. 'Everyone knows what she did. Changing her name doesn't make it any different.'

I was curious. 'What business are you talking about?'

'The music-room fire was all her fault,' said Eric. Seeing my blank expression, he added, 'The music room in the east wing. Julie was caught smoking. The whole house nearly went up in flames. Then there was all that trouble with her dad poaching . . .'

Of course, I'd heard rumours about the Jones clan being evicted but I'd never known the reason why.

'I thought Julie Jones left the estate decades ago,' I said. 'You would have still been a kid.'

'My dad told me,' said Eric. 'You could say Julie and I are related.'

I was surprised. 'Related? How?'

'Her grandfather and my grandfather were both married to her grandmother,' he explained.

'Not at the same time,' I joked. 'It sounds a little incestuous.'

'Oh, it was incestuous all right,' said Eric darkly, 'in more ways than one. And then my wife Vera – God rest her soul – she was Julie's niece.'

'So . . . you and Julie must be cousins?' I said.

Eric shrugged. 'Half–grandkids? Half-cousins? What the hell do I know?' he said. 'But what I do know is that Julie causes trouble wherever she goes.'

When I thought of all that had happened with the production so far, it seemed he could be right.

'I think we should call Julie Lucia now,' I said. 'After all, that is her name.'

'She'll always be Julie to me.'

'When did you last see *Lucia*?' I said pointedly.

'Me?' Eric seemed incredulous. 'I've never met her, but I know she's a bad sort.'

I felt a tiny bit of sympathy for the greatest soprano of all time and wondered if the gossip was true. Most of all, I wondered what on earth had possessed her to return to Little Dipperton.

'I'd better get on,' I said and made to close the window but Eric slipped his hand into the gap, and, had I not reacted so quickly, he would almost certainly have lost a couple of fingers.

'And then there's the bats,' he said. 'They always roost in the roof above the ballroom.'

'Yes, I heard about those, but they're not back yet,' I said. 'Maybe they won't come this summer.'

'They'll come,' said Eric firmly. 'Do you know that the greater horseshoe bat population has fallen by ninety per cent in the last hundred years? And do you know why?'

'I have no idea,' I said.

'It's mostly because of the explosion of lights in cities and whatnot. Especially the LED lights that folks use these days,' Eric explained. 'And it's not just the bats that are affected by this. All nocturnal creatures are. It's a crying shame.'

'Yes, it is,' I said. 'I suppose it's the price of progress.'

Eric's explanation was distressing and I didn't intend to sound flippant. Ever since I'd moved to the countryside, I'd become much more conscious of the environment. As well as the greater horseshoe bats, Honeychurch was home to another endangered species, the adorable dormouse.

'I'd like to hear more,' I said. 'But I'm meeting someone at the gatehouse and I don't want to be late.'

Reluctantly, Eric withdrew his fingers from my window. 'We're always looking for bat monitors. I'll let Simon know you're interested.'

'Great!' I said, although inwardly I could have kicked myself. I had a lot on my plate at the moment but in this instance, it was for a good cause.

Thankfully, Eric let me leave but I still had to wait for him to double- and triple-check that the ladder, poles and banner were secured with ropes on the trailer. Eric set off down the service road, and I crawled along behind him at five miles an hour all the way to the tradesman's exit and into Cavalier Lane. Then, with mind-numbing slowness, I followed the tractor-trailer along the stone boundary wall to the main entrance.

As the crow flies, Jane's Cottage – the place I called home and the former summerhouse that was built on the foundation of an old hunting lodge – was only about five minutes from the Hall. But, back in the halcyon days of country-house estates, one of Edith's ancestors had created an elaborate network of service roads that were tucked discreetly behind dense banks of laurel and rhododendrons. As a result, it could take me ten to fifteen minutes to get from A to B; today it seemed to take for ever.

We reached the main entrance to the estate, which was marked by a pair of towering granite pillars topped with stone hawks with their wings extended. The words 'Honeychurch Hall' were engraved on one, lending a grandiose air that was echoed by the pair of eighteenth-century gatehouses.

A convoy of trucks came into view emblazoned with the logo 'Backstage Movers' and turned in to the main drive. This production seemed to be serious stuff.

Opposite the main entrance was a field with an open five-bar gate. Eric drove in and stopped. I parked my car in the crescent-shaped apron that hugged the west gatehouse, surprised to find that another car was already there: a metallic-blue Kia. At first I thought it must be Douglas Jones but then I recognised my colleague from the Dartmouth Antique Emporium where I rented a space.

Fiona Reynolds was out of her car before I had even turned off the engine. I noted her usual attire of neat navy suit, pearls and low-heeled pumps, but I could tell by her worried expression that something was wrong.

'Is everything okay?' I asked.

'No, it's not,' she said. 'I need to talk to you.'

Fiona waited while I unlocked the door to my showroom and disconnected the alarm. She followed me inside.

'Nice place,' she said, giving the showroom a cursory glance. 'But too far out of town.'

'That's why I'm happy to be renting a space from you,' I said. 'I'm sorry I only have a few minutes. I have someone coming for a valuation at noon.'

'Then I'll get straight to the point,' Fiona said. 'Do you remember the night that the theatre caught fire?'

'Nightingales?' I said. 'Vaguely, yes. Why?'

'The police – specifically your *boyfriend*, Detective Inspector Shawn Cropper – again seem to think that I had something to do with it.'

'What? But . . . gosh!' I was shocked. Shawn hadn't said anything to me, but then he wouldn't. He always kept business and pleasure separate; even so, he knew that Fiona was a friend of mine – even if we weren't particularly close.

'I had a falling-out with Olga – or rather, Victor did,' said Fiona.

I had to think for a moment. It was Fiona who had recommended Victor Mullins to file taxes for Mum and me, but I hadn't realised that she knew the Russian countess and said so.

'Why would you?' Fiona said. 'The theatre is just a hobby of mine. Reggie does a bit of PR for D.O.D.O. and I've been making costumes and helping backstage for years – well before Olga came on the scene.'

'O-kay,' I said slowly, not sure how this could possibly warrant her unexpected visit. And then I remembered. 'Wasn't the fire the night you and I went out for dinner?'

'Yes!' Fiona exclaimed. 'You have to tell Cropper that I was with you.'

'That's easy enough, you were,' I said. 'But there were other people in the restaurant. You used your credit card. Why is he making such a fuss?'

'The fire started in the early hours,' she said. 'You know how obsessive the police can be with details.'

'But . . . what about Reggie?' I said.

Fiona bit her lip. 'The thing is . . . this is so embarrass-ing . . . Reggie and I have been having some problems and . . .' She forced a smile. 'He's staying with a . . . friend. So you see, I don't have an alibi. All I need is for you to say that you came back to our house for coffee afterwards.'

Even though I didn't think for a moment that Fiona could possibly be involved in the fire, this request was awkward on so many levels. I loved renting the space at the Dartmouth Antique Emporium and would hate to put either my personal relationship with Fiona or our business relationship in jeopardy. Plus, I would be flat-out lying to Shawn!

'Why do the police think it was deliberate?' I said. 'And why are they accusing you?'

'There's some question about finding an accelerant in Victor's office. And . . .' She took a deep breath. 'Someone saw my car parked outside the theatre that night.'

I was reluctant to ask but I just had to. 'And . . . *was* your car parked outside? *Did* you go there after we left the restaurant?'

'I did not set fire to the theatre,' Fiona said. 'That's what's important, isn't it?'

'You didn't answer my question,' I said.

She seemed annoyed. 'The less you know, the better. You have to trust me on this.'

Unfortunately, Douglas Jones chose that precise moment to appear in the open doorway. He was carrying an old-fashioned brown leather suitcase.

'Sorry. This is my appointment,' I said to Fiona. 'Can we talk about this later? I'm coming to the emporium this afternoon.'

Fiona regarded Douglas with a sneer and said in a low voice, 'I can't imagine he'll have any family heirlooms.' And with that, she covered her nose with her hand and slid past Douglas as if he had the plague.

'What's her problem?' said Douglas.

If only I knew.

Douglas was a stocky, unpleasant man in his sixties with a florid face and the tell-tale veins of a heavy drinker. Dressed in his usual tweed flat cap and tattered jacket, he carried a distinct unwashed aroma, which made sense now that Mum had told me he lived in a yurt.

I invited him in.

Noticing there was no visible form of transport, I asked, 'Did you walk here?'

Douglas regarded me with suspicion and said, 'Mind your own bloody business.'

He looked around the showroom. 'Blimey,' he said. 'Bit fancy. Not like I remember.'

I knew that several of the Jones clan had lived in both gatehouses, but that was years ago. It had never occurred to me that Douglas might have been one of them.

I had spent a lot of money on converting the buildings. The west gatehouse was my showroom and office and I used the east gatehouse as a stockroom-cum-store.

Mum's stepbrother Alfred had built the shelves and display cabinets for my antique dolls, vintage teddy bears and an odd assortment of items that took my fancy. My day-to-day business was at the Dartmouth Antique Emporium. I tended to use the showroom only for private meetings with collectors.

The west gatehouse consisted of one large living area, one-and-a-half storeys high with a gabled ceiling and two tiny dormer windows. There were three bay windows that looked out on to the driveway and surrounding parkland. A galley kitchen and tiny bathroom were tacked on to the rear. At one point there had been a mezzanine level with a ladder that led up to a sleeping area, but the floorboards had been rotten and Edith agreed that I could take them out. Just as I leased Jane's Cottage from the estate, I leased the gatehouses from it too.

'All you twats coming down here and buying up our properties,' grumbled Douglas.

I was startled. 'Excuse me? Twats?'

'That's what you are,' Douglas went on. 'Up in London Tuesday, Wednesday and Thursday. T.W.A.T. Down here at the weekends, pushing up the house prices,' he said. 'We locals can't afford to buy anything now.'

I thought of Douglas living in squalor in his yurt. He made a good point.

Often those who bought second homes changed them into holiday accommodation, which meant that the winter months were very quiet. It was one of the main reasons why village life was struggling to survive.

'Twats?' I said lightly. 'I thought you called us D.F.L.s.'

I knew that the derogatory term stood for Down From London, with the added insult that those offenders drove around in smart 'Chelsea tractors' – a dig at the expensive cars that were seen clogging up the narrow lanes in the summer months.

'As it happens,' I said mildly, 'I lease the gatehouses from the estate.'

'This should be *my* house, not yours.' Douglas puffed up his chest and jabbed a finger in my face. 'There's been Joneses living in these gatehouses for centuries!'

I knew that was not true. I certainly didn't want to get into a conversation I couldn't win but I could definitely deflect it. 'I assume that Lucia Lombardi is one of your cousins.'

'You mean our Julie?' Douglas scowled. 'It's her fault we got evicted. She's got some nerve coming back. I can't believe her ladyship is putting up with it.'

'Well, she is,' I said and swiftly changed the subject. 'You wanted to show me something?'

Douglas sneezed and wiped his nose on his sleeve. He lifted the suitcase on to the top of my walnut partners' desk, sending a pencil holder and a sheaf of documents flying.

'Careful!' I picked them up and put everything back. 'Do we have to open that on here?'

After some difficulty, Douglas managed to unsnap the brass clasps. The lock looked as if it had been tampered with.

'Presumably there's no key?' I said.

'Don't need one.'

As he flipped up the lid my senses were instantly assaulted by the pungent smell of mould. The brown silk lining bore watermarks and was coming away at the seams. Inside was an odd assortment of items – a crumpled faded red and white kimono decorated with pagodas, a worn beaded purse, an Estée Lauder lipstick and an old-fashion powder compact inset with roses on the lid. A red and gold Hermès scarf decorated with horses was wrapped around a large object.

'Well?' Douglas said. 'What do you think?'

When he flagged me down in the lane a few days ago, Douglas claimed he'd got some treasures to sell. Right away my expectations had been low, but I'd felt sorry for him. I knew I should have followed my instincts.

Feigning disappointment, I said, 'Oh, Douglas! I am so sorry. These aren't the kinds of things that I buy.' I gestured to the showroom that was lined with dolls and bears. 'I wish I could, but I can't.'

But Douglas didn't seem offended at all.

'Maybe not that rubbish but you'll want to buy *this*.'
He carefully picked up the object that was wrapped in the
scarf and offered it to me. 'Reckon this is worth a fortune.
I'll take cash.'

Chapter Four

'This' turned out to be a Matryoshka or Russian nesting doll – a common souvenir that was easily available in any Russian market and online, too. EBay had a huge selection, which could be bought for as little as ten pounds or as much as five thousand, depending on the year and quality.

Unfortunately there was nothing spectacular about this particular doll. She was painted in generic gold with red flowers that would have been popular in the USSR in the 1970s and '80s.

Douglas's excitement was almost childlike. I knew he would be very disappointed so I resolved to let him down gently.

'This is a Russian nesting doll,' I said. 'She's called a Matryoshka.'

'Russian, eh?' he said. 'I thought it was foreign. There's a price label on the bottom.'

He was right, there was. It looked like the doll had actually been bought in Russia.

'Mothers play a big role in the traditional Russian family,' I explained. 'They are seen as the bearer of life. You see her shape? Her big belly? She is nesting her "children" inside.'

Douglas looked confused.

'Families back then usually had more than three children, and they'd also have members of their extended family all living under one roof,' I said. 'Each family member had their own unique role in the household, symbolised by one of the dolls. Have you opened it?'

'Eh? Opened it?'

'There should be more dolls inside.' I tipped the mother doll upside down and gently rotated her middle. She was a little stiff, but without too much force I was able to open her to reveal another doll.

I told him that each female doll would have her own characteristic feature and attire. Often the traditional designs and patterns of the wooden dolls illustrated scenes that once existed in nineteenth-century Russia.

'There could be as few as three or as many as twelve inside this one. More would be better.'

'Well, I'll be blowed!' Douglas seemed in awe. 'Let me do it.'

So I did. Douglas carefully unscrewed each doll, marvelling at how they fitted so snugly inside each other. In the end there were eight dolls lined up in descending height on my desk. The last doll was so tiny she was no bigger than a postage stamp.

'Will you look at that!' Douglas beamed. 'Eight dolls!

Reckon they'll be worth a bob or two. These are the real thing!'

'Real, but fairly common, I'm afraid,' I said. 'What chiefly determines their value is the time period in which they were made. Their clothing often gives a clue to a period of Russian history.'

'Who invented them dolls, then?' Douglas seemed genuinely interested so I told him that the original set were crafted in 1890 by a woodworker named Vasily Zvyozdochkin and painted by an artist called Sergey Malyutin. Vasily wanted to make a wooden doll with hidden toys inside. They created a wooden peasant girl in traditional Russian attire wearing a headscarf and holding a black rooster in her arms.

'They called her "Matryoshka",' I said, 'meaning "little matron".'

Douglas nodded. 'How much is it worth, then?'

'Why don't you take her to the community shop in the village?' I suggested.

I may as well have told Douglas to set fire to it. He was so outraged that his protests sparked a coughing fit. I fetched him a glass of water from the galley kitchen.

When I returned he had just about recovered and was trying, unsuccessfully, to put the dolls back together.

'Let me!' I said sharply. 'You'll break them.'

Douglas sank on to the two-seater sofa, seemingly defeated. He looked up at me through rheumy eyes. 'I just need the money, Kat,' he whispered. 'Can't cook on my camping stove because I've run out of meths. All I've eaten this week are cold baked beans out of the tin. Can't you show some Christian charity?'

I was about to protest when I caught myself. Douglas wasn't a well man. I noted the elbows were out on his jacket and his trousers had definitely seen better days. He lived alone in a yurt in the woods. He had no car and, as far as I knew, he didn't have a job. Douglas's life couldn't be easy.

The dolls were in excellent condition. There were no cracks or signs of wear. Maybe I should just buy them and be done with it. 'I'll give you thirty pounds.'

And that was on the generous side.

'Thirty *pounds*?' Douglas was incensed. 'Thirty pounds! You'll mark it up three hundred per cent. I know your type.'

'Fine. Forty, and that's my final offer.' I had a sudden thought. 'Where did you say you got this suitcase?' Up until that moment it hadn't crossed my mind, but now the contents seemed strange.

Douglas refused to look me in the eye. 'Car boot sale. Cost me five pounds.'

'So you've made a profit,' I said lightly.

'Sixty and I'll throw in the suitcase,' said Douglas.

'Fifty. I don't want the suitcase.'

Douglas dissolved into yet another coughing fit and grunted something that I assumed meant he agreed.

Even as I counted out five ten-pound notes from my purse, I was having second thoughts. I only had Douglas's word about using the meths for his camping stove. He was probably drinking it.

Douglas, all smiles now, got to his feet.

'Fifty pounds,' I said sternly and kept hold of the notes. 'And don't go complaining if you see it for sale in the community shop for more.'

'I knew it,' he said, disgusted. 'I knew you'd screw me over.'

'Oh, for heaven's sake!' I rolled my eyes in exasperation. 'Then forget it. The deal is off.'

He snatched the money out of my hand and headed for the door.

'The suitcase!' I called after him. 'I don't want it!'

But he had already gone.

Despite telling myself I'd done a good deed, I knew I'd been ripped off. I picked up the Matryoshka and took all the dolls out again. It was just as I'd first thought. There was nothing extraordinary about these wooden figures, but I knew they would make a nice present for someone.

Perhaps it would be wiser to take it to Dartmouth Antique Emporium rather than the community shop, where I could guarantee that Douglas would kick up a fuss if he saw it there or, worse, someone paid more than fifty pounds for it.

As for the suitcase, I would throw that out for the dustman.

I put all the children back inside the Matryoshka and set her aside on my desk. But when I moved the suitcase, the clasps popped open and deposited the contents on to the carpet.

As I shoved the contents back in, I noticed a white man-sized cotton handkerchief embroidered with the initials

E.R.H. and a crumpled Valentine card bearing the male figure from Kim Casali's *Love Is* . . . cartoon strip. He was wearing devil's horns. The tagline said, 'Your bad boy with a heart of gold.' I found two champagne corks, a handful of miniature soaps and a menu from The King's Arms, a five-star hotel in Sherborne, Dorset.

The randomness of the items made me think of a teenager's treasures or perhaps mementoes from some love affair.

I often came across boxes of personal possessions included as part of a job lot at an estate sale. Sometimes there would be old photograph albums and items of sentimental value that, now, no one wanted. I found that depressing. Perhaps Douglas *had* found the suitcase at a car boot sale after all.

I spent what was left of the morning packing up an adorable Steiff miniature unicorn to send to a collector in Scotland. As I locked up the showroom and turned on the alarm, a flatbed truck bearing the company name of Oakman Event Hire and a Bristol telephone number turned into the drive. It was jammed with dozens of plastic chairs spray-painted in gold and tied down with ropes.

The driver opened the window and gestured for me to approach.

'Honeychurch Hall?' he asked.

'It's about a mile up the drive,' I said. 'When you get to the fork, turn left.'

He paused to stare at me. 'Wait a minute. Shouldn't I know you?'

'I don't know,' I said politely. 'Should you?'

'Antique girl from the telly, right?' He snapped his fingers. 'Rapunzel! Your hair!'

The days of being recognised as the former TV host of *Fakes & Treasures* were now a rare occurrence. 'That's me.'

'I knew it.' He beamed. 'What's going on, then? A wedding? You getting married?'

'Hardly.' I pointed to the event banner overhead. 'They're performing *The Merry Widow* here. It's an operetta.'

'Nah . . . not my thing. I went to see *Cats* with the missis and that was bad enough. All that caterwauling.' He laughed at his own joke. 'Who's going to come down here? I could hardly find the place myself and I've got satnav.'

'Fans of Lucia Lombardi,' I said.

'Never heard of her! Well, good luck. You're going to need it.' And with those prophetic words, he gave a nod of thanks and moved away just as another Oakman Event Hire flatbed truck appeared. This one was carrying enormous stone urns bearing live rose bushes.

As I watched the departing trucks trundle up the drive and disappear from view I couldn't help wondering whether this five-night performance was worth all the upheaval and hassle, let alone the extortionate expense. Live roses from Bristol? Wouldn't artificial flowers do?

Whatever the relationship between Countess Olga Golodkin and Edith, it seemed a very big favour to ask of the elderly lady. The only reason I could think of was that Olga must have paid her a lot of money.

Chapter Five

Armed with my package and three bottles of Mum's Honeychurch Gin, I headed for the village of Little Dipperton.

It was a typical chocolate-box Devonshire village consisting of a series of whitewashed cottages, some in dire need of re-thatching, others with slate stone roofs. Encompassed by a low stone wall, the cottages formed a crescent around the Norman church of St Mary's and its graveyard. Ancient yew trees and dense hedges flourished among the dozens and dozens of lichen-covered gravestones that commemorated the names of the families who had been born, died and still lived in a village that was mentioned in the Domesday Book.

Naturally, the Honeychurch dynasty had their own mausoleum embellished with hawks in flight and bearing the family motto of *ad perseverate est ad triumphum* – to endure is to triumph.

Little Dipperton boasted a seventeenth-century pub

called the Hare & Hounds, a greengrocer, Violet Green's tearoom and the community shop and post office.

At one time the Honeychurch Hall estate owned the entire village of Little Dipperton but now only a handful of cottages were tenant-occupied; their low front doors and window frames were painted in a distinctive dark blue and opened directly on to the one-lane road that snaked through the village.

Twenty-something Bethany Davis and her partner Simon Payne lived in the flat above the post office and community shop. The industrious couple had done a great job of keeping the spirit of the original shop alive – using the old-fashioned cash register and brass counter bell – but at the same time, they embraced the diverse demands of twenty-first-century consumers.

Volunteers from the village gave up an hour or two of their time every week to help out. In return, the shop carried homemade wares ranging from honey, local cheeses and artisan bread to handmade pottery, jewellery and knitted scarves. And, of course, Mum's gin.

Simon boasted that there was nothing that their shop did not sell; he called it Aladdin's Bazaar.

Bethany had also started a White Elephant corner where unwanted items or gifts could either be swapped or purchased with a donation to BatWatch being strongly encouraged. And if there was any doubt about the presence of the greater horseshoe bats in the area, a large map showed the maternity roosts in the South Hams. Honeychurch Hall was circled in red with the caption:

Little Dipperton: Proud Protectors of the Greater Horseshoe Bat.
The map was edged in black with a BatWatch logo that
looked remarkably like the cartoon bat from the comic
strip *Batman.*

Many of the objects in the White Elephant corner were
just plain weird and always provided a source of amusement.
Someone once left an inflatable sheep that generated a few
bawdy comments from the farming community. And of
course the annual Naked Farmer calendars, photographed
by local photographer and bestselling author Nicola de
Pulford, were hugely popular. My mother had one hanging
in her office and claimed it helped her describe the physical
attributes of the heroes in her books.

Behind the counter were shelves filled with large glass
jars containing sweets that were now coming back into
fashion – Sherbet Pips, Fruit Chews, Black Jacks and the
kind of treacle toffee that removed dental fillings in one
bite.

In front of the counter stood a low bench spread with a
selection of local newspapers – the *Dipperton Deal,
Dartmouth Packet* and *Totnes Times* – as well as national
newspapers and trashy magazines, including the dreaded
Star Stalkers!, which used to be the bane of my life when I
worked in TV as it reported everything I did – and wore –
in print.

Mum's Krystalle Storm novels were displayed on a
carousel next to picturesque postcards of the South Hams.
It was easy to see why the South Hams had been designated
an area of outstanding natural beauty, with spectacular

Dartmoor, stunning coastal beaches and breathtaking rolling fields and forests, as well as being home to many National Trust and English Heritage properties. I was very happy living here.

When Mum first saw her books in the community shop, she panicked. Her identity was a closely guarded secret – only Shawn and I knew the truth. One of these days this secret would come back to bite her. Secrets always did.

I headed for the Plexiglas window that encased a small cubbyhole that served as the tiny post office and slid the package under the window for Bethany to stamp and post.

With her large Bambi eyes and cloud of blonde hair, Bethany was a dead ringer for Blondie, the 1980s pop icon. She knew it too and preferred to wear 1980s clothing. Bethany was the least likely village postmistress you would ever expect to find.

Bethany finished stamping my package. She leaned in and lowered her voice. 'Can you get Iris to bring some more of her homemade gin?'

Gesturing to my tote bag, I said, 'I have three bottles in here.' I found I was whispering too, which made me think I was doing some kind of drug drop.

What had started as Mum and Delia's light-hearted endeavour to make homemade gin as Christmas gifts had grown into a little cottage industry. Selling without a licence was illegal, but my mother had convinced Shawn that it was just a 'few' bottles and Shawn had turned a blind eye. Bethany had seemed only too happy to bend the rules a little and sell it under the radar.

She gestured to the parcel window and said, 'Quickly! Through here.'

Checking that no one was watching, I passed the bottles over and realised that, in fact, I was my mother's accomplice.

Selling gin wasn't the only illegal thing Mum was doing either. The copious amounts of money she earned from her Krystalle Storm books was kept in an offshore account in the Channel Islands. Mum was predictably cagey about this and when she'd hired Victor Mullins to file her tax return, she had flat-out lied when he asked her if she received any income other than the pension that Dad had set up for her before he died.

Luckily, I was distracted from dwelling on my mother's shady lifestyle by Bethany's partner, who called out a greeting. Simon came over carrying a bag of birdseed, two canisters of red paint and a bottle of antifreeze.

Simon was built like an American football player and had to stoop because of the low ceiling. Two of the beams had foam taped to their undersides and someone had written 'Ouch!' in a blue Sharpie pen.

'I just got off the phone with Eric,' he said. 'He tells me that you're interested in getting involved in BatWatch. Can you hang on a mo?'

I waited while Simon put the items in their appropriate places, thinking that Eric hadn't wasted any time.

I liked Simon. He had worked on the fishing trawlers out of Brixham until a nasty injury with a trawl winch put an end to that. Although he walked with a permanent limp he always seemed to be in a good mood.

'Would you be interested in being the spokesperson for Little Dipperton BatWatch?' Simon asked.

'I'm intrigued,' I said cautiously. 'But I honestly don't know the first thing about bats.'

'No need to worry about that,' said Simon. 'You've got Eric on your doorstep and, of course, Harry is a walking encyclopaedia.'

I smiled as I thought of the precocious – yet adorable – eight-year-old Harry Honeychurch, who would one day become the 16th Earl of Grenville.

'We want to raise public awareness and you're still a household name,' Simon went on. 'We'll shoot a few very short informational videos for YouTube. I've already got someone to write the copy. You just need to read it for the camera and look beautiful.'

I acknowledged the compliment. 'How can I refuse? When does all this start?'

'Brilliant!' Simon beamed. 'It could be any time now. I'll be in touch. Do I have your mobile?'

I gave him my number, adding the usual warning about the signal being spotty, and turned to leave just as Delia Evans – dressed in a Marks & Spencer outfit of neat plum skirt and matching cardigan – wandered in with a sheaf of flyers. I thought she'd gone a bit overboard on the colour of her wig this afternoon.

Poor Delia suffered from alopecia and rather than be embarrassed by it, she'd decided to broadcast it by wearing a variety of stylish wigs. Today's choice was a vivid auburn.

The moment Delia saw me, her cheerful expression

turned to a scowl. Ever since my relationship with her son Guy hadn't worked out, she'd been decidedly frosty towards me. Apparently, Guy had been devastated and believed that I had used him to make Shawn jealous enough to reveal his true feelings over that fateful Christmas. Although it had never been my intention, Shawn *had* got jealous and he *did* confess his feelings.

'Hi, Delia,' I said brightly. 'How are you?'

'Are you going to Dartmouth today?' she said rudely.

'Yes. Why?'

Delia thrust a bunch of flyers into my hands. 'These need to go up everywhere. Telegraph poles, shop windows, bus shelters – anywhere there is an empty space.'

I would have thrust them right back at her if it weren't for her friendship with my mother. Plus, I knew that Delia didn't drive and went everywhere by bicycle. I was surprised that she'd been commandeered to do such a chore but not surprised enough to ask why. With Delia, the less I had to do with her, the better.

The glossy flyers were for *The Merry Widow* and had 'New Venue! New Tenor!' and the words 'Honeychurch Hall' splashed diagonally across them in heavy black font. Along the bottom was printed 'Sold Out'. Lucia Lombardi's glamorous headshot – she was wearing a *Sunset Boulevard*-like blood-red turban – bore the caption 'Greatest Soprano of All Time!' and 'Hear her hit the High G10!'. The poster also stated it was Countess Olga Golodkin's final production and that it was dedicated to the memory of Lady Suzanne Stubbs-Thomas.

'I'll put up as many as I have time for,' I said.

'Oh!' said Delia. 'I meant to tell you: Guy has met the most gorgeous French model. She's adorable. Taller than you, definitely thinner than you and she has such lovely short hair. It's so *pert*. Long hair can look such a mess, don't you think?'

Delia's barbs were so obvious that it was amusing. Yes, I'd gained a few pounds after decades of having to starve myself for the camera; yes, I was a modest five foot five; and yes, my hair could be unruly – hence the nickname Rapunzel.

'I'm happy for him,' I said. And I was. 'Guy deserves the best.'

'Yes.' Delia nodded vehemently. 'He most certainly does after all his heartache.' She paused as if expecting me to say something or, perhaps, to apologise yet again, so I changed the subject.

'How is everything going at the Hall?'

'Lucia Lombardi is arriving today,' said Delia. 'I am run off my feet. And poor Peggy Cropper! All she seems to do is make gallons of tea. It's been non-stop with builders and the production crew working flat out. The ballroom hasn't been used for decades. Not since the music-room fire.'

With a nod to the heap of flyers she'd just dumped on me, I said, 'Well, I'd better get going.'

Delia laid a hand on my arm. 'Wait,' she said. 'Is Iris still doing the Honeychurch family tree?'

I nodded. Somehow, my mother had become the official archivist for the Honeychurch dynasty, whose lineage could be dated back to Henry V's reign in the 1400s.

Delia lowered her voice. 'What about the servants? You know, the folks below stairs.'

'I think so,' I said. 'Why?'

'Peggy Cropper told me that Lucia was born plain Julie Jones,' Delia went on. 'She lived in one of the gatehouses. Was one of the Jones lot. The ones who were evicted.'

I tried to disengage her hand but she held on. 'I really need to get going,' I said. 'There are a lot of flyers here to put out.'

'Would you know anything about it?' Delia tightened her grip on my arm.

I refused to be drawn into Delia's penchant for gossip and was quite sure that she knew as much as anyone. I was also sure that whatever had happened had been blown out of proportion and, in the way of any village gossip, the story had been exaggerated as the years had passed by.

'And she's been married four times. She's very rich.' Delia gave a nasty laugh. '*The Merry Widow* . . . very apt, don't you think? Although, aren't we all merry widows? There's Iris, Peggy, me . . . and, of course, now you.'

'I'm not a widow,' I protested.

'Well . . . widows and one spinster, then,' said Delia cattily. 'Apparently Julie slept with everyone in the village, including his lordship!'

'Lord *Rupert*?' I didn't believe it. Anyway, was it actually possible? Quickly I made a mental calculation that since Reynard claimed not to have seen Lucia for nearly forty years, and she had left the area in the late seventies, Rupert would have been around fourteen!

'I don't know where you heard that,' I said.

'Everyone knows that his lordship has an eye for the ladies,' Delia went on.

In that she was right. Rupert had been married twice, the first time to Kelly Jones, who – good grief – must have been related to Julie in some way, and now to poor Lavinia Carew, who was always worried that he was about to have an affair or was in the middle of one.

'Whatever happened was years ago and it's obviously been forgotten.' I was desperate to escape but still Delia held on.

'Rupert would only have been a lad. I think he might have been under age!' she said with relish. 'That couldn't happen now, could it? She'd be put in prison. Peggy Cropper said that she remembered Julie slept with anything with a pulse.'

Now I *knew* that Delia was just being spiteful. Approaching the age of eighty, Peggy Cropper would never use that kind of language.

'I bet she changed her name to escape her past, but you never can,' Delia declared. 'Trust me. I know all about that.'

Finally I was able to prise her fingers free but Delia *still* blocked my escape.

'And yet she's putting on the airs and graces,' said Delia. 'Insists on bottles of Evian water. Bet it's to wash her hair like J. Lo – Jennifer Lopez—'

'I know who J. Lo is,' I said.

'*And* she's coming with an entourage! A personal

assistant, a driver, her own cook! *And* she's demanding a private room to rehearse because apparently she only sings with the entire company at the dress rehearsal.'

'Oh,' was all I managed to say.

'If you ask me, she sounds like a total diva.'

'Do I?' a female voice said, and there, standing behind Delia, was the greatest soprano of all time: Lucia Lombardi herself.

Chapter Six

Delia was mortified. 'I was talking about Jennifer Lopez,' she said quickly. 'Wasn't I, Kat?'

I didn't answer but, instead, made a point of greeting Lucia with a warm smile. 'I hope you had a good journey. I'm Kat Stanford; I live in the area.'

Lucia was petite and voluptuous and wore a tightly belted leopard-print coat, heavy make-up and a lot of gold jewellery. Her dyed hair fell in soft curls to her shoulders. She carried herself with an air of such superiority that I thought Delia's comment about her being a diva might be true.

Lucia seemed a few years younger than my mother. I wondered if their paths had, indeed, ever crossed. Bushman Travelling Fair and Boxing Emporium had camped in the Hall grounds every summer and Mum would have been fifteen when they left for good. It was distinctly possible.

'Why Olga couldn't find another venue in somewhere like Plymouth is beyond me,' Lucia said with a sniff. 'This is the back of beyond. My driver kept getting lost. There are no signposts and the lanes are so narrow.'

'I expect you've forgotten what the roads are like around here,' said Delia. 'Where is your driver now?'

'Waiting outside in the Mercedes,' said Lucia. 'There is nowhere to park.'

'Oh!' Delia exclaimed. 'You can't let him do that. He'll block the traffic.'

'Excuse me? I can do what I like, dear,' said Lucia.

'Yes . . . yes of course you can.' Delia nodded. 'I think we've got off to a bad start. I'm the housekeeper at Honeychurch Hall. We've got everything ready for you and your entourage.'

'Oh dear,' said Lucia with a sigh. 'I suppose that means we'll meet again. What's your name?'

'Delia Evans.'

'Well, Delia Evans,' said Lucia, 'please make sure there is plenty of Evian water at my disposal.'

Delia looked blank. 'Excuse me?'

'Don't I use it to wash my hair?' Lucia caught my eye. I couldn't be certain but I thought I caught a glimmer of amusement in her own.

I was desperate to leave but by now a handful of villagers must have heard that the local-girl-made-good was back and I couldn't get to the door.

I heard, 'used to live on the estate' and 'went to Italy to make her fortune' and 'what about the greater horseshoe bats?'

'Who is going to replace Victor Mullins?' said one bold soul. 'The show can't go on without him.'

'The doctor's standing in,' piped up Doreen Mutters, landlady at the Hare & Hounds. 'He's got a lovely voice.'

There was a chorus of agreement about Reynard's dulcet tones and how he had enthralled the patrons at the local pub last weekend with his spontaneous rendition of 'Ave Maria'. I looked to Lucia for a sign that they were talking about her childhood sweetheart, the man who had broken my mother's heart, but her face gave nothing away.

One woman stepped forward and proffered her a scrap of paper. 'Would you autograph my shopping list for me, Miss Lombardi?'

Lucia snapped her fingers and, as if by magic, a dashingly attractive little Italian man of around my age materialised with pen in hand. How he'd got through the crowd was a mystery – perhaps he'd crawled between their legs?

'Signora,' he said and handed Lucia a pen.

He then turned away from her and leaned over so that she could use his back – clad in an expensive Italian suit – to rest on. It was obvious that he had done this a gazillion times before.

I heard Doreen say, 'I wish I could get my Stan to do that.'

There was a ripple of laugher.

'Men are so easy to train if you know how.' Lucia had a straight face but again, I caught that glimmer in her eye. 'This is Paolo Carerra. He is my everything.'

Paolo had to be at least twenty-five years her junior. He was devastatingly good-looking with dark brown eyes, a mass of tousled dark hair, broad shoulders and a tapered waist. He looked as though he could easily belong among the pages of a Krystalle Storm novel, despite his lack of height.

Maybe Peggy Cropper had a point about Lucia's reputation. She clearly liked younger men. Reynard could be out of luck.

A car horn sounded outside from an impatient motorist. Presumably Paolo was Lucia's driver and had left the car unattended.

'Go back to the car,' Lucia said.

But Paolo didn't respond. He seemed transfixed and, unfortunately, he seemed transfixed by me. His dark brown eyes looked me up and down with ill-disguised admiration. I was so embarrassed I had to look away.

'Paolo!' Lucia said sharply.

'I am sorry, Signora, but I am struck by such beautiful hair,' he exclaimed. '*Che bellissimi!*'

Before I could say a word, Delia chimed in, 'Kat is famous too. Not as famous as you, Miss Lombardi, but she used to be on the telly.'

'Of course! *Fakes & Treasures*?' Paolo said eagerly. 'You are Rapunzel.'

'I've never heard of it or of you,' said Lucia.

The impatient motorist sounded his horn again, which was accompanied by two different horns and a shout of, 'Who is the idiot with the Mercedes?'

Paolo vanished – confirming my suspicion that he was able to escape through small spaces.

'Kat's got a showroom in the west gatehouse at Honeychurch Hall,' Delia declared.

'The *gatehouse*?' Lucia's eyes widened. 'I'll come and visit. You never know, I might buy something.'

Simon elbowed his way through. He was carrying a case of Evian water. 'Where would you like this?'

'You can take it outside to my car,' said Lucia.

Delia shot me a look of triumph and mouthed, *J-Lo*.

But Lucia and Simon didn't make it to the door because suddenly there was a deafening crash, a loud bang and the sound of a car alarm going off.

We all poured into the street to find Violet Green's Morris Minor had struck the door on the driver's side of a black Mercedes S Cabriolet. Poor Paolo was barely visible as he fought the exploded airbag.

Unfortunately, Paolo had moved the car across the entrance to the narrow alley between the community shop and Violet Green's teashop, where she always parked her Morris Minor. A large sign in red lettering said, 'Do Not Block Entrance'; Paolo had done just that.

Violet, who couldn't see too well, must have reversed out without checking her rear-view mirror.

Everyone clustered around the elderly lady, who remained in the driver's seat, still gripping the steering wheel. She was obviously in shock. The only damage to her car seemed to be to the rear bumper.

It was chaos. Someone was calling for an ambulance, another, to get hold of Eric and his tractor, and Simon was placating the growing line of motorists queuing behind the stricken vehicles.

I managed to help Paolo out of the damaged car through

the passenger door. He was shaken and covered in white powder from the airbag.

Next I went to Violet's assistance, where several of her friends were in a quandary as to whether to move her or not.

'We should wait for the ambulance to come,' Doreen Mutters declared.

I squeezed in to see how Violet was faring and, to be honest, she seemed fine to me.

But then strong fingers pushed me aside.

It was Lucia and she was livid. 'You did that deliberately, Violet Green!' She followed that up with a torrent of Italian that did not sound complimentary.

There were gasps of disbelief from the handful of villagers who had gathered around to enjoy the unfolding drama.

Violet just sat there with a mutinous expression on her face.

'Leave her alone, Julie,' Doreen Mutters snapped. 'Haven't you done enough damage?'

'Oh, for heaven's sake,' Lucia said. 'It was years ago and don't call me Julie. My name is Lucia.'

'No one wants you around here,' Doreen hissed. 'You're bad news. Go back to Italy.'

There was a deathly hush until a lone voice said, 'Does this mean that the show won't go on?'

'Signora?' Paolo popped up from behind Lucia's elbow. 'We need a new hire car.'

Lucia snapped her fingers and turned to me. '*You!*' she barked. 'You can take me to the Hall.'

I didn't have a chance to protest because Lucia was already demanding that Paolo get her luggage and transfer it to my car. 'And don't forget my Barolo!'

Chapter Seven

As we left the village behind us, Lucia said, 'Thank you, Kat. It is Kat, isn't it?'

'Yes. And it's fine. It's not far.' I smiled but it was far from fine. I had been put on the spot and could hardly have said no.

I glanced over at my passenger, surprised to see her hands were clenched tightly on her lap. Her nails were very long and painted a deep red. It suddenly occurred to me that maybe Lucia was nervous. She'd been away for a very long time.

A police car appeared with its light flashing. I was certain it was Shawn and felt a sudden rush of butterflies.

Following what had transpired at Christmas when he almost lost his life, we had seen a fair amount of each other but had never moved to the obvious next level. Even when his mother-in-law had taken the twins overnight, Shawn always seemed to have an early start the next morning. I'd respected his request to take it 'slow', but things had been moving at such a glacial pace that I was beginning to wonder if he was losing interest in me – especially since his recent return from a training course in London.

True, Shawn had his boys to think about, but I was getting impatient. I liked him a lot. I had even caught myself thinking big-picture plans involving them all, and at one time I was certain he had felt the same way.

When Mum had mentioned the *Mars and Venus* book earlier, the truth was that I had been putting those tactics into practice. I'd taken a step back. I'd stopped initiating the phone calls and text messages, but Shawn seemed oblivious.

Had I scared him off? Was I too aggressive? Had it just been the thrill of the chase for him?

What was all the more confusing was that he remained attentive, kind and sweetly flirtatious. It was ironic. When I was dating Piers Carew, Lady Lavinia's brother, it was the other way around. Now I was having a taste of my own medicine and I didn't like it one bit.

I pulled my Golf in tightly against the hedge. As I hoped, Shawn stopped his car and opened the window. I opened mine too and smiled at the dishevelled policeman with his dark brown eyes and mop of curly brown hair.

'We must stop meeting like this,' he joked.

My eyes were drawn to today's tie, which sported a bat design. 'Nice tie.'

When we first met I thought that Shawn's penchant for wearing unusual ties rather odd, as was his fascination for trains. Now I found both endearing.

'BatWatch,' said Shawn. 'The twins have moved on from dinosaurs. Bats are their new obsession— Oh.' Shawn reddened. 'I didn't realise you had company.'

'This is Lucia Lombardi,' I said, gesturing to my passenger. 'I'm taking her to the Hall.'

'Welcome home,' said Shawn. 'It must seem strange to be back in the area after so many years.'

'That was a lifetime ago,' said Lucia briskly. 'We all need to move on from our past but unfortunately some people can't.'

'And some people can. And they do.' Shawn smiled and looked right at me, confusing me yet again. What exactly did he mean?

'You should tell that to Doreen Mutters and that bitch Violet Green,' said Lucia. 'She deliberately reversed into my car.'

I was taken aback by Lucia's venom and wondered if it was nerves that provoked it.

'Were you hurt?' Shawn said politely.

'I wasn't in the car at the time,' said Lucia, 'but that's not the point. Paolo – he's my driver – almost suffocated under an airbag.'

'But presumably he didn't,' Shawn said.

'Paolo is strong. He'll be fine,' said Lucia. 'But I can assure you that I will be pressing charges.'

'Kat?' Shawn said. 'Did you see what happened?'

I admitted that I had not. In fact, I wasn't sure if anyone had seen what had happened since we had all been in the community shop at the time.

'If I had been sitting in the front seat I would have been killed,' Lucia pointed out.

I thought that highly unlikely given the fact that the Mercedes had been stationary at the time and Violet's Morris Minor rarely went more than twenty miles per hour even on a main road. But I kept quiet.

'I'm beginning to think our production is cursed,' Lucia continued. 'First of all Victor has a fatal car accident and then the theatre burns down.'

'It's fortunate that our local doctor is able to take on Victor's role,' said Shawn. 'Dr Reynard Smeaton is one of the finest tenors in the West Country. He could easily have turned professional but apparently he was called to the stethoscope.'

'Let's hope he really can sing.' Lucia scowled. 'Amateurs. All amateurs.'

'Right . . . well . . . I know where to find you should you really want to press charges,' said Shawn. And, with a few pleasantries, he put his car into gear and drove away.

Lucia was annoyed. 'God! Why did I come back? What the hell was I thinking?'

I wasn't sure if she expected an answer so I asked the obvious question. 'So why did you?'

'Money,' she declared.

'Oh,' I said. 'At least you're honest!'

'Olga made me an offer that I couldn't refuse – or, should I say, Monty did. Sorry – it's just . . . it's quite strange coming back here,' said Lucia. 'And to tell you the truth, I came back to sing for Suzanne.'

'That's Sir Monty's wife, isn't it?' I asked.

'Suzanne was my very first fan,' said Lucia. 'She started the Lucia Lombardi fan club. I knew her a long time before she married Monty. I was fond of her. She was an opera groupie. Knew all the lyrics to every opera in Italian and in German. She was wealthy in her own right. It's not Monty's money that funds D.O.D.O. It was hers.'

'I didn't know that,' I said. 'And what about the Countess Golodkin?'

'We go back a long way,' was all Lucia said. 'And now she's retiring – for the second time. And, by the way, I did recognise you.'

I shot her a quizzical look.

'It was that housekeeper,' said Lucia. 'Delia Evans. She just put my back up.'

I desperately wanted to say how much I agreed with her on that score but restrained myself.

'Do *you* remember your first fan?' Lucia said suddenly.

I actually did and told her so. 'Barbara from Canada. We're still in touch even now.'

'You're not from here, are you?'

'Is it that obvious?' And, just for something to say, I found myself telling the greatest soprano of all time why I had ended up living in Little Dipperton.

'Your mother is very lucky to have you around,' said Lucia. 'Just be careful and watch what you say. You'll get sucked into the gossip and backbiting. These people will twist the truth any chance they get.'

It had been no different when I worked in television and

I told her so. I knew what it was like to be in the public eye and have my personal life dissected among the pages of *Star Stalkers!*. But whereas most readers of tabloids took the contents with a pinch of salt, those in small communities tended to believe them as truths.

'I try to be Switzerland,' I said, 'and not get drawn in or take sides.'

'I assume the policeman is Robert Cropper's son,' said Lucia. 'He's the spitting image of his father.'

'I've never met Shawn's father,' I said. 'He retired and moved to Spain.'

'Well, Shawn likes you,' she said.

'He's a nice man,' I said carefully.

She laughed again. 'What's the matter? No ring on that finger? Had your heart broken? Is that it?'

'Something like that,' I said.

'Time is marching on. I've had four husbands and loved every one of them. But as I grow older, I don't want the hassle,' said Lucia. 'I like being married and I like not being married. Take lovers. That's my advice to you. You'll be much happier.'

Despite my first impression of not liking her, I found I actually did. I couldn't help wondering if the diva thing was all an act. 'How did you meet Countess Golodkin?'

'I met Olga here.'

'Here?' This was unexpected. 'In Little Dipperton?'

'At Honeychurch Hall,' she said. 'Oh yes. Olga and her mother spent two summers staying as her ladyship's guests. I still call the dowager countess her ladyship. She used to terrify me.'

'She terrifies everyone.' I grinned. 'But she's got a heart of gold.'

'Yes,' Lucia said quietly. 'Yes, she really has. I had no intention of coming back here. The production was in Dartmouth.'

'But that's only a few miles from here,' I said.

'Believe me, when you are born in a tiny village, Dartmouth is like going up to London,' she said. 'There are still folks here who have never left the county, let alone the country.'

'But you escaped,' I said lightly. 'That takes courage.'

'I was talent-spotted. Trust me, I needed no encouragement to get away.'

We had turned into Cavalier Lane and were drawing close to the Hall. I saw the narrow potholed road through Lucia's eyes, with its towering hedgerows filled with wild flowers. As we took another blind corner I recognised Douglas Jones wandering in the middle of the road carrying a large plastic shopping bag.

'What is that idiot doing?' Lucia said.

I honked the horn but Douglas made no attempt to stand aside to let us pass. I honked the horn again.

'Is he deaf?' Lucia opened the window and yelled, 'Out of the way!'

Douglas looked over his shoulder.

'Is that . . .? Good God,' Lucia exclaimed. 'Is that . . . is that *Dougie*?'

'Yes,' I said. 'Related, I assume.'

'Everyone is related to everyone around here,' she said. 'But that doesn't mean we have to like each other.'

'Do you want me to stop?'

'Good God,' she said again. 'No!'

As we slowly eased by, Douglas's scowl turned to one of recognition then horror. He shrank into the hedge and turned his face away, as if doing so would render him invisible.

'Don't tell me that branch of the family are back on the estate,' said Lucia.

'They're not,' I said. 'Douglas is living in the woods.'

'You mean . . . Honeychurch Woods?' Lucia said slowly. 'Interesting.'

'The woods are stunning at the moment,' I said. 'There are carpets and carpets of bluebells.'

'Yes, it's the right time of year for bluebells,' said Lucia. 'I remember those woods well. When I was a girl I made a fairy ring in a clearing in the hope that the fairies would visit. I'd leave flowers, marbles, coloured shells and that plastic tat you find in Christmas crackers.'

'And did the fairies come?'

'Of course not,' she laughed. 'But that didn't stop me wishing they would.'

We didn't speak again until we took the left fork where the drive split in two. Lucia rummaged in her handbag and pulled out a lipstick.

'Is there . . . do you have . . .? Oh, it's here.' She flipped the sun visor down and reapplied her lipstick in the vanity mirror. I stole a look and noticed that her hand was actually shaking.

'We're here,' I said.

Chapter Eight

Lucia gave a little gasp of dismay. 'It's so run-down!'

She was right. Honeychurch Hall was very run-down.

Even though the discovery of the Honeychurch mint and the subsequent sale of several rare seventeenth-century silver coins had gone a long way to repairing a small portion of the roof and moving the fallen cornices and broken roof tiles out of sight, the Hall still carried a neglected and abandoned air. True, the stone water fountain with its rearing horses in the centre of the turning circle now worked, but many of the twelve-pane casement windows on the ground and first floors remained shuttered and the house was in desperate need of a good coat of paint.

'How small it is,' Lucia mused. 'But of course, when you are a child, things seem so much bigger.'

The architecture could be described as 'classic revival'. It had a Palladian front but, judging by the four banks of tall chimneys topped with decorative, octagonal pots, it encased a much older building – most likely a Tudor manor house. The main entrance was very grand, with a central porte cochère and Tuscan columns.

'I doubt if Peggy Cropper is still alive,' said Lucia. 'She was a nasty piece of work.'

I told her that Peggy was, but that her husband Seth had died just a few months ago.

'Did he fulfil his lifelong dream of becoming a butler?' she sneered. I pretended I hadn't heard and didn't answer. Lucia was an enigma. One moment she could be so nice – especially when she had spoken about her fondness for Suzanne. But the next, she just seemed downright mean.

I parked next to a new Porsche 911 in dark metallic grey. It sported the number plate Mir 777.

'That will be Olga's car,' said Lucia. 'Impractical at her age, but then she does have an image to live up to.'

'What does Mir stand for?' I asked.

'It was the nickname her father gave her,' said Lucia.

'When did you last see her?' I said.

'I really can't remember.' She pulled down the visor to check her reflection again.

At that moment Edith emerged from the porte cochère and came to greet us. She'd changed out of her usual riding habit and into a green tartan skirt and matching jacket. Her scarlet lipstick gave her pale complexion a ghostly air. I thought of the village gossip and decided that there was no way that Edith would be so welcoming if everything that was said about Lucia were true.

A petite woman a little older than my mother stepped out of the shadows behind Edith.

Countess Olga Golodkin wore a wide-brimmed black hat and a bright red swirling cape that dwarfed her small frame. Compared to Edith's bolt-upright stance, she seemed very frail and walked with a cane.

Lucia was right: getting in and out of a Porsche 911 would be a challenge, let alone driving it. She wouldn't be able to see over the steering wheel without sitting on a cushion.

'Here we go,' Lucia muttered and slipped out of the front seat. 'Darlings! Darlings!' she gushed. 'I am here! *Sono arrivata!*'

She rushed up to Olga and engulfed her in a warm embrace while Edith looked on. I went to join them. Although Edith's smile didn't falter, I saw coldness in her eyes, which surprised me. I was wrong. Edith had not forgotten the past at all.

Lucia thanked me for driving her. She was different now. She was a star – all flamboyance and huge gestures.

Since Lucia made no move to get her luggage, it looked like it was going to be up to me. I made two trips into the Hall with her suitcases and a box of wine – presumably, the Barolo – and dumped them in the vestibule.

When I returned I heard Lucia say, 'It was a Morris Minor.'

'My darling, how terrible!' Olga exclaimed. 'What on earth happened?'

'Violet Green deliberately reversed into my Mercedes,' Lucia said.

'Good grief! Not *another* car accident,' said Edith.

'Are you hurt?' Olga said. 'Whiplash? Can you still sing?'

'Fortunately I wasn't in the car at the time,' said Lucia. 'Paolo is dealing with it.'

Olga looked blank. 'Paolo?'

'*Il mio braccio destro*, Paolo is my everything,' Lucia replied. 'He's a divine cook. A little expensive but I refuse to go anywhere without him.'

'I don't recall you mentioning this Paolo person to me,' said Olga.

'I have to be very particular about what I eat on tour,' Lucia declared. 'I can't afford to be ill. Paolo told Brooke, your personal assistant, that he would be accompanying me.'

'And your personal assistant told Delia,' said Edith smoothly. 'It won't be a problem, Olga dear.'

If Olga was annoyed she didn't show it. 'Monty will have to take care of the extra expense,' she said. 'And the housekeeper will need to sort out another bedroom for him.'

'Make it next to mine. Adjoining rooms preferred,' said Lucia. 'Unless that's a problem, milady – um . . . Edith.' Lucia blushed.

'Delia will take care of it,' said Edith. 'That is, if I knew where she was.'

I was about to say that I'd seen Delia in the village but Olga beat me to it. 'She's distributing the new flyers.'

'Perhaps you should have checked with me first, Olga dear,' said Edith tightly. 'Delia is run off her feet.'

'Oh, I am sorry,' said Olga, not looking sorry at all. 'I assumed she was my servant.'

Edith stiffened. 'We don't call them servants here,' she said. 'They're part of the family.'

'Did you bring your riding clothes, Lucia?' Olga asked suddenly. 'Edith is going to show us the estate tomorrow.'

'I'm afraid we don't have a horse for Lucia – my horses are too valuable for amateurs,' said Edith. 'But if she would like to accompany us on foot she's very welcome.'

The put-down was subtle but I caught it and so, clearly, did Lucia, who just shook her head. Whatever she was going to say was prevented by the sound of an approaching car.

A red Mini appeared with my mother at the wheel. She parked next to my Golf. This was completely unexpected and a little worrying. What on earth was she doing here?

My mother got out of the driving seat and reached back inside to grab two bottles of her homemade gin, each bearing a red ribbon. She was dressed up to the nines with a jaunty French beret and black stilettos – the type of shoe that I'd never seen her wear in my life – and seemed a shadow of the spurned woman I had comforted just hours before.

'I come bearing gifts!' she trilled.

Unfortunately, Mum wasn't watching where she was walking, missed her footing and only just managed to save herself – and the bottles of gin – by ricocheting off the wing of Olga's Porsche. The car alarm went off.

For several moments we were entertained by an array of different whoops and sirens as Olga fumbled for her car keys – dropping them twice – in a frantic attempt to turn it off.

Suddenly, all went silent just as Mum bellowed, 'And I made the gin myself!'

There was an awkward moment before she thrust a bottle at Olga and then at Lucia. 'Welcome, welcome,' she said.

'I never touch hard liquor,' Lucia said, and gave her bottle to Olga. 'I only drink Barolo and I'm most particular about the vintage.'

Olga peered at the label on the bottle of gin. 'Is that a *sheep*? And what's this . . .? "Made by Iris." Who on earth is Iris?'

'I'm Iris,' said Mum. 'And yes, you are quite right. The animal covered in white fluff called wool is a sheep. It's my logo.'

'My mother's gin is very popular in the West Country,' I said.

'It is *frightfully* good,' Edith agreed. 'It's made on the estate in the henhouse.'

'The henhouse!' Lucia exclaimed. 'Goodness!'

Olga sniggered. 'How quaint.'

'Well, Reynard *loves* my homemade gin,' Mum declared.

Lucia frowned. 'Reynard who?'

'Smeaton.' Mum's eyes widened. 'The doctor. Your new co-star, Count Danilo Danilovitsch.'

'Dr Reynard Smeaton,' said Olga. 'I told you all about him, Lucia dear. He's Victor's replacement.'

'Reynard refuses to drink anything else,' Mum went on. 'And I happen to know that he detests red wine.'

'How thoughtful of you, Iris,' Edith said. 'Let's go inside now and see if Peggy will rustle up a late lunch for our star.'

And with that, Edith and Olga retreated to the Hall. Lucia was about to follow when my mother barred her way.

'It's very nice to meet you,' Mum said with blatant insincerity. 'I'm such a fan. Reynard speaks about you all the time.'

Lucia seemed confused. 'Well. Good. Excuse me—'

'I know you're great friends with Reynard on Facebook,' Mum went on quickly.

'I have a lot of friends on Facebook,' said Lucia. 'But I don't handle my Facebook page. Paolo does all that awful social media stuff.'

Mum's jaw dropped. 'You mean . . . this Paolo person answers all your private direct messages?'

'That's what he's paid for,' said Lucia. 'I don't have time for all that nonsense. Why?'

Mum caught my eye and I could tell from her expression that she couldn't believe her luck. 'So . . . you don't remember a Reynard Smeaton at all?'

Lucia seemed impatient. 'I am not sure what you are asking.'

'Not even when you lived here?' My mother cleared her throat. 'Apparently you were boyfriend and girlfriend.'

Lucia gave a heavy sigh. 'I have had a lot of boyfriends, my dear, but I am quite certain that I would have remembered someone with such a ridiculous first name. Now please excuse me, travelling makes me very tired.'

I wanted to point out that she'd only travelled from Dartmouth and even then she'd been chauffeur-driven.

'Of course, of course,' Mum said happily. 'Go and take a nap. Do!'

And with that, Lucia was gone.

My mother was ecstatic. 'Just wait until I tell Reynard! I've been so silly! It just goes to show you can't believe everything you read on Facebook. And who is Paolo?'

'He's Italian. He is her driver and whatever other services she requires,' I said. '*And* he's at least twenty-five years her junior.'

'How very Joan Collins!' Mum beamed. 'Is he handsome?'

'Very. In fact, he'd look right at home on the cover of one of your novels.'

'Then Reynard won't stand a chance,' Mum gloated. 'He's going to be devastated.'

'And you'll be there to mend his broken heart,' I said. 'That's all well and good, but you are forgetting something.'

'I am?'

'The fact that Lucia seems indifferent doesn't change the fact that Reynard still holds a torch for her.'

Mum's face fell. 'Oh.'

'Speaking of which, don't *you* remember her? You must have been here at the same time as she was.'

'It's hard to tell,' said Mum. 'It was so long ago. Alfred might, though. We should ask him.'

'Now, if you'll excuse me, I need to get on,' I said. 'I have to get to Dartmouth and I still haven't had lunch.'

'Nor have I,' said Mum. 'I'd lost my appetite but now I find I'm quite peckish. Do you have supplies at the gatehouse?'

'I have bread and cheese,' I said, 'and a few tomatoes.'

'Good. Because there is something I need to tell you.'

Chapter Nine

'**Lucia Lombardi has not sung a note for the past ten years!**' Mum declared as we tucked into our hastily made sandwiches. 'There was even a rumour that she pulled a Beyoncé in her last concert.'

'I have no idea what "pulling a Beyoncé" means,' I said.

'Lip-synced!' Mum exclaimed. 'I think she's lost her nerve.'

'You mean you hope she has,' I said. 'And where exactly did you get this information?'

'The Internet,' Mum said proudly. 'According to Google, Lucia has sung with the greatest – Paris, New York, Moscow and, of course, Italy. So, as I said before, why on earth would she choose to come out of retirement to sing with a bunch of amateurs?'

I filled my mother in on Lucia's friendship with Sir Monty Stubbs-Thomas's deceased wife, who had founded Lucia's fan club.

'I bet the fan club will be on Facebook,' said Mum. 'I'll take a look.'

'And Lucia's getting paid a lot of money.'

'The Countess Golodkin has got an interesting background,' Mum went on. 'Apparently, she defected from the Soviet Union with her mother in nineteen seventy-five. Her father, who just happened to be a famous Russian opera singer, never made it out.'

'That's sad,' I said. 'What happened?'

'It doesn't say,' said Mum. 'But the Countess found fame in her own right and has served as the artistic director for the Sydney Opera House, La Scala in Milan, The Royal Opera House in London, the Palais Garnier in Paris. She's worked in Stockholm, Vienna, Hungary, Buenos Aires. You name it. She's been there.'

'I get the idea,' I said. 'TMI.'

Mum frowned. 'What?'

'Too much information,' I said. 'You really need to get savvy with your acronyms.'

'Anyway, in a nutshell, the Countess became known for her lavish productions, exquisite costumes and the use of live animals on stage until she retired from professional opera at age sixty-five.'

I raised an eyebrow. 'Live animals? Seriously?'

'Oh yes. In Rimsky-Korsakov's *The Maid of Pskov* – however you pronounce it – a storm and chase scene featured two horses at full gallop that tore across the stage from one wing to another.'

'I can't see that happening in the ballroom here,' I said drily. 'So how did Olga end up in deepest Devon?'

'Sir Monty and his wife Suzanne begged her to take

over as the artistic director for D.O.D.O. The company is regarded as one of the best semi-professional opera organisations in South West England, so she agreed.'

'I'm impressed,' I said. 'Well done. You've missed your vocation as a walking encyclopaedia. Did you learn that off by heart?'

Mum tapped her forehead. 'Mind like a steel trap.' She finished up her sandwich with a satisfied sigh. 'Google is incredible! I can't think why I was so reluctant to give it a go.'

'Can I say I told you so?' I teased.

'It's amazing what you can find out,' said Mum. 'Do you know what a castrato is?'

'Excuse me?'

'It's a male voice that used to be inbetween a soprano and an alto.' Mum gave a mischievous grin.

'O-kay,' I said slowly.

'Guess why it's extinct.'

'You know I hate guessing games,' I said. 'And I really need to get on with my day.'

Mum started to titter. 'I'll give you a clue. It was originally intended for use in church, but moved into the opera domain for much of the eighteenth century. Guess?'

'No, Mother,' I said, exasperated. 'Just tell me.'

'The voice was produced by castrating the unfortunate singer, and I can honestly say that if Reynard doesn't behave himself—'

'I get the idea,' I said wearily. I got up and cleared our

plates. 'Go on, off you go now. Go and finish your manuscript. Shoo!'

But then Mum spied the Russian nesting doll on my
desk and, with a cry of delight, picked it up.

'Oh!' she exclaimed. 'I've always wanted a Babushka.'

'It's actually a Matryoshka,' I said. 'There's a difference.'

'Matryoshka, Babushka, Matryoshka, who cares? I
love it.'

'The name has a different meaning, Mum,' I said.
'Babushka means grandmother or old woman. Matryoshka
symbolises fertility. And you can have it, with my
compliments.'

Mum unscrewed the doll and happily began arranging
the smaller dolls in descending order of height. 'Where did
you find it?'

I pointed to Douglas's battered suitcase that I'd set on
the floor. 'In that. Douglas Jones bought it at a car boot
sale.'

'How can he have done that?' Mum said. 'He doesn't
have a car.'

'I have no idea,' I said and went on to tell her that I had
paid fifty pounds for the privilege.

'You were ripped off,' said Mum. 'This Russian doll is
charming, though.' She pointed to the suitcase. 'Anything
else interesting in there?'

'See for yourself,' I said. So she did.

Mum wrinkled her nose. 'It smells of mould.' She
pawed through the contents. 'Just seventies tat. How
disappointing.'

I put the suitcase back in the corner. Mum popped her new treasure into her tote bag and we left the gatehouse together just as Rupert's black Range Rover sped on by with – to my surprise – Lucia riding shotgun.

Rupert didn't even slow down at the entrance; unfortunately neither did Paolo, who suddenly turned into the drive at the wheel of a silver Camry.

Brakes screeched, tyres skidded on gravel, and then came the sickening sound of metal hitting metal followed by three loud bangs.

Lucia and Rupert vanished under a sea of airbags. And, for the second time in less than four hours, Paolo did too.

It was bedlam. Mum and I raced over to help.

The Range Rover had struck the Camry with such force that it had spun sideways and now blocked the main entrance. We helped Lucia out of the front passenger seat. She wore wellington boots and what looked like a borrowed Barbour jacket, judging by the length of the sleeves. There was white powder in her hair.

Rupert yelled at Paolo, who was beside himself with anger and let loose a torrent of Italian before it registered that Lucia had actually been sitting in Rupert's car.

'Why is the Signora in your car?' Paolo demanded. 'Where are you taking her?'

Rupert didn't answer. He was already on his mobile.

'Let's all have a brandy,' Mum exclaimed.

And then Lucia fainted – very, very carefully. Paolo uttered a cry of dismay and more Italian language followed.

'We must call the doctor!' he exclaimed. 'Is she dying?'

Mum was horrified. 'No, we can't call the doctor!'

But it seemed that Rupert already had. 'Smeaton is on his way,' he declared.

Mum darted back into the gatehouse muttering the word lipstick. I stayed to help but wasn't really sure what I could do.

Fortunately, Lucia seemed to rally and allowed Paolo to help her to her feet. I pointed to the gatehouse and gestured for them to wait inside.

Turning back to Rupert I said, 'Are you hurt?'

But Rupert was already making a second phone call. 'Eric, bring the tractor,' I heard him say, along with some other unflattering comments that included 'little Italian fool'.

Rupert's moustache was bristling with fury as he paced back and forth, waiting for help to come. Brushing off the white powder that had coated his green tweed jacket, he checked his watch. 'Goddamit. I've got an appointment with my solicitor in Exeter at three. I'll never make it in time.'

'I'm sure Eric will be here in a moment,' I said. 'You know, it could have been worse.' I pointed to my Golf and to my mother's Mini. By some miracle, both had escaped being struck.

But Rupert was too angry to care. He peered up and down the drive. 'If that fool's car isn't moved in the next five minutes I shall move it myself.' He started pacing again. 'The world has gone mad! It's chaos at the Hall. I don't know what Mother was thinking.'

We heard the roar of an oncoming car that sounded like it needed a new exhaust pipe. Seconds later, Reynard's dirty red Saab swung into the drive at high speed.

There was no time for him to stop.

I clapped my hands over my ears and braced for the sound of impact.

Reynard hit the horn, hit the brakes and – with an ear-splitting crash – hit the Camry broadside.

Paolo burst out of the showroom, jumping up and down in dismay, but Reynard didn't seem to care. He scrambled out of the Saab with panic written all over his face.

'Where is she?' Reynard demanded. 'Oh God! Where is she? Is she alive?'

I was right behind the doctor as he ran to the showroom. I saw Mum's anguished face as he burst inside and zeroed in on Lucia. He flew to the sofa where she was seated, nursing a brandy balloon, and dropped to his knees at her feet.

I half expected him to burst into song.

'Julie, oh Julie.' He reached for Lucia's hand, but since she was holding the brandy balloon, he knocked that instead. Brandy spilled on to her borrowed Barbour jacket.

'Careful!' she snapped. 'And don't call me Julie. My name is Lucia.'

Reynard recoiled as if she'd slapped him.

'I'll get a cloth,' Mum proclaimed loudly and dis-appeared into the kitchen.

Lucia's rebuke seemed to have brought the doctor to his senses. 'Do you need an ambulance?'

'I'm fine, you idiot,' she spat. 'It's my lovely Paolo who is not. This is the second time he has been struck by an airbag today. I fear he may have a concussion.'

'Paolo is Lucia's *boyfriend*,' Mum trumpeted from the kitchen.

'Boyfriend?' Reynard's face fell. 'You have a boyfriend?'

'And he's young!' Mum trumpeted again.

'Where is my Paolo?' Lucia demanded.

'He's with Rupert,' I said, 'sorting out the cars. I think he'll be okay.'

My mother returned with a dripping-wet dishcloth and handed it to Reynard. 'Here, use this.'

'Why would I need that?' Lucia batted his hand away. 'This jacket is waterproof!'

'Your s-s-status on Facebook says you are single,' Reynard stammered. 'I don't understand.'

'Paolo attends to my social media,' said Lucia dismissively. 'Why?'

Reynard looked horrified. 'Do you mean . . . are you saying that it was *Paolo* who sent me a friend request and not you?'

Lucia seemed incredulous. 'Paolo? Of course it was Paolo. He is under strict instructions to friend everyone.'

Mum couldn't hide her glee, and even I felt an uncharitable surge of *schadenfreude*. Reynard had been incredibly cruel to my mother. It served him right.

Another cacophony of horns sounded from outside my window.

Rupert stuck his head in the door. If anything, his bad

mood had got worse. 'Eric is here, Reynard. We need you to help push these cars out of the entrance. There's another wretched delivery truck waiting to get in.'

Reluctantly, Reynard followed Rupert outside, shooting a longing glance over his shoulder, but Lucia didn't notice. She was on her feet – still holding what was now an empty brandy balloon – roaming around my showroom and inspecting the vintage bears and dolls that lined the shelves.

'I've never been interested in this sort of thing,' she said. 'I suppose there must be money in it. But I've never felt the attraction of grown-ups playing dolls.'

'Kat is one of the most respected dealers in the country,' Mum said coldly. 'And these items are not played with. They're collectibles. You see that doll – the one with the pink cap – that's a Jumeau. It's worth thousands.'

'Thousands?' Lucia seemed astonished. 'Really and—' She spied the old brown leather suitcase. 'Is *that* worth thousands?'

'It is to the man who brought it in,' Mum retorted. 'Beauty is in the eye of the beholder, you know.'

'And who was that?' Lucia asked mildly. 'Who brought it in?'

'Apparently, he is a relative of yours. Douglas Jones. Why? Are you interested?' Mum said. 'I'm sure Kat would give you a good price.'

'No, thank you.' Lucia handed my mother the empty brandy balloon. 'Wait – I feel I should know you.'

'I don't see how,' my mother said. 'I only moved here last spring.'

'No. I'm certain of it.' Lucia cocked her head. 'I always remember a fan. No need to be shy. I don't bite.'

I could see Mum making a super-human effort to bite her tongue.

'Ask Paolo and he will give you one of my autographed photos,' said Lucia. 'If you'd like to come backstage after the performance, I will be glad to give you a tour.'

'I'm sure my mother would love that,' I said, barely able to keep a straight face.

Mum and I followed Lucia outside as two more Backstage Movers trucks thundered up the drive. Eric finished unhooking the tow hitch from Paolo's rental car, which he had moved to the field on the opposite side of the road.

Thanks to the rhino grill that Rupert had bolted on to the front of his Range Rover, the Camry looked as if it belonged on the scrapheap.

'I'll give you fifty quid for that,' said Eric to Paolo.

Paolo was hysterical. 'No! No! It is Enterprise! They come. They come.'

Rupert and his offending car had already gone but the doctor was inspecting the front bumper of his Saab, which would have to be repaired along with the exhaust pipe that had fallen off and was lying in the road.

Reynard spotted Lucia and hurried over. 'Where are you going?'

'For a walk,' said Lucia. 'I always walk at this time in the afternoon. I'm going to look at the bluebells.'

'As your doctor, I don't think that's advisable,' said Reynard. 'You've just been in an accident.'

'Don't be ridiculous,' she snapped. 'I'm fine.'

'And I thought we should discuss our roles,' Reynard ventured.

Lucia frowned. 'Our roles?'

'I've taken Victor Mullins's place as Count Danilo Danilovitsch,' said Reynard, 'Hanna Glawari's true love. How life imitates art.'

Mum turned green.

'What does he mean by that?' I whispered.

'In *The Merry Widow* the widow and the count were lovers many years before,' Mum whispered back to me.

'Then it looks like he's in for a disappointment,' I said.

But to our surprise Lucia stopped and gave Reynard a once-over. He puffed out his chest and held in his stomach.

'Wait . . . *you're* Victor's replacement,' said Lucia. 'I didn't realise.'

'We have met before, you know,' said Reynard nervously. 'A long time ago. When we were teenagers. When I went off to university and then to medical school, we lost touch. My name is Reynard. Named after the fox.'

'Good God.' Mum blanched. He had said the exact same thing to her.

And then the most peculiar thing happened. Lucia's frown was replaced by a dazzling smile. 'Why on earth didn't you say so at the beginning!'

She stepped forward and gave Reynard a warm embrace, held his cheeks in her hands and gazed into his eyes. 'Darling, how could I have forgotten you? Of course we've met. And you will be singing with me? How thrilling.'

Lucia looked to my mother and there was triumph in her eyes. 'We should have dinner in my suite tomorrow night,' she went on. 'We'll get food sent up.'

'I think that's highly unlikely,' Mum snapped. 'The Hall isn't a hotel—'

'Maybe not, but my Paolo is a wonderful cook,' said Lucia.

'Won't he mind?' Mum said pointedly.

'I pay him not to mind,' said Lucia.

Reynard was over the moon. 'You used to call me Rey, Julie.'

'Don't call me Julie!'

'Sorry. It's a bad habit. I've just . . . I've just dreamed of seeing you again,' gushed Reynard. 'After all this time. I can hardly believe it. We can rehearse together, make soft music.'

'Oh, good grief,' Mum muttered with disgust.

'*A domani, mio caro,*' said Lucia, and, following a quick word to Paolo on her way out, she set off on foot and was soon lost from sight.

Reynard promptly ignored my poor mother, got into his Saab and drove away, leaving the exhaust pipe abandoned in the lane.

It was then that Mum noticed Paolo. Her face that just moments before had been a picture of misery changed to one of unbridled admiration.

'Good heavens,' she said, 'I see what you mean! A little vertically challenged but definitely book-jacket material. Why on earth would Lucia prefer Reynard? In fact, why on earth would I?'

Mum got into her Mini and drove away too, leaving me to help Paolo as he attempted to open the boot of the Camry.

'She is stuck,' he wailed.

'I'll get a screwdriver,' I said. 'Perhaps we can jimmy the lock. Wait here.'

In the end we were able to do just that. The boot popped open.

Paolo gave a cry of alarm. *'Il bagalio!* The luggage!' He turned to me, utterly panic-stricken. 'The Signora will never forgive me! The Signora will kill me!'

'What on earth is the matter?'

'Oh . . . oh . . .' He shook his head in despair. 'It has gone! It has *gone.*'

Chapter Ten

'But I already took Lucia's suitcases and a box of wine to the Hall,' I said calmly. 'Was there more?'

'Yes, yes,' Paolo exclaimed. 'There was one more. She was behind the back seat on the floor of the Mercedes.'

'That should be easy enough,' I said. 'Let's go inside and call Enterprise. I bet they'll still have it.'

As we trooped back into the gatehouse I realised that, just like the condition of the Camry, my day was starting to be a write-off too.

After a flurry of phone calls Paolo sank on to the sofa and gave a heavy sigh. 'They only have a small car left. The Signora won't be happy. It is a Smart car.'

'Better than nothing,' I said. 'And Lucia's luggage?'

'They look. We wait.'

'I'm sorry,' I said. 'I can't wait. I have to go out now, but would you like me to run you to the Hall?'

We moved Paolo's small suitcase into my Golf and I found myself heading back to the Hall for the third time that day. We made small talk about the beauty of the English countryside. I was surprised to learn that Paolo had only been working for Lucia for less than six weeks.

'How did you get the job?' I asked.

'My *zia* – my aunt, she used to be Lucia's housekeeper in Florence when the Signora had a big, big villa,' he said. 'The Signora retired but then my *zia* says the Signora is offered a lot of money to sing in London so she says, yes! And then she changed her mind and says, no! And then she changes her mind again . . . and *eccoci*. Here we are.' He gave a rueful smile. 'But not in London.'

'You must be disappointed that it's not in London,' I said.

Paolo shrugged. 'I don't mind and it is only for a little longer.'

'Just for this one production?' I said.

He grinned. 'Yes. That is all. Just one.'

'Honeychurch Hall,' I said as I drew up to the front entrance yet again.

'*Il castello e abbandonato*,' Paolo exclaimed. 'It is derelict. Is that the right word?'

I laughed. 'Well . . . not exactly derelict. It's just a little run-down.'

I left him at the front door, ringing the bell. I doubted anyone would answer but I left him there all the same.

Returning down the drive I pulled over so that a Silver Cloud Rolls-Royce bearing the number plate 'Monty 1' could pass.

I'd met Sir Montgomery Stubbs-Thomas many times on the auction circuit. He dabbled in antiques and was notorious for pushing up the prices and then dropping out at the last minute. At one time there was a rumour that he was part of a shill bidding ring.

Sir Monty stopped, opened the window and squinted at me through his monocle. Like most English country gentleman, he sported the usual green tweed jacket and flat cap.

'Looking for the Countess,' he demanded rudely.

'Hello. Lovely day, isn't it?' I said. 'Do you mean Lady Edith Honeychurch or the Countess Golodkin?'

'Golodkin.'

'The drive splits about half a mile further on,' I said. 'Take the left fork to the front of the house. You can't miss it.'

'Do I know you?'

For a moment I was tempted to deny it. 'We've met many times, Sir Monty,' I said. 'Kat Stanford.'

With just a nod, he closed his window and drove on and, finally, I headed for the Dartmouth Antique Emporium just as the dark clouds on the horizon opened and heavy rain began to fall.

Sometimes I still pinched myself to make sure I wasn't dreaming and that I really had left London for the countryside and that I really *did* live in Devon.

When I first realised that my initial trip to Little Dipperton to persuade my mother to move back to London was going to turn out to be a permanent stay, I was horrified.

Being just days away from signing a lease on a shop in bustling and trendy Shoreditch, I'd traded my life in

London for a remote corner of the South Hams where, without telling a soul, my mother had upped sticks and impulsively bought the Carriage House.

At first I was lonely. I missed hosting *Fakes & Treasures* and sharing my days with kindred spirits – the fans, the collectors and the production crew. Plus, I had a very busy social life thanks to my decade-long relationship with international art investigator David Wynne.

But it had always been a dream to have my own antique business, so I was thrilled when Edith offered to lease me the gatehouses for Kat's Collectibles & Mobile Valuation Services.

Unfortunately, I quickly discovered that despite paying a fortune for advertising in the *Antiques Trade Gazette* and online, I was too far off the beaten track and, even with satnav, the showroom was difficult for customers to find.

In the end I decided to make visits to the showroom by appointment only and found that it was the best way to attract serious collectors, and those that made the effort always bought something.

Even though my mobile valuation service was going well, it was when I decided to rent a space at Dartmouth Antique Emporium that my business really began to pick up.

The Dartmouth Antique Emporium was on the outskirts of Dartmouth town centre, just ten miles away from Little Dipperton.

Dartmouth was steeped in history and a popular tourist destination. Nestled on the estuary of the River Dart and with narrow streets, overhanging medieval buildings and old quays, the town's origins could be traced back to the Norman Conquest.

Dartmouth had been an assembly point for ships to set sail for the second and third Crusades in 1147 and 1190. When England was under threat from the Spanish Armada, eleven ships set off from Dartmouth and captured the *Nuestra Señora del Rosario*, which was anchored in the Dart for over a year. The Spanish crew who were captured worked as slaves at Greenway House – once Agatha Christie's summer home and now in the hands of the National Trust.

Dartmouth was also home to the magnificent Britannia Royal Naval College, the Dartmouth Steam Railway and a fifteenth-century castle. Summers were filled with so many events – the Dartmouth Regatta, the Music Festival and the Food & Wine Festival to name just three. It was a thriving town and I loved it.

The Dartmouth Antique Emporium was housed in a newly converted barn with its own dedicated car park for customers. There was also a coffee shop with plenty of outdoor seating in the courtyard surrounded by planters overflowing with geraniums.

Inside the building, a skylight spanned the gabled roof that stretched the length of the Emporium where over thirty dealers sold their stuff in individual spaces. Some dealers were there every day but most of us worked on a rota, taking care of each other's areas – a set-up that suited me since it gave me the flexibility I needed to go to auctions, do my mobile valuations and, of course, to meet collectors back at my showroom.

Kat's Collectibles & Mobile Valuation Services had a space close to the main entrance. It was beautifully light, with a large arched window that overlooked the court-yard. Matching walnut bookshelves and glass cabinets lined the partition walls displaying vintage bears and a selection of porcelain dolls. The floor was covered in an Afghan rug in blues and reds. In the corner next to the window was a pretty Queen Anne oak bureau and a Queen Anne walnut and leather desk chair. In another was a leather wingback chair.

Mum called the space my 'lair'.

As I parked my car next to Fiona's metallic-blue Kia, I felt a twinge of anxiety. On the drive over I had decided I'd have to tell her that I needed to be honest with Shawn and the only alibi I could give her would be the truth. Surely she would understand.

Picking up the pile of flyers that Delia had given me this morning – I'd distribute those later – I headed inside. Set back in an alcove was a unit of old-fashioned key pigeon-holes where mail and notes could be left for dealers. I grabbed my very small stack just as Shawn entered with his sidekick Detective Constable Clive Banks, or, as my mother nicknamed him because of his heavy beard, Captain Pugwash.

I was pleased to see Shawn but rather than returning my smile of welcome, he looked grave.

'Sorry,' he said grimly, 'we're on police business. Looking for Fiona Reynolds?'

I pointed to the door marked 'Manager'. As I thought of Fiona's hurried visit to my showroom this morning, I felt a horrible sense of foreboding.

Shawn knocked but didn't wait for an answer. He and Clive entered.

By now, a small crowd had gathered. Through the open entrance I saw Shawn's police car had the light on and it was actually flashing.

I was in a dilemma but common sense won out. I knew what I knew and nothing else. With any luck it would turn out to be a misunderstanding. I ducked into a space that sold mid-century kitchenware and waited to see what would happen.

Ten long minutes later, Shawn and Clive emerged with – I couldn't believe it – Fiona in handcuffs.

Her face registered shock. When she saw me she called out, 'There's Kat. I told you I was with her that night. Kat! Tell them!'

Shawn kept her walking. 'Then you have nothing to worry about, Mrs Reynolds. I will make sure to take Miss Stanford's statement. But for now, we need to go to the police station.'

They left and I just stood there, more than a little shaken.

I composed myself and knocked on the office door. Fiona's husband Reggie was on the phone. He raised a finger and pointed to the ladder-back chair in front of his desk. I took a seat and waited. My stomach was in knots.

Both in their late fifties, Fiona and Reggie had moved

down from London a decade ago. They'd traded the PR world in the capital for a quiet life in the country. Fiona told me once that Reggie had missed their glamorous social life and the perks that went with having high-profile clients. She'd often mentioned that she felt he'd never really settled in Devon.

'Right,' he said, finishing up the call. 'I'll meet you at the police station in an hour.' He disconnected the line.

'What on earth is going on?' I exclaimed.

'That was my solicitor,' he said. 'Fiona has been arrested for setting fire to the theatre.'

'But of course she didn't do it,' I said. 'You must know that.'

But Reggie didn't answer. 'Fiona told me that on the night of the fire she was with you until the early hours.'

I was annoyed that Fiona would have put me in such an awkward position. 'We had dinner at the Castle Hotel, yes, but . . .'

Reggie's eyes narrowed. 'But what?'

'I was home by eleven thirty,' I said. 'Look, Fiona told me you were taking some time apart so I do know that you can't give her an alibi.'

'You're right. I can't,' said Reggie.

I felt a flash of anger. 'And that's it? You just *can't*?'

Reggie refused to meet my eye.

'Fiona gave *no* indication that she was upset about anything when we had dinner that night. Nothing at all.'

'She wouldn't,' said Reggie. 'She's very good at hiding her feelings.' He looked up from his desk. 'Look, Kat . . . I know you and Fiona are friends, but she was seen at the theatre that night. There's a witness.'

'That makes no sense,' I said. 'She'd walked to the restaurant and I dropped her home so she could have a drink. You're telling me that when she got home she decided to risk her licence and drive out to the theatre? I don't believe it.'

Reggie got to his feet. 'I need to go to the police station.'

I was thoroughly rattled. 'I'm going to have to make a statement. You do know that, don't you?'

Reggie paused. 'Then tell the truth.'

He ushered me out of the office and turned to lock the door. I watched him leave, horribly unsettled. It was as if he didn't care.

I plonked a handful of flyers on the hospitality table and headed for my space. My friend Di, who ran the jewellery booth opposite mine, was there waiting. 'I suppose you've heard.'

'Of course I have,' I said.

Tall and rangy and with a pixie cut and elfin face, she reminded me of a young colt. Usually she was smiling, but not today.

'Let's have some tea,' she said. 'Then I'll fill you in on what I know.'

Chapter Eleven

Ten minutes later we were sitting at a table under a green awning out in the courtyard with our mugs of hot tea and a chocolate brownie each. Rain fell steadily.

'Frankly, I'm not surprised,' said Di.

I decided not to mention that I'd had dinner with Fiona that night. 'Why would you say that?'

'Listen . . . I've been here longer than you and you just see the nice side of Fiona because she's impressed by your fame.'

'Fame?' I snorted. 'Hardly.'

'You're a celebrity!' Di scolded. 'I've heard Fiona brag about you to her friends. Oh, and in case you wondered, I have never exploited our friendship.'

I grinned. 'I'm glad to hear it.'

'That's the problem with you,' Di went on. 'You always see the best in everyone.'

'Nothing wrong with that, is there?'

Di took a sip of tea and pulled a face. 'No sugar.' She took three sachets and tipped them into her cup.

'And still you stay so thin,' I said. 'I'm jealous.'

As she stirred her tea, Di said, 'Did I tell you that I used to help Fiona with the costumes for D.O.D.O.?'

'No.' I was surprised. 'Really? When?'

'Years ago,' she said. 'That's how I came to rent a space here. Everything went well until Olga became the director and made all these big changes. She didn't seem to accept that D.O.D.O. was just a bit of light-hearted fun for opera fans. Olga got a salary – and poor Victor, of course. She has a paid personal assistant, too. Everyone else did it for love or free tickets. She put a lot of people's backs up with her demands and expectations.'

Although I had only met Olga for all of five minutes, I could see how she might do that.

'Most of us had proper jobs,' said Di. 'I couldn't hack it so I stopped volunteering. I mean, who needs that kind of aggro?' Di took a bite of chocolate brownie. I'd already devoured mine.

'I still can't see Fiona setting fire to the theatre,' I insisted.

'Fiona and Victor were close friends . . .'

'I gathered that,' I said. 'He was my tax adviser and accountant. My mother used him too. Fiona gave me his number.'

Di raised an eyebrow. 'So you knew what he was like.'

'Like? In what way?' I said.

'He played everything by the book.'

I thought of how my mother had lied to Victor's face about only living on her widow's pension and the furious row that we'd had when she told me. Filing her taxes had been yet another thing that Mum hadn't given much thought to after Dad passed away. My mother's earnings from her royalties were huge. She would almost certainly face prison time if it all came out.

'Victor used to be the treasurer for D.O.D.O. until Olga took that role over as well. She's such a control freak.' Di looked over her shoulder as if to make sure we weren't being overheard. 'Fiona told me that Victor hadn't trusted Olga's financial expertise – she had no budgets whatsoever for any of the productions. She just kept on spending.'

'Sir Monty didn't seem to mind,' I said. 'Isn't he the one who's footing the bill?'

'And to get Lucia Lombardi out of retirement and *pay* her to sing?' Di seemed astonished. 'D.O.D.O. may be one of the best semi-pro companies in the country but, *Lucia Lombardi*?'

'Sir Monty's wife and Lucia were friends,' I said.

'Suzanne? Oh, yes. That's right.' Di nodded. 'She's one of those weird groupies that follow their idols all over the world. Absolutely loaded.'

'Suzanne died, Di,' I said. 'Lucia agreed to sing in her memory.'

Di reddened and seemed embarrassed. 'I didn't realise. As I said, it was years ago and obviously you know more about it than I do.'

'I don't,' I protested.

But Di seemed miffed. She checked her watch. 'Got to

go. Oh – did you see the message about a doll's house valuation? I left it in your cubbyhole.'

I was too agitated to do much, so I spent what was left of the afternoon walking around Dartmouth, replacing the old flyers with the new, until it was time to do the valuation.

The address was out on the Kingsbridge road. An elderly lady was going into a nursing home and her daughter had to sell her cherished toy collection to pay for it. These kinds of valuations always made me feel sad.

The Victorian doll's house was in excellent condition and had belonged to the elderly lady's grandmother. I ended up giving them a very generous price because I loved it and toyed with the idea of keeping it for my showroom. It had a painted redbrick façade, white quoining and glazed windows and all the original contents, including a coal scuttle, washstand and tin-plate bath.

As I headed back home, the road took me past the ruined theatre. There's something horribly fascinating about a burned-out building. I slowed right down to a crawl so I could look.

Set back from the road, the theatre had been a converted petrol station that had been built in the 1940s. The original petrol pumps had been restored and stood mournfully out front. The front of the building had rollback glass-paned wall-to-wall doors that would have opened into the service bays behind. But a closer look showed that the roofline and the glass-paned doors were scorched. If it hadn't been for the heavy-duty red and white striped barricade tape and signs to Keep Out, it would have been hard to tell that there had been a fire in there at all.

On the left-hand side of the building was a Portakabin. I assumed that this was where the costumes had been stored.

I just couldn't accept that I'd dropped Fiona at her house in Dartmouth, only for her to get into her car and drive out here in the middle of the night. It would have meant that she'd been thinking about coming back all evening. Unless something had happened when she got home?

I replayed her ominous comment when she left the gatehouse. She'd said that the less I knew, the better. What had she meant by that? Reggie said that there had been a witness. This wasn't even a residential neighbourhood – there were no houses about – it was just an old filling station on a stretch of deserted country road surrounded by belts of trees.

I headed for home.

If I thought that my day was over, I was wrong. For a start, someone had sprayed graffiti in red paint on both the granite pillars – 'Go Home! Save Our Bats!' – and Paolo was waiting for me, perched on the bonnet of a white Smart car.

I pointed to the graffiti. 'You didn't happen to see who did that, did you?'

'I just arrive.' Paolo pointed to the car. 'Small. Yes?'

'Did you find the missing luggage?'

'No. The Mercedes has gone to *l'auto riparazione*,' he said. 'I have solved the problem but I need your help, Signora.'

'And I need yours,' I said. 'Help me take this doll's house inside, will you?'

He waited while I unlocked the door and disabled the alarm. For someone so small, Paolo was remarkably strong. He insisted he needed no assistance and carried the whole thing without any help from me. He set it on the floor next to Douglas's leather suitcase.

'Charming house, yes?' he said. 'You leave it on the floor?'

'For now.' I had to photograph everything and it was easier that way. 'You wanted my help?'

'I will make it up to you, I promise,' Paolo said eagerly. 'It is more than my life is worth to anger the Signora.'

'What do you need me to do?' I asked.

'You will be here tomorrow for a delivery? Yes?'

'Oh, Paolo,' I groaned. 'I can't. I have a busy schedule. Why can't whatever it is be delivered to the Hall?'

'Please, Signora, I am begging you,' he pleaded. 'Leave the door unlocked, perhaps?'

'Are you mad?' I said. 'I've got all my stock in here!'

His face fell. I had an idea and gestured for him to follow me around the side of the gatehouse. At the back was a small potting shed that I hadn't cleared out yet. It was full of broken terracotta pots and the random bits and pieces that always seemed to mysteriously appear in small potting sheds.

'You can tell whoever it is to leave whatever it is in there,' I said. 'But I'm not taking any responsibility if it goes missing.'

'Thank you, thank you,' Paolo gushed. He picked up my hand and began to kiss it voraciously.

'Okay, no problem.' I laughed. 'But can I have my hand back, please?'

I watched him drive away happy. For the next couple of hours I was absorbed in my new acquisition. I took photographs and catalogued everything, not just to keep track of my stock but for insurance purposes.

Thinking of insurance made me think about the fire. I wondered if the theatre had been insured.

The phone rang and – speak of the devil – it was Fiona. To my shock, she was calling me from the actual police station.

'They're keeping me in overnight,' she said miserably. 'Shawn will want a statement from you.'

My heart sank. 'What did you tell him?'

'That I was with you,' said Fiona. 'I need you to find out what he knows—'

'Fiona . . . I just, I just can't do that.' I felt wretched. 'Shawn is extremely professional. He never discusses a case with me.'

'But he's going to take your statement,' Fiona said again. 'At least find out who claimed to see my car there.'

'I'll try,' I said.

'Look . . . I just need to buy some time.' She sounded close to tears. 'I could lose everything. The Emporium, my marriage . . . You do believe me, don't you?'

'Fiona . . . it's not that I don't, it's . . .' The line was quiet. 'Are you still there?'

'Victor's death wasn't an accident,' she said quickly. 'I know I can prove it. He found something he shouldn't have done – he was murdered. I have to go.'

And with that shocking revelation, she disconnected the line.

I was stunned. How could Victor Mullins have been murdered? He'd been driving drunk and had a car accident. Everyone knew that.

I could certainly ask Shawn, but Shawn didn't call me that night and, putting *The Rules* into practice, I certainly wasn't going to call him.

And then I had an idea. Tomorrow, I was riding out with Edith and Olga.

Surely there couldn't be any harm in asking Olga a few questions?

Chapter Twelve

After a night of heavy rain, the morning air smelled amazing. The blossom was out, the hedges were filled with an abundance of wild flowers, and I woke up feeling cheerful until I remembered my conversation with Fiona. Victor had been murdered.

I left my Golf on the service-road side of the stable block. Unlike the condition of the Hall, the quadrant of redbrick buildings with their neat white trim was immaculate. Horses peered over green-painted split-stable doors.

I loved coming here and felt incredibly lucky. I had ridden a lot as a child but my parents had never been able to afford a horse, let alone keep one in the middle of London. Edith had generously told me to treat Duchess, a dapple-grey mare, as my own. It was a dream come true for a townie like me, and another reason why I could never imagine returning to live in a city.

As I tacked up Duchess, Alfred Bushman, the stable manager and Mum's stepbrother, led Tinkerbell, Edith's chestnut mare, out of her box. I'd hoped to ask him if he remembered Lucia, or Julie as she was back then, but Edith – dressed as usual in her side-saddle habit – was already waiting on the stone mounting block.

Alfred stood at Tinkerbell's head while Edith lifted her right leg over the top pommel and slid gracefully on to the saddle, adjusting her habit as she did so. Edith had taught me to ride side-saddle but I had never felt completely safe and always rode astride.

I led out Duchess and mounted then waited alongside Edith while Alfred fetched Jupiter, a sweet-natured bay mare, from her box for Olga.

Alfred was still an enigma to me. With his thatch of white hair, wire-rimmed spectacles and a mouth with very few teeth, it had taken a while to get to know this myster-ious wiry character. Over the past year, I'd grown to admire Alfred's gift, not just with horses: he had an uncanny intu-ition that he attributed to his 'Romany' blood.

Olga emerged through the archway wearing jodhpurs. She leaned heavily on her cane and I wondered if it was wise for her to ride.

Even using the mounting block, she had difficulty getting on to Jupiter.

Edith must have felt the same reservations because she said, 'Olga dear, are you sure you want to do this?'

'Stop fussing,' Olga snapped. 'I'm sure if you can ride out, I can.'

'I didn't get a new hip,' Edith said. 'And we don't want any more accidents, do we?'

'And you shouldn't be riding side-saddle at your age,' Olga retorted. 'When you come off you'll break your neck.'

I was taken aback by Olga's rudeness and stole a glance at Edith, who didn't seem so warm towards her friend this morning either. I couldn't help wondering what on earth had happened between them.

We rode out of the yard in single file, with Edith in the lead and me bringing up the rear, accompanied, of course, by Mr Chips, Edith's beloved Jack Russell terrier.

Instead of heading down the main drive, we took the service road and then cut up to Hopton's Crest through a twitten that ran between a hedge and the Victorian walled garden.

Hopton's Crest was named after Sir Ralph Hopton, who had been a Royalist commander in the first Civil War and who had secured the South West of England for King Charles I. I loved riding up there. The views were spectacular.

Below, on one side of the ridge, nestled the village of Little Dipperton and on the other, tucked between trees and centuries-old dry-stone walls, lay the magnificent Honeychurch Hall estate, with the quirky equine ceme- tery, ornamental grounds, Victorian walled garden, sunken grotto and stumpery. Mum's Carriage House stood adja- cent to Eric Pugsley's hideous scrapyard.

From afar, it all looked deceptively grand.

At the end of the ridge, the track narrowed to a steep path that wound down through sloping woodland where we stopped at a five-bar gate that marked one of the many entrances to Honeychurch Woods. The scent of bluebells was intoxicating. All I could see was a carpet of blue.

I remembered how Eric had scolded me once when I brought back a bunch of these beautiful flowers. As a townie, I had no idea that it was against the law to intentionally pick English bluebells. When he explained that it takes bluebell colonies between five and seven years to get established, I immediately understood my misdemeanour and felt really embarrassed.

We picked up the bridleway. It was a well-trodden short cut from the Hall to the village on foot or bicycle. The bridleway being wider, I was able to urge Duchess to move up alongside Olga so I could talk to her.

'How are the changes to the ballroom coming along?' I asked. 'Have you started rehearsing yet?'

'Frankly, the acoustics in the ballroom are only just about acceptable,' said Olga. 'I've had to cut the chamber orchestra down to the bare minimum. The dressing rooms are too far away from backstage, meaning that my artistes will have to wait in a dark passageway.'

'How lucky you were able to find somewhere so quickly,' I said pointedly.

'Lucia's suite is far too cold and not suitable accommodation for the greatest soprano of all time,' Olga grumbled on. 'And to answer your second question – we're hoping to have our first company rehearsal on Monday. Of course we've been rehearsing at Nightingales for weeks but now we have to adjust to a new space.'

I felt disappointed by Olga's lack of gratitude.

'I must say that the Hall is in the most appalling state,' she continued. 'Edith is clearly going senile. She is so forgetful.'

In my experience, Edith's mind was as sharp as a tack. She had to be the most energetic octogenarian I had ever met. She was definitely not forgetful.

I sprang to Edith's defence. 'I don't see Edith like that at all,' I said firmly. 'I don't think you realise what a huge thing it is for her to open the Hall to strangers.'

'For which she's being paid,' Olga declared. 'I'd hoped we could use the former music room as our green room but it appears that no one ever bothered to rebuild it.'

Olga had given me the perfect segue. 'I was so sorry to hear about the theatre fire. Thank heavens no one was hurt.'

'Yes,' said Olga. 'At least that's something to be grateful for.'

'Hopefully the building was insured,' I said.

'Unfortunately, it wasn't,' said Olga. 'Our treasurer had let the insurance policy lapse. We've lost a great deal of money.'

'Oh!' This wasn't what I'd expected to hear at all. What's more, Di had told me that Olga had appointed herself as treasurer, but I didn't let on that I knew.

'Was that Victor Mullins?' I said innocently. 'I heard about his car accident. He was my tax accountant.'

'Victor seems to have been everyone's tax accountant,' Olga replied.

'Well, that's because it's his profession,' I said.

'Unfortunately, Victor is no longer around to explain

himself,' she said. 'It's all very distressing. And of course his computer and all the financial records were lost in the fire. It's going to take a lot of time to untangle the mess he left behind.'

'But you're retiring,' I said lightly. 'So at least it won't be your problem.'

'I have my reputation to consider,' said Olga. 'I'm most displeased about the way that everything is being handled.'

'Perhaps it would have been better to have cancelled the production?' I ventured.

'Absolutely not,' said Olga. 'Not only is it the last opera I shall ever direct, Lucia is world-famous and a massive draw. Our ticket sales have gone through the roof and, besides, Lucia is paid whether she sings or not.'

This was very interesting. Perhaps I had misjudged Olga. She must be under a great deal of stress. It was her last hurrah and regardless of who was footing the bill, to have to pay Lucia for not singing at all would be humiliating. With no insurance and patrons demanding their money back, of course the show must go on.

'I hear the police suspect arson,' I said carefully. 'Do they have any leads?'

'Not only a lead. A suspect,' Olga declared. 'A disgruntled volunteer who I fired a week ago.'

My heart sank. Fiona hadn't mentioned anything about being fired.

'I didn't know you could fire volunteers,' I said.

'Fiona Reynolds's car was caught entering the theatre car park on CCTV on the night of the fire.'

'*CCTV*?' I was shocked. Was this the so-called witness that Reggie had mentioned?

'Are you sure it was Fiona driving?' I demanded.

'The police have the video footage,' said Olga. 'It caught her entering the Portakabin where she set about destroying some costumes first.'

Fiona *had* gone back after all. Fiona had lied to me.

'Was she seen entering the theatre?' I asked.

Olga didn't answer. I knew that she was becoming agitated because Jupiter had picked it up. The mare started snatching at her bit and throwing her head around. Olga sank down into the saddle and struck Jupiter with her whip.

I decided I didn't like Olga very much at all. In fact, if anyone was a diva it was the Russian Countess.

Suddenly Mr Chips came tearing back to find us, barking maniacally, before disappearing into the undergrowth. Then he was back again and then disappeared once more.

Edith drew rein. She pointed through the trees with her riding crop. 'He must have seen something.'

Mr Chips returned for a third time. He was definitely trying to tell us something.

'What on earth is wrong with that wretched dog?' Olga exclaimed.

'I'll go and find out.' I dismounted and had to tie Duchess to a tree. I knew that neither Edith nor Olga could get off because I'd never be able to get them back on again.

Tinkerbell was pawing at the ground and snorting. 'Can you smell something?' Edith asked anxiously.

I took a deep breath. 'It smells like burning.'

'I can't see smoke, can you?' said Edith.

I listened for any telltale crackles but could hear only the sound of the wind rustling through the trees. 'If there was a fire, wouldn't we know by now?'

Mr Chips returned again. He kept spinning in circles and nipped at my ankles before plunging into the undergrowth only to bounce back yet *again*!

I went after him, pushing my way through thick scrub, brambles and stinging nettles to emerge on to a footpath that showed signs of regular use. Mr Chips stopped to make sure I was following.

I'd only walked a few minutes when the little dog darted down a narrow animal track.

My heart began to thump and the hairs on my arms began to prickle. Something felt very wrong.

We came to a break in the trees where there was a clearing.

Mingled with last night's rainfall, the smell of burning was overpowering.

And then I saw the charred remains of what had definitely once been a campsite and, judging by the scorched and twisted metal poles, all that remained of a tent.

A blackened camp stove stood among the mounds of ash and broken glass.

I looked inside the tent and saw a charred collection of cooking utensils – a saucepan, a frying pan, teapot and mug, scorched baked bean tins, melted plastic bottles and random containers. A heat-warped truckle bed was piled high with blackened bedding.

And then I realised that it wasn't bedding at all.

It was a body.

I staggered backwards in shock, tripping over Mr Chips and landing heavily on the ground.

I didn't need to go any closer. I already knew who it was. It was Douglas Jones.

Chapter Thirteen

It took over an hour for help to come. Douglas's yurt was deep in Honeychurch Woods and only accessible on foot. Fortunately, I had been able to call Shawn from my mobile, but I left it up to Edith to explain exactly how he could find the clearing.

As I sat on a tree stump waiting for him, I couldn't help but wonder if in some way Douglas Jones's death was my fault. Had he used my fifty pounds to buy meths, got drunk and accidentally started the fire?

'Kat!' Shawn stepped into the clearing, closely followed by Clive.

'I thought you'd never get here,' I exclaimed and just fell into his arms.

He gently tipped my chin up and I saw concern in his dark brown eyes. 'Are you all right?'

I nodded but I found I wasn't all right at all. In fact, I was shaking. 'I feel cold.'

'You're in shock,' he said gently. 'Here, come and sit

down for a moment.' He led me back to the tree stump then took out a pocket-sized disposable heat-retaining foil blanket and undid the wrapper. He draped it around my shoulders.

'Since Edith and the Countess have taken your means of transport back to the Hall,' Shawn continued, 'I can take you home after we secure the area. Do you mind waiting?'

I nodded again. 'What do you think happened?'

'That's what we're going to find out,' said Shawn.

He and Clive donned disposable plastic gloves, produced a handful of Ziploc evidence bags and got to work.

While Clive inspected what remained of the tent, Shawn studied the campfire, sifting through the ash and making notes in his police notebook. Using a stick he began to pick out large shards of glass, pushing them into a separate pile.

I told him about Douglas coming to see me at the gatehouse the day before and that I'd bought a worthless suitcase from him for fifty pounds.'

'Fifty pounds! What was in the suitcase?'

'Just bric-a-brac and a Matryoshka – a Russian nesting doll,' I said. 'He told me that he bought it at a car boot sale.'

'Fifty pounds,' Shawn said again. 'That must have been some doll.'

'Trust me, it isn't,' I said. 'I suppose I felt sorry for him. Maybe if he hadn't had the money he wouldn't have bought the meths. Do you think he drank it? Maybe he accidentally knocked the stove over?'

'Well . . . the heavy rain certainly prevented the fire

from spreading.' Shawn paused for a moment. 'Douglas used a Trangia stove which uses methylated spirits and yes, he might have drunk some, but we won't know how much because it was vaporised by the heat. There'll be an autopsy, of course.' Shawn worked on the perimeter of the campsite and started poking around in the undergrowth. He disappeared behind an oak tree.

'Hello! What have we here, guv!' Clive called out.

Shawn's head popped out from behind the tree trunk.

Clive raised a spiked stick that held charred paperback novels. 'Someone reads Krystalle Storm,' he said with a chuckle. 'I wouldn't have thought Douglas was the type.'

Instinctively, my stomach clenched as it always did whenever my mother's secret pseudonym was mentioned.

Much to my confusion, Shawn beckoned for me to join him behind the tree.

'Speaking of Krystalle Storm,' Shawn said in a low voice, 'what do you think of that?'

'That' happened to be a red plastic milk crate containing empty gin bottles with ceramic flip-top lids. Each bottle bore the incriminating blue label of a sheep and the damning words 'Honeychurch Gin, Made by Iris'.

I didn't know what to say.

'Iris told me that she and Delia Evans only made a few bottles to give away at Christmas,' Shawn said sternly. 'It's now May.'

'Blimey!' said Clive as he joined us. He was holding a scorch-marked tin with the Oxo trademark. 'Those bottles are expensive. The missis makes sloe gin at Christmas and they're about two pounds each, although if you buy them on Amazon, you can—'

'Thank you, Clive,' Shawn cut in. He thought for a moment. 'What does Douglas do with the empty bottles? Return them to Iris?'

'I have no idea,' I said. And I really didn't.

'Here,' Clive said, handing him the tin. 'Take a look.'

Shawn removed the lid. Inside was a roll of banknotes that had escaped the fire. Shawn tipped them out, flattened the roll and counted.

I didn't draw breath. A peculiar feeling began to grow in my stomach. A thousand things were racing through my mind, primarily the Krystalle Storm novels, the empty gin bottles in the same kind of red plastic milk crate that I'd spied in Mum's kitchen only yesterday, and the money – especially the money.

'Three hundred and seventy-seven pounds and a handful of change,' Shawn declared. 'Do you remember what denomination you gave him?'

'Five ten-pound notes,' I said. 'But why on earth did he tell me he was broke? I believed him!'

'Why indeed?' Shawn said drily. 'Where do you think he got all this money from?'

I shrugged but inside my mind was spinning. Had Douglas found out who Mum really was and decided to blackmail her?

'Anything else, Clive?' Shawn asked.

'Well . . . it looks like Douglas was holding his mobile

phone,' said Clive. 'But – apologies to you, Kat – I wouldn't be able to get it out unless I broke his fingers.'

'A mobile, eh?' Shawn mused. 'Probably a pay-as-you-go.' He looked at me. 'It'll be interesting to see who Douglas liked to call.'

There was a rustle and a loud cough and suddenly Rupert burst into the clearing brandishing an envelope. He stopped in shock. 'Good God, what on earth happened here?'

'Douglas Jones is dead, milord,' said Shawn.

Clive pointed to the burnt-out tent. 'What remains of him is over there.'

'Well, that saves me the trouble of evicting him.' Rupert waved the envelope again. 'An eviction notice with immediate effect.'

'Milord!' Shawn gasped. I was shocked at Rupert's callousness too.

'Don't look at me like that.' Rupert was defiant. 'I spoke to Jones last week and he was downright rude. He claimed this was common land but that is not the case. Just because there is a public footpath through my woods does not give anyone free licence to pitch a tent.'

'It's actually a yurt, milord,' said Clive. 'Or rather, it *was*.'

'Is that why you're here?' Shawn asked.

'I saw your police car parked by the gate and assumed you'd got my message,' said Rupert.

'Message, milord?' Shawn looked worried.

'I left a message on your mobile this morning requesting

assistance to serve this eviction notice in case Jones turned violent.'

'He has – or should I say *had* – got a temper,' Clive agreed.

Shawn pulled out his mobile and seemed to be scrolling through his call list. 'Ah yes, I see. A missed call but no number was listed.'

'I don't list my number,' said Rupert.

Shawn regarded Rupert with curiosity. 'But you knew exactly where to find Douglas Jones's camp?'

'Of course I knew,' said Rupert. 'I followed him here last week on foot. Why do you ask?'

'We've yet to establish whether the fire was an accident or deliberate,' said Shawn.

'Deliberate!' Rupert and I chorused.

'I can think of a lot of people who would like him out of the way,' Rupert went on. 'But . . . surely . . . are you talking . . . *murder*?'

'We'll know more after the autopsy,' said Shawn.

'Wretched family,' Rupert said. 'Father ordered the lot of them off our land years ago. Douglas Jones had some damn cheek.'

'And what about Julie?' Shawn asked quietly.

Rupert looked blank. 'Who?'

'Julie Jones,' said Shawn.

'He means Lucia Lombardi,' Clive chimed in. 'You know, the greatest soprano of all time.'

Rupert's jaw dropped in amazement. 'I'm sorry? What? I mean . . . are you telling me that Julie Jones is Lucia *Lombardi*?'

I looked at him in astonishment. Even Shawn had to stifle a cry of surprise.

Had Rupert seriously no idea that Lucia Lombardi had been born on the estate? My mother always said that men never listen. It would seem that she was right.

'Good grief! Julie Jones is Lucia whatever her name is.' Rupert still seemed in shock. 'Are you quite certain?'

'When did you last see the deceased, milord?' Shawn asked.

'I told you. Last week,' he said. 'Wait – are you *mad*? Do you think I would risk setting fire to my own woods?'

'It rained heavily last night, milord,' said Shawn. 'So that wouldn't have happened.'

'The fire was last night, was it?' Rupert said. 'Well, you can ask my wife. I was home with her all evening.'

'I'll need to stay here a little longer,' said Shawn. 'Would you mind running Kat back to the Hall, milord?'

'I'd appreciate a lift, thank you,' I said.

'Kat, a word?' Shawn nodded for me to step out of earshot. As we did, I caught a snatch of Rupert asking Clive if *he* had known Lucia Lombardi's real identity.

'I assume you know that we've arrested Fiona Reynolds in connection with the fire at Nightingales Theatre,' Shawn said.

My stomach turned over. Of course I knew. I prayed that he wasn't going to question me right here, right now.

'Yes, I heard,' I said.

'Fiona mentioned that you had dinner with her that night,' he said. 'So I'll need a statement from you. Speaking of dinner, there is something else I need to discuss with you. I thought we could meet tonight.'

Great. I could guarantee it concerned my mother and the empty gin bottles and Krystalle Storm.

'Are you sure you'll be able to get away?' I said. 'We could make it another time. Really.' I gestured aimlessly to the campsite. 'Isn't this more important?'

Shawn cocked his head. 'In this instance, no.'

'Then that will be lovely,' I lied.

'But you're right,' he said. 'I am working on a couple of cases at the moment so why don't we meet at the Royal Castle Hotel at seven thirty in case something comes up and I get called away.'

It was only when I followed Rupert back to his car that my eye was drawn to a splash of colour and something shiny sparkling in a sudden shaft of sunshine at the base of a tree.

I hung back to take a closer look. 'I'll catch you up in a minute,' I called out to Rupert but he didn't seem to hear and plunged on ahead.

Just a few yards off the beaten track was an old oak. Nestled among the gnarled roots were freshly picked wood columbines and pink harebells, a shiny piece of slate and what looked like a brass curtain ring. When I took a closer look the newer items seemed to have been placed on top of dirty crushed shells, several tarnished marbles, a grimy plastic ring from a cracker and dead pine needles.

Was this Lucia's fairy ring? Had she been to visit Douglas?

A gust of wind sent the leaves rustling through the trees once more and I was struck by a dreadful sense of foreboding.

I raced to catch up with Rupert. I needed to get back to Honeychurch Hall immediately.

I absolutely had to talk to my mother.

Chapter Fourteen

'He's dead?' Mum gasped. 'Douglas Jones is *dead*?'

My mother had not been happy to see me. I had found her in her writing room in the converted piggery and after I'd tapped out our secret code on the door she had reluctantly let me in.

'Of course I'm sorry he's dead, don't get me wrong, but I honestly don't have time for this right now,' she went on. 'And I can't see what it can possibly have to do with me.'

'Well, let's hope you're right and it has nothing to do with you,' I said. 'But we really need to talk. You could be in real trouble. Tea?'

'You sound so serious,' said Mum. 'Should we have something a little stronger? What's the time?'

I ignored her and headed for the little mini-kitchen area she'd set up in a corner.

Mum didn't speak as we waited for the kettle to boil. I scanned the small room, impressed with everything my mother had accomplished in her writing life. She'd done it all by herself and with no encouragement from anyone, simply because Dad and I just hadn't known.

Floor-to-ceiling custom-made bookshelves covered one wall, displaying all her writing awards. Mum's first-edition books ran for entire shelves, and I knew that she had boxes of copies up in the attic in the Carriage House, too.

A grey metal filing cabinet five drawers high stood in one corner. In another, a standard lamp, Dad's battered wingback chair and a hexagonal table piled with magazines. My father's Olivetti typewriter sat on a walnut partners' desk beneath a window that looked out on the forest beyond, which was currently carpeted in bluebells. I thought again of the wild flowers left at the fairy ring in Honeychurch Woods.

A corkboard stretched the length of another wall, showing the official Honeychurch family. The Earl of Grenville title had been passed down the male line until Edith's brother, the 13th Earl, was killed in a romantic duel in 1959. It was Edward, an American cousin, who then inherited the Earldom and persuaded a fiercely independent Edith to marry him. Rupert, the current Earl, was born soon afterwards. Edith's husband died in 1990. She'd been a widow for more than three decades.

I noticed that Mum was working on another family tree and had labelled it 'Below Stairs'.

I made two mugs of tea – no coronation china in here – and grabbed an open packet of digestive biscuits. In all the upset I'd forgotten to eat lunch.

We took our tea to the sofa in front of the wood-burning stove.

'Right,' I said, 'you'd better start talking.'

Mum cleared her throat. 'I haven't been anywhere near Honeychurch Woods.'

'I didn't mention where Douglas Jones died, Mum,' I said wearily.

My mother reddened and shrugged. 'Well, I assume it was in the woods because that's where Douglas lived. What happened? Did he have a stroke?'

'No, Mother,' I said. 'Douglas's yurt burned to the ground with him inside. I saw the body. It was horrible.'

'That must have been awful.' Mum reached over and patted my knee. 'I'm so sorry, darling.' She took a sip of tea. Either my mother was an excellent actress – which was possible – and really didn't know what had happened to Douglas or she did and she didn't care.

'Aren't you curious?' I said. 'Don't you want to know how his yurt burned down?'

'Not really.' Mum picked up a digestive biscuit and took a nibble.

'Mum,' I said, 'Shawn thinks the fire might have been deliberate and he will be asking you some questions about your, um . . . friendship with Douglas.'

'*Me?*' Mum's eyes widened. 'Whatever for? I barely know the man.'

Exasperated, I took her mug of tea away and set it on the coffee table in front of us.

'Pay attention. This is important,' I said. 'Shawn found a plastic crate full of empty gin bottles – *your* gin bottles – at the campsite.'

'Oh,' said Mum. 'Was Shawn cross?'

I regarded my mother with astonishment. 'Yes. Extremely. But that is not the point. Shawn implied that you might have had something to do with Douglas's death.'

'But that's ridiculous! Of course I didn't.'

'Can you prove otherwise?' I demanded.

'Fine.' Mum rolled her eyes. 'Douglas and I had an arrangement. He would return the bottles and I would give him some money. Have you any idea how much those bottles cost?'

'As a matter of fact, I do,' I said.

'I gave him fifty pence for every bottle he returned.'

I thought back to the roll of banknotes in Douglas's Oxo tin. There was no way that he could have returned that many bottles – or was there? Was my mother's gin production that huge? The dread I'd felt earlier increased.

'I'm sorry but I don't think you're telling me everything,' I said.

'Douglas was a horrible little man,' Mum went on. 'He told me to raise the price to a pound or he'd report me to the police. But I refused.'

'Oh, Mum!' I wailed. 'Does anyone else know about your arrangement?'

'Of course not!'

I thought for a moment. 'But . . . how did Douglas return the bottles to you?' I demanded. 'He doesn't have a car. I can't see him carrying that crate along Cavalier Lane.'

Mum picked her mug back up and took a sip.

And then I remembered the pay-as-you-go phone that

Douglas had been clasping in his hand when he died and which, at this very moment, was being studied by some very clever techno-savvy forensics.

'The phone,' I said. 'Douglas had a mobile phone. Did *you* buy it for him?'

Mum looked sheepish. 'It's a burner— Oh! Sorry. No pun intended.'

'Not funny,' I said coldly. 'Well, the police have that phone now and I can guarantee that your number will be on it. They'll realise that you met him and gave him the money.'

'I'm not breaking the law,' Mum said hotly. 'It's not a crime to recycle the bottles.'

'It's not just about the bottles,' I said. 'It's also about Krystalle Storm.'

'What about her?' said Mum.

'Douglas Jones had a few of your novels in his yurt.'

'Really? Well I never,' said Mum. 'Which ones?'

'It doesn't matter which ones!' I said exasperated. 'Was Douglas Jones blackmailing you, because if he was, you need to tell Shawn straight away.'

'Oh.' Mum ate a whole biscuit.

'Was he?' I demanded.

My mother just shrugged, which infuriated me even more.

Yet again I recalled my father's last words before he died – and the only reason why I had decided to stay in Devon. I had promised to keep an eye on my mother. I had assumed it was because she had failing health – especially as I had grown up believing that her migraines were indications of a terminal disease – but it was increasingly obvious that someone needed to keep her out of trouble and that some-one was me.

'You've *got* to tell Shawn, Mum!' I said. 'And sooner rather than later.'

'All right,' she said grudgingly. 'But after I turn in my manuscript. And you were right that I should change the title. I'm going with *Dangerous*. Do you think that little Italian might be willing to pose for my cover?'

'Sometimes I think I'm talking to a brick wall.' I gave a heavy sigh and got to my feet. 'And for the record, Rupert turned up at the campsite and he had no idea that Lucia Lombardi is Julie Jones. No idea whatsoever. So whatever malicious rumours your friend Delia is spreading about the two of them having a fling when he was underage, they are completely unfounded.'

'Ah,' said Mum. 'I thought as much. Come and take a look at this.'

Mum got up, grabbed a pen and a block of Post-its from her desk and beckoned for me to join her by the corkboard.

'You did hear me about Shawn, didn't you?' I persisted.

'Yes, yes, of course I did,' Mum said dismissively. 'Now see here. This is the below-stairs family tree.'

I studied the inter-linking branches of the five main families that had worked on the estate for centuries – Pugsley, Banks, Stark, Cropper and the infamous Jones clan.

'Rupert can be a bit thick,' said Mum, 'but he would have been around fourteen years old when Julie was still living here. Even so . . . maybe he'd like an older woman to show him the ropes, but I don't think so.' Mum jabbed her pen at the Jones branch of the family tree. 'But then Rupert goes on to marry Julie's niece Kelly, two decades his junior, who was poisoned. Remember her?'

I vaguely remembered the story but Kelly's demise had happened years before Mum and I moved to the area.

'I'm telling you,' I said, 'Rupert hadn't a clue as to who Julie was. If Julie had shown him the ropes, wouldn't he have remembered?'

'Exactly my point!' Mum exclaimed. 'I think Julie Jones was having a fling with the fourteenth Earl of Grenville – Edith's husband!'

'But . . . he would have been far too old for her,' I said.

'The fourteenth Earl – that's the American chappy, Edward Rupert – would have been about twenty-five to thirty years Julie's senior,' said Mum, warming to her theme. 'I mean, look at Michael Douglas and Catherine Zeta-Jones? Their gap is twenty-five years and they're still together.'

'I don't know, Mum.' I was doubtful. 'Edith would never have had her back here if she knew.'

'But maybe her ladyship never found out? Or maybe she just assumed it was Rupert?'

I shook my head. 'No. And let's not forget the music-room fire.'

Mum gave a gasp. 'Fire!' Her eyes widened. 'Don't you think there's a recurring theme here?'

'What do you mean?'

'The music-room fire, the theatre was set on fire and Douglas's yurt . . .' she said. 'I don't believe in coincidences, do you?'

'Olga told me that the insurance policy on the theatre had lapsed,' I said. 'Victor had forgotten to renew it.'

'Victor? Our little Victor?' Mum shook her head vehemently. 'He did love my gin. But no, Victor would never do that. He was extremely conscientious. All those questions he asked me about any other income. He reminded me of your father – very much a dot all the i's and cross all the t's kind of man.'

Which made it all the more ironic that Dad had been a tax inspector. In fact, my parents had got together when he was actually auditing the Bushman Travelling Fair and Boxing Emporium. I had told Mum many times that she needed to come clean but still her thousands and thousands of pounds languished in a bank in the Channel Islands.

'Well, right now, Fiona is being blamed for the fire.' I went on to tell Mum about Fiona's arrest and how she had asked me to give her an alibi.

'You can't do that, darling,' said Mum. 'Especially not with Shawn.'

'I wasn't going to,' I said. 'And don't change the subject. We're talking about you.'

'I wasn't. You were.'

I headed for the door. 'Well . . . looking on the bright side, you seem a lot more cheerful now. At least this is distracting you from Reynard.'

'Yes,' Mum said rather too brightly. 'I'm completely over him. When I washed my hair I washed him right out. Wait – Kat, before you go. Would you . . . will you . . .?'

I gave a heavy sigh. 'Why do I think you're going to ask me a favour?'

'Just find out what else Shawn knows before I phone him and commit perjury.'

'Oh God,' I groaned. 'Fine. I'm meeting him tonight for dinner. I'll see what he has to say.'

Chapter Fifteen

The Royal Castle Hotel was one of my favourite places in Dartmouth.

Built in the 1600s, the building had a white castellated façade and overlooked the harbour. Inside there was ancient panelling and beams of hand-hewn timber reputedly salvaged from the wreck of a Spanish Armada vessel.

Shawn was already seated in the restaurant but he stood up when I walked in. He looked very nice in a dark green jacket and an open-necked shirt. I rarely saw him without a tie, which meant, just maybe, that this was going to be a social occasion after all.

But moments later I sensed something was amiss. Shawn wouldn't quite look me in the eye. And then I saw the bunch of daffodils wrapped in brown paper and tied with a yellow bow sitting on my chair. I immediately thought of Reynard's 'confused-need-a-space' speech to my mother the day before.

Shawn must have seen something in my expression. 'Don't you like daffodils?'

'Yes,' I said. 'They're beautiful but . . . what's going on? It's not my birthday. It's not your birthday. Are we celebrating something?'

I was aware of my heart thumping in my chest. Something felt wrong. I should have guessed. When Shawn came back from London I thought that he had changed towards me and it seemed I was right.

From the table behind us I heard a female voice say, 'Isn't that Kat Stanford? You know, the *Fakes & Treasures* girl?' I didn't turn around but I didn't need to. I could feel her eyes boring into the back of my head.

'And he's given her daffodils,' her friend chimed in. 'Bit cheap, if you ask me. Probably picked them by the roadside.' They gave a nasty laugh.

I placed the daffodils under my chair.

'I didn't,' said Shawn.

'Didn't what?' I said.

'Pick them by the roadside,' he said. 'But I admit I rushed into Morrison's and that was all they had so late in the day.'

'It's the thought that counts,' I said. 'I love daffodils. They remind me of my dad.'

An uncomfortable silence fell between us.

Fortunately the young waitress in tight black leggings and sporting the nametag 'Carol' came over to give us our menus.

Shawn beamed at her and she smiled back. I felt an unexpected twinge of jealousy. What was wrong with me? Ever since Shawn and I had met I'd felt so confident in his affections, despite a few false starts. I knew I sounded conceited but it had never occurred to me that he would lose interest in me first. It served me right.

Carol asked what we'd like to drink. I knew I'd be driving so I just ordered a glass of house white wine. Shawn had a Perrier.

'A Perrier?' I said. 'No wine?'

'I'm on call.' And, as if to prove a point, he brought out his iPhone and set it face up on the table.

'Why don't we leave it for this evening?' I said. 'I can tell that you're distracted, especially with all that distressing business with Douglas.'

'Did you talk to your mother?' Shawn said.

'She's going to call you first thing in the morning.' I stared blindly at the menu. 'Gosh. This all looks very yummy.'

'You're reading it upside down,' Shawn said gently.

'Oh.' I turned it right side up and gave a nervous smile. 'It looks even yummier this way around.'

'I do need to ask you a few questions about Fiona Reynolds,' he said. 'But not tonight. I'll come by sometime tomorrow. Tonight . . . well . . . tonight I really need to talk to you about something important.'

So this was it. Shawn was going to break up with me. My mother's conversation with Reynard flashed through my mind and how she dealt with his rejection with such dignity and disdain. I would do the same.

Carol returned with my wine. I downed half a glass straight away.

Shawn seemed startled. He leaned in. 'Are you all right?'

I desperately didn't want to talk about 'us'. I also didn't want to talk about Fiona and I definitely didn't want to talk about my mother. I had this wild urge to dash to the loo and climb out of the window and run away.

'Yes, fine,' I said brightly. 'It's Douglas Jones. I can't stop thinking about him.' What on earth had possessed me to bring up the one topic I wanted to avoid?

Shawn sat back in his chair. 'We'll get a formal report, of course,' he said briskly, 'but I'm afraid my suspicions have been confirmed. He was murdered.'

'That's terrible,' I whispered. 'But I know this is nothing to do with my mother. She wouldn't hurt a fly.'

'Since it seems that you want to know, I'll tell you,' said Shawn. 'Douglas Jones was alive during the fire due to the presence of carbon monoxide in his blood, soot in his airways and evidence of scorching below the vocal cords.'

'Oh gosh. That's terrible,' I said again. 'Perhaps he was drunk and fell asleep? Maybe he left the campfire burning and a gust of wind blew an ember on to the canvas—'

'Or he deliberately hit himself over the head with a jeroboam,' said Shawn.

'*What*?' I exclaimed.

'You really want to talk about this now?' Shawn said.

'Yes, I do.'

'We found a large piece of glass embedded in his skull.' Shawn said the word *skull* with relish. 'Further inspection showed that the broken glass salvaged from the campfire all came from the same object. I believe a bottle of that size is called a jeroboam. Not a common sight.'

It was over. Mum was screwed. I distinctly remember that she and Delia had made an extra large bottle of Honeychurch Gin for the silent auction in December.

'We have reason to believe that the glass shard retrieved from Douglas's skull came from the same bottle that was discovered in the ashes in the campfire,' said Shawn. 'We have deduced that he was knocked out, therefore giving the perpetrator time to set a fire to make it look like it was an accident.'

Carol chose that moment to return to take our order. She chattered on about the specials but I couldn't possibly eat anything. Shawn, however, declared he was starving. When I told him to order for me he didn't even ask for my preferences, but picked one of my favourites – the West Country Beef Sirloin with baby carrots.

'Just because my mother's gin bottles were found at the scene doesn't mean—'

'And her phone number was programmed into Douglas's mobile,' said Shawn.

'It would have been,' I said quickly. 'My mother gave Douglas money for returning the empty bottles. As Clive pointed out, they get expensive.'

'Really? All three hundred and seventy-seven pounds?' said Shawn. 'That's a lot of bottles.'

'Fifty pounds of that would have been mine,' I pointed out. 'Minus the meths, I suppose.'

A flicker of annoyance crossed Shawn's face. 'And when were you planning on telling me about your mother's arrangement with Douglas Jones?'

'It's not for me to tell you,' I said. 'I think you're being unfair.'

'Unfair?' Shawn stiffened. 'I'm being *unfair*?' Shawn leaned across the table, clearly annoyed. 'Your mother is an international bestselling author and it's my belief that Douglas Jones found her out.'

'Because he had a few books in his yurt?' I scoffed, but deep down I feared the same thing, too. 'You do know that you can buy her books in the community shop.'

'Yes, I know you can,' said Shawn. 'But I think he was blackmailing her.'

'My mother is definitely not someone who would succumb to blackmail,' I protested.

'Of course she wouldn't,' said Shawn. 'She'd put a stop to it one way or another. She's got far too much to lose.'

'That's not what I meant!' My voice was louder than I intended and unfortunately at that moment, the Frank Sinatra compilation in the background stopped playing and there was an unexpected lull in the conversations coming from the surrounding tables. I felt that everyone was looking at us. They probably were.

'Loyalty,' said Shawn, 'is a very commendable quality, but not when you are protecting someone for . . . for . . .'

'For *what*?' I hissed. 'Go on. Say it.'

'I really didn't want to have this conversation tonight and I definitely didn't want to have it with you,' said Shawn.

'I've kept her secret, but sooner or later someone will find out. I wouldn't want to go to HMRC.'

I was appalled. 'Now who is using blackmail!'

Shawn reddened and started rearranging the cloth napkin on his lap. We fell into an excruciating silence. I was in a total panic and downed the rest of my wine. Had my mother killed Douglas? Not deliberately, of course, but it was distinctly possible that there had been some kind of scuffle.

Finally, Shawn took a deep breath. 'Look, I'm sorry. Sometimes it's hard for me to switch off. It was very unprofessional of me to put you in such a terrible position. Of course you are going to protect your mother. I have to remind myself that you aren't Iris.' He reached for my hand across the table and I let him take it. 'Will you forgive me?'

'I'm sorry too,' I said. 'It's been a horrible day.' But the knot in my stomach was growing by the second.

At that moment our food arrived, saving us both from saying anything more. It looked delicious but I wasn't hungry. Shawn ordered me another glass of wine, which I shouldn't really have accepted given that I was driving.

'You can mix it with some of my Perrier,' he said.

Shawn tucked into his fish voraciously. I always marvelled at how men could just change the subject and act as if we hadn't had one of the most harrowing conversations of my life. My mother said that men were able to put their emotions into boxes and I was beginning to see that she was right. When Shawn downed his knife and fork, he didn't even seem to notice that I had barely eaten.

He cleared his throat. 'Can we start the evening again?'

'Um. Yes. Okay,' I said.

'You look beautiful tonight.' Shawn gazed into my eyes. 'You are very special to me, Kat, and I'm sure you know how I feel about you.'

Good grief. Seriously? Did he really think I could flip a switch? Unless . . . oh no! My poor stomach lurched again. I'd thought that Shawn was going to break up with me but what if it was the complete opposite! Was he going to *propose*?

Shawn reached across and took my hand in his. 'I feel I owe you an explanation.'

'Of course you don't,' I said quickly.

He laughed. 'You don't know what I'm going to say!'

I picked up my wine glass with my free hand and took a big gulp. 'This wine is so good!'

'Kat! I'm trying to talk to you!' Shawn said, exasperated. 'Promise that you'll hear me out before you say anything?'

I nodded. 'Okay.'

'When I was on that course in London I realised that things needed to change,' he said. 'There are too many memories here for me.'

I felt an unexpected surge of anger. *Here we go yet again.* Now he's going to play the Helen card. Why did Shawn constantly keep me off-balance?

'I feel like I've not been completely honest with you,' Shawn went on. 'Ever since the incident at Larcombe quarry.'

'When you nearly drowned,' I reminded him. And then,

with a pang, I thought of the Christmas that had followed. It had been so magical. I had spent time with the twins and then Shawn had gone off on his wretched course to London and everything had changed. It was obvious. The enforced break had given him time to think about us and he must have realised he'd made a mistake. I'd been so sure that the feeling was mutual. And right now I was so confused.

'I knew that something had made you change your mind towards me, Shawn,' I said quietly. 'I could sense it. The thing is, I'll never be Helen—'

'Helen? This isn't about Helen, Kat.' Shawn turned pink. He suddenly seemed nervous. He took a deep breath. 'I've put in for a transfer to the Met to work in counter terrorism.'

I wasn't sure if I had heard him properly. A transfer? To the Met? In London?

I snatched my hand away and put them both on my lap out of reach.

So he was breaking up with me after all. What a fool I'd been.

'You're right,' Shawn ran on quickly. 'I *had* withdrawn from you because I wasn't sure how things were between us. I'd put you in a box. I admit it.'

My mother was right about boxes.

'So you're leaving Devon,' I said flatly. 'What about the twins? What about your mother-in-law? She'll miss her grandkids terribly.'

'That decision was a heavy one to make,' he agreed.

I could feel my anger rising again.

'But if they need to change schools, now is the best time for it to happen,' he said. 'Lizzie is prepared to move with us.'

'And when are you planning on leaving?' I said coldly.

'In the summer,' said Shawn. 'They'll start their new school in September.'

To my dismay, I felt a lump in my throat. Good grief. I hoped I wasn't going to cry. 'Why didn't you tell me you were thinking about doing this?' I whispered. 'What about . . . what about us?'

'I'm very fond of you, you know that.' Shawn sought a hand but then realised both were staying firmly on my lap. 'But you blow hot and cold.'

I was incredulous. '*I* blow hot and cold! It's *you* that blows hot and cold!'

Shawn seemed genuinely surprised. 'I've always felt I was your back-up plan.'

'That's not true!' I protested.

'Isn't it?' Shawn's voice was gentle. 'First, I have to watch you going out with Lavinia's idiotic brother—'

'Piers Carew pursued me,' I said.

'And you seemed happy to let him do that.'

I remembered how mortified I'd been when the two men had had a schoolboy punch-up outside Jane's Cottage, breaking all my garden furniture in the process.

'And if I remember correctly,' Shawn went on, 'you said you never wanted to see me after that.'

'I didn't say never; I didn't want to see either of you,' I said. 'I needed to get my head straight.'

'Let's see,' said Shawn. 'And then there was that arrogant twit. The helicopter pilot.'

'Guy Evans,' I said.

'Have you any idea how jealous I felt seeing you two together?' Shawn said. 'Hearing all the comments from the locals in the pub about what you were up to?'

'Nothing physical ever happened with either Piers or Guy,' I insisted and I wanted to add, *Or with you*!

'I don't care if it did or if it didn't,' he said. 'That's irrelevant. The point is you were considering giving your heart to them.'

'Now who's being unfair!' I exclaimed. 'You know how I feel about you.'

'Do I?' Shawn folded his arms. 'That's the thing, Kat, it's only when you think you're going to lose me that you get interested.'

Carol returned with the dessert menus.

'Can you come back in a few minutes?' Shawn asked and she went away.

I was upset and incredibly confused. The problem was that Shawn's comments had hit a nerve. Perhaps he was right.

'You've taught me so much,' Shawn went on. 'And I'm grateful for that. When I met you I was still unable to move on from Helen. She was the love of my life—'

'I know Helen was the love of your life,' I snapped. 'All this time I've felt I've been competing with *Helen*. I've held back because of *Helen*.'

Shawn frowned. 'But how can she be a threat to you?'

My jaw dropped. 'Seriously? Her memory is a threat.

All the time! She's always there. In fact, she's here right now because we're talking about her!'

'You're asking me to forget the mother of my children?' Shawn seemed distressed.

'No!' I was exasperated. 'Of course not. I don't want you to forget her in any way at all. That's what's so difficult for me. One of the things that I love about you is your loyalty.'

'So you *do* love me?'

'I didn't actually mean it quite that way,' I said quickly and then realised that I had just dug my own grave. 'Or maybe I do. I don't know.'

Shawn gave me a wry smile. 'And that's the thing, Kat. You just don't.'

I blinked back tears. How had this happened between us? Why hadn't I told him how I really felt before?

'I'll need some time to adjust to my new role,' he said crisply. 'It's going to be very different. We'll see how things go. I'll still be down in Devon occasionally. You make regular trips to London anyway, don't you? And you still have your flat in Putney.'

I couldn't believe it. I just hadn't seen this coming at all.

'And if things work out . . .' He leaned in and sought a hand again but they stayed where they were in my lap. 'You can come and join me and the twins.'

'I don't want to move back to London,' I said coldly. 'I like it here.'

'Well then . . .' Shawn sat back in his chair, his face etched with disappointment. 'I didn't realise. I thought you'd be excited about London.'

'Excited about *London*?' I looked at him with incredulity. 'Why would I want to move back to London? You just don't know me at all. Excuse me.' I grabbed my tote bag and got up from the table, accidentally treading on the daffodils in the process.

'For heaven's sake! *Katherine*, sit down,' Shawn hissed. 'Now you're being childish. And people are looking. Don't create a scene.'

The two women on the table behind stared at me open-mouthed. I had no doubt whatsoever that they had heard every word.

'I hope you enjoyed the show,' I said to them and made a beeline for the Ladies.

Chapter Sixteen

I looked at my reflection in the mirror above the basin. Green eyes stared out of a pale face surrounded by a mane of unruly chestnut hair.

What had just happened out there? Was my relationship with Shawn over?

Not once had I thought that Shawn would move away. I'd always wanted a family. I adored Shawn's twins and had only recently allowed myself the fantasy of being a surrogate mother to them.

Shawn was right. I did blow hot and cold – at first, because I had been cautious following the end of my relationship with David, but also out of respect for Shawn's feelings for Helen. I hadn't wanted to compete with a dead wife. I'd had to compete with a live one, even though David and Trudi had been estranged.

True, it must have been hard for Shawn to see me with other boyfriends, but he could have spoken up. He'd never seemed that bothered.

I was deeply hurt and more disappointed than I thought I would be, but I couldn't get away from the fact that I should have seen this coming. I should have asked questions. I'd just assumed too much. He was a good man, a good father. He deserved a good life and if he wanted a big career in London, I should wish him well and let him go.

I splashed my face with water. He hadn't left yet. It wasn't until the end of the summer. I could either sulk and lose him for ever or just be the best I could possibly be. But most of all I had to be certain that a life with Shawn and his boys was what I really wanted. Could I move back to London? Could I ever leave my mother to her own devices?

I wondered what Dear Amanda would make of all this.

I reapplied my lipstick and pinched my cheeks to bring back some colour, then I returned to our table. To my dismay, Shawn's chair was empty.

'He's gone, Kat luv,' said the woman on the adjacent table. This time I looked at her. She had brassy hair and piggy eyes.

'Yeah,' her friend agreed. 'Bad luck. But never mind: plenty more fish in the sea.'

The brassy woman took out her iPhone. 'Mind if I take a photo?'

'Yes, I do mind,' I said, but it was too late. She already had. It was all I could do not to snatch the phone away and hurl it out of the window, but Carol the waitress saved me.

She appeared with a note and handed it over. 'Shawn asked me to give you this.'

'Thank you. The bill? I need to settle—' I fumbled in my tote bag for my purse. 'I'm not sure if he—'

'He already paid,' said Carol. 'He told me he knew you had your car.' Spying my untouched meal she added, 'You didn't like your steak?'

'I'm not feeling well,' I lied. 'There's nothing wrong with the food at all.'

'She's lovesick,' the brassy woman called out. 'Aw. Sad Kat.'

'Excuse me,' I said to the waitress and fled.

I sat in my car for a good five minutes, desperately trying not to cry. I *had* to get a grip. These tears couldn't just be to do with Shawn, could they?

I was dealing with so many things at the moment: my mother's lies, Fiona Reynolds's lies and then the horror of finding Douglas's dead body.

Shawn obviously didn't understand me at all – or I him. Maybe this was for the best.

With a heavy heart, I pulled the note out of my handbag and braced myself for a goodbye letter but it wasn't what I expected at all.

> *Break-in at your gatehouse. See you there.*
> *Shawn x*

My mind was racing as I sped home. The Hall had seen a constant stream of activity, with all the stage trucks coming and going. Yes, I had installed a high-tech burglar alarm that was connected directly to the police station but, even so, there would be precious minutes wasted before a

response of any kind could get there. That would give a
burglar plenty of time to snatch and grab my most expensive stock, nicely displayed in plain sight.

Could the evening get any worse?

The drive back from Dartmouth seemed to take for ever
but soon I saw blue lights flashing on the brow of the hill,
lighting up the night sky. Both the west and east gatehouse
lights were ablaze. There were two cars parked outside –
Clive's panda and Shawn's silver run-around.

I hurried inside just as my mother emerged from the
galley kitchen holding two mugs of steaming-hot liquid.
'Tea, boys?'

'Mum!' I exclaimed. 'What on earth are you doing here?
I didn't see your car outside.' I took in her appearance. 'And
why are you dressed like that?'

My mother looked glamorous in a nice cream coat from
Marks & Spencer. I caught a glimpse of cleavage in a low
V-necked jersey top. She was wearing tights and the same
stilettos that she'd worn on Wednesday at the Hall.

'I disabled the alarm. You gave me a set of keys, darling.'
Mum handed the mugs to Shawn and Clive, who were
inspecting the locks on the windows.

'Your mother managed to startle the intruder,' Shawn
said, showing no indication of our earlier conversation. He
was in full-on business mode. He'd even put on a tie. 'It
doesn't seem that anything has been taken but only you can
be the judge of that.'

I knew every inch of my showroom and every item on
every shelf and in every display cabinet. I opened and

closed the drawers on my desk, checking the contents. My laptop hadn't been taken and the safe was still locked. It had a combination that was high-tech and definitely hadn't been tampered with.

To my relief, there seemed to be nothing missing at all.

'And there was no sign of a forced entry in the east gatehouse,' said Clive.

'Good, so no harm done,' Mum said.

'But, where *is* your car, Mum?' I asked her. 'Surely you didn't walk here at this time of night? And in those shoes?'

'I left it in the lane,' Mum said. 'I was just passing by.'

'I didn't see it in the lane,' I said.

'Your mother was very foolish to try to stop the intruder,' said Shawn. 'But it's just as well that she did.'

'You mean you saw someone?' I said sharply.

'I heard the alarm go off,' said Mum.

My suspicion deepened. 'You heard the alarm when you were driving by?'

'It's very loud.' Mum smiled and showed too many teeth: a dead giveaway that she was up to something.

'The intruder seems to have broken in through the rear toilet window,' Clive put in.

'I don't have an alarm in there,' I said. 'But I have motion detectors—'

'Which were tripped when the intruder entered the showroom,' said Shawn. 'The back door was open, indicating that the intruder let him or herself out that way.'

I thought for a moment. 'The toilet window is tiny. Someone very small would have had to have squeezed in through there.'

'Someone small obviously did,' said Shawn.

'There have been so many people roaming around the estate,' Mum went on. 'Delia said that her ladyship has been very worried about the silver.'

'Did you see anyone walking along the lanes earlier, Iris?' Shawn's notebook was out and his pen was poised. 'Or an unfamiliar car?'

Mum shook her head.

'Nor did I,' I said. 'And there is only one lane that leads up from Little Dipperton to the Hall.'

'Whoever it was could have been on foot,' Clive suggested. 'Or perhaps on a bicycle?'

'But there's only Paolo, Olga and Lucia staying at the Hall,' I pointed out.

Mum frowned. 'Wait . . .'

'Yes?' Shawn said eagerly. 'You are remembering something?'

'Why did you both arrive separately?' Mum demanded. 'I thought you were having a romantic dinner tonight.'

'I was in the Ladies when Shawn got the call,' I said quickly.

'We had driven to Dartmouth separately,' Shawn said equally quickly. 'It was a burglary so time was of the essence. I left immediately.'

Mum frowned. 'But, Katherine . . . you were at least ten minutes behind Shawn.'

'I had to walk to my car, why?'

'I just wondered.' Mum caught my eye and mouthed, *Is everything all right*?

'So nothing was stolen?' Clive reappeared. 'Because I'm going home, if you don't mind. I'm on the early shift tomorrow.'

'Let's switch cars,' said Shawn. 'I'm on police business now.' The two men exchanged car keys. Clive thanked Mum for the tea, handed her his empty mug and left the three of us alone.

Shawn made no attempt to leave. My heart sank. Was he going to grill Mum about Douglas Jones *now*? It wouldn't surprise me in the least if he did.

'Iris,' Shawn began, 'that was a brave and very foolish thing to do.'

'I didn't think twice about it,' Mum declared. 'As I said, it was just lucky that I happened to be passing by.'

'Yes, I wanted to ask you about that,' said Shawn.

'I heard the alarm and stopped the car and came here immediately,' Mum said. 'Guns blazing, so to speak.'

Shawn cocked his head. 'And where were you passing by to – or from?'

'The Hall.' Mum smiled, showing too many teeth *again*. 'I offered Countess Golodkin my needlework expertise in case there were any problems with the costumes. Delia mentioned that some were damaged in the fire.'

'They weren't damaged in the fire. They were damaged in the Portakabin, which did not catch fire,' said Shawn. 'It's interesting that even though the alarm was going off, you decided to open the five-bar gate opposite the main entrance and reverse your car in.'

'Five-bar gate?' I echoed. 'You parked in the field *opposite*?'

Mum reddened. 'I had to pull over . . . to . . . to . . . spend a penny.'

So my mother was lying about all this, too. Suddenly moving to London with Shawn seemed appealing.

Shawn gave a heavy sigh. 'Iris, I do want to talk to you about another matter but for right now, I'm just trying to get an idea of timing. You must have heard the alarm after you had parked the car to . . . to . . . spend a penny, since I would have thought it highly unlikely that you would have taken the time to park so beautifully – facing the main drive, no less.'

'That's right,' Mum agreed.

'So . . . you didn't see anyone anywhere around that time, which suggests to me the intruder must have come across the fields from the village,' said Shawn.

'I suppose so,' said Mum.

Shawn thought for a moment. 'You said you were on your way *back* from the Hall. So – correct me if I'm wrong – you got to the gatehouses and yet, even knowing that you were a short five-minute drive from home—'

'Seven minutes,' Mum said. 'Or possibly ten.'

'You suddenly decided you wanted to er . . . spend a penny.'

'That's right,' Mum agreed again.

'So . . . rather than use Kat's facilities,' said Shawn. 'You opened the five-bar gate, reversed your car in there so you could . . .?'

'Go behind the hedge. Yes. Exactly. Wait! Quiet!' Mum froze. 'Can you hear a car?'

Sure enough we could hear the crunch of tyres on gravel. The car stopped right outside and the engine was turned off. There was the slam of a car door.

Mum's expression was tense.

There was a knock and the door slowly opened.

Reynard Smeaton popped his head in.

Mum gave a strangled cry. Even Shawn muttered, 'Bloody hell.' I just stood there in shock.

'Good grief!' Mum said angrily. 'What on earth has happened to you!'

Chapter Seventeen

Reynard could hardly stand upright. He had to hang on to the doorjamb to keep his balance. 'Saw the p'lice car,' he mumbled. 'S'everything 'right?'

Reynard's eyes were glazed; his lips were bruised and swollen. His hair was all dishevelled and there seemed to be bits of pasta stuck into his beard. He was minus a tie and it was hard to miss the red lipstick stains on his white-collared shirt.

'You're drunk!' Mum snapped.

'I hope you aren't considering driving home in that condition, sir,' said Shawn.

'I was but . . . don't feel very well.' The doctor struggled to focus as he looked at the three of us standing there before slowly recognising my mother.

'Iris? Is that really you?' he slurred. 'You look stunning. Gorgeous. Beautiful. Oh, sweetie, my darling—'

'I've been on a date,' Mum said coldly. 'Rather like you.'

Reynard looked blank and slapped his own cheek in an effort to get a grip.

Shawn regarded my mother and then Reynard with surprise. 'I thought you were an item.'

'I thought you and Kat were an item,' Mum retorted.

My suspicion as to exactly what my mother had been doing parked in a field directly opposite the main entrance to the Hall was becoming all too clear.

She had been stalking her former boyfriend. I was sure of it.

'Have you been at the Hall, sir?' Shawn enquired.

'I was having dinner with Lucia.' Reynard yawned and rubbed his forehead. 'Tired.'

'I see, so . . .' Shawn looked first to my mother, and then back to Reynard. 'You must have seen each other at the Hall?'

Reynard frowned. 'I didn't see you.'

'It was very quick. In and out,' said Mum. 'Then I had a date.'

'A date?' Reynard seemed shocked. 'You had a *date*?'

'You and I are having a break.' Mum's tone was icy. 'I can do what I like.'

'I really need to lie down,' Reynard whispered, eyeing the sofa with longing.

'No,' Mum shouted. 'Go home!'

'Yes, I think Iris is right,' said Shawn wearily. 'I think we've had enough for this evening.' He closed his notebook. 'I'll take the doctor home. He can come back tomorrow to pick up his car.'

'No, no!' Reynard said airily. 'I'm fine to drive . . . absolutely fine. I only had one gin and tonic. Wanted to keep a clear head.'

'One *bottle*, more like,' Mum spat.

Mum's gin was notoriously strong but it had never affected Reynard in the past. In fact, my mother – not that I wanted to think about this too much – said that they often played strip poker and Reynard could drink her under the table and still manage to recite the alphabet backwards.

'I'm going to overlook the fact that you have already been behind the wheel of a car drunk,' said Shawn sternly. 'You do know that you could have had – or caused – an accident?'

'Pity,' muttered Mum.

'But you'd better come with me now.' Shawn took Reynard's arm, who, with one long mournful glance at my mother, allowed himself to be borne away.

'I'd better get going too,' Mum said and made to follow them.

'I don't think so,' I said, barring her way. 'You and I need to talk.'

'You can be so oppressive, Katherine,' Mum grumbled. 'But yes we do. Did you speak to Shawn about me?'

'Yes I did and it's not looking good,' I said. 'You'd better pour yourself a brandy.'

We headed to the galley kitchen. Mum perched on a barstool while I fixed the drinks.

'Did you see the state of Reynard?' she said miserably. 'It's as if that *harlot* devoured him. No tie! Lipstick on his collar! What's the name of that deadly spider? The one that kills after mating.'

'A black widow,' I said. 'But fortunately, Reynard is still very much alive. Anyway, I thought you washed him right out of your hair.'

'I lied.'

We returned to the showroom and settled on the sofa with our drinks.

'Speaking about lying,' I said, 'what were you really doing lurking in the field at the top of the drive?'

'Don't judge me, Katherine,' she said. 'I was going insane. Delia called and couldn't wait to tell me that Reynard was dining in Lucia's suite tonight.'

'But you knew that already,' I said. 'You were there when she invited him.'

Mum gave a dismissive wave of her hand. 'She was gloating! Told me what the little Italian was preparing for them in the kitchen – oysters, figs, celery—'

'Celery?' I raised an eyebrow.

'Celery is an aphrodisiac as well. I googled it.'

Despite my mother's obvious pain, I had to laugh. 'Well, it obviously didn't work otherwise he would still be in her suite.'

She brightened. 'Oh yes. That's true.'

'Delia told me that there was a big kerfuffle because Reynard wouldn't drink her fancy red wine,' Mum went on. 'He'd only drink my gin.'

'There . . . you see. You were with them in spirit,' I said. 'And whilst we are on the topic of gin—'

'I couldn't stand not knowing,' Mum went on. 'I *had* to know if he was going to stay with her all night. It was killing me.'

I was aghast. 'You were going to sit in your car *all* night?' I studied my mother's attire. She had removed her cream coat and was looking very nice. 'So why bother to dress up and pretend you were going on a date?'

'I just wanted to be prepared in case he *didn't* stay all night,' she said.

I was beginning to fear for my mother's sanity. 'Um. Okay. So what was your plan if he didn't stay the night – which he didn't? Were you going to throw yourself in front of his car?'

'Not exactly. But I was going to pretend to have car trouble.'

'Parked in a field.'

'It was in the entrance to the field,' Mum reminded me. 'Oh, what does it matter? I wanted to make him jealous but he seemed too drunk to care. I can't believe he was actually going to drive home in such a terrible state.' She shuddered with revulsion. 'She must have kissed him.' She frowned then brightened. 'Or perhaps they had a fight? Maybe she punched him in the mouth and that's why he left?'

'Maybe,' I said doubtfully.

'Talking of fights,' said Mum, 'I noticed a distinct frost between you and Shawn.'

So I told her everything. If I'd expected any sympathy, I was wrong.

'You can't blame him,' said my mother. 'You haven't exactly been that enthusiastic, dear.'

'I was just being cautious,' I said. 'But it also shows that he doesn't understand me at all. Why would he think that I would want to live in London again? I can't think of anything worse. I love it here! And besides, someone has to keep an eye on you.'

We both fell quiet for a moment and it was then that I realised that something *had* been stolen after all. Douglas Jones's suitcase was missing.

'Are you positive?' Mum said when I told her.

'Yes.' I pointed to the corner. 'It was over there between my desk and the bookshelf.'

'But who on earth would want it?' Mum echoed my thoughts. 'There's nothing in there worth stealing.'

'Well obviously, since Douglas is dead, it wasn't him,' I said.

'Then that leaves Lucia,' said Mum. 'Don't you remember? She seemed to take an interest in it.'

'But Lucia was with Reynard tonight,' I said.

'Actually, I did see a car tonight,' Mum said suddenly. 'It was Olga's Porsche. She left the Hall around eight thirty.'

'Olga's Porsche?' I was confused. 'I thought you talked to her about helping with the costumes.'

Mum blushed. 'Well . . . I had thought about talking to her but what with one thing and another—'

'Oh Mum!' I wailed. 'You told Shawn that you met with her! What if he asks her to verify your story?'

'Why would he do that?' Mum seemed genuinely surprised. 'You know . . . Olga hasn't come back yet either.'

As if on cue, we heard a car engine slow down and turn in through the entrance. Light from the headlamps flared across the window blinds that I always kept lowered at night.

Mum hurried to the window and pulled the blind aside. 'It's her. She's back. I wonder where she went.' Mum yawned. 'I think it's time for bed. What was it you wanted to talk to me about?'

The thought of talking to my mother about the broken jeroboam meeting Douglas's skull and her phone number in the dead man's mobile was just too much for me this evening. I'd had enough drama for one day.

'It can wait,' I said.

Mum got up and took the brandy balloons into the kitchen. When she returned she said, 'Are you going to tell Shawn about the suitcase?'

'I suppose I'll have to,' I said.

'What should we do about the alarm?' Mum said.

We tested it a couple of times and found it was still working. 'I'll deal with all this tomorrow,' I said. 'Let's go.'

Chapter Eighteen

When I arrived at the gatehouse the next morning a DHL delivery van was parked out front with the engine idling. The uniformed driver was pacing outside my door carrying a large cardboard box.

I parked my Golf and went to greet him. 'You'll be wanting the Hall?'

The driver looked up at my showroom sign and then consulted his electronic proof of delivery tablet. 'Nope,' he said. 'This is the right place. Kat's Collectibles & Mobile Valuation Services. Need a signature from Kat Stanford.'

I knew I hadn't ordered anything but then I remembered Paolo and his favour. 'Will you wait a moment while I make a call? It's not for me.'

'Sorry. No can do,' said the driver. 'Says your name right here. Only you can sign for it.'

'I know. But I'm positive it's not for me.'

'Look, you've got to take it,' he said. 'The routes are all timed these days. I'm already behind with my next delivery because first of all I got lost and second of all, I had to wait for you.'

I pulled out my iPhone then realised that I didn't have Paolo's mobile number. I only had the main number at the Hall. By the time someone answered the phone, let alone tried to find Paolo, the best part of a half-hour or more would have gone by.

'Come on, luv, give me a break,' the driver pleaded. 'I've got sixty-five more deliveries to do today.'

'Fine.'

He handed me the digital pen and tablet and I duly scrawled my name. The driver snatched them back, jumped in his van, reversed out of the main gate and roared away as if he was competing in The Great Race.

I unlocked the gatehouse, glad to see that the alarm was still working, and set the box down on my desk. Maybe it was for me after all. I hunted for some scissors.

I heard the sound of another car.

Suddenly, Paolo burst through the door brandishing his iPhone as I stood poised over the box with my scissors. The return label said 'Soundscapes'.

Dressed in sweatpants, a hoodie and trainers, I could feel the heat radiating from Paolo's body and detected thin beads of sweat under his curly hairline.

'No!' he shouted wildly and snatched the scissors from my grasp. 'No! Do not touch it, Signora! I had *un avviso!* You see!'

He showed me a map on his iPhone screen with a little blue dot moving away from a large asterisk, which I assumed was where we were standing right now. 'Clever, yes?'

'Very,' I agreed. 'But the box is addressed to me. Can I have the scissors back please?' I was teasing, of course, but Paolo freaked out.

'No! No! Signora.' Paolo grabbed the box off my desk and darted to the other side of the showroom.

'I was joking, Paolo,' I said. 'What's in the box?'

He shook his head vehemently. 'I am sorry. I cannot tell you on pain of death.'

'Of course you can,' I said. 'Come on, it'll be our secret.'

'No, Signora.' Paolo shook his head again. 'I cannot.'

I had a sudden thought. As Lucia's 'everything', wouldn't he keep her diary? Paolo would know of Lucia's movements the night the yurt caught fire. He'd also know where she was when the theatre caught fire, too.

'I was about to make some coffee,' I said slyly. 'Would you like some?'

'No, no,' said Paolo. 'The Signora will be expecting her breakfast – but okay. Yes. Quick. You have espresso?'

'I do.' I had treated myself to a Nespresso machine at Christmas.

Paolo waved his iPhone. 'You make coffee. I take box to car. I call her.'

I headed for the galley kitchen and made the coffee. Moments later, Paolo joined me.

'Well?' I smiled. 'Have you been given permission?'

'Yes,' Paolo said. 'She is tired from last night and not

happy. I fear the doctor was a disappointment to her. She told him to leave.'

'And why was that?' I asked.

'He was drunk. I mix him cocktail – just one! He is no man. In Italy we call him *una mezza femminuccia*: a man who is half a woman.'

I laughed.

'The Signora *mangia uomini*,' Paolo went on. 'She eats men.'

'And are you and the Signora . . .?'

'No!' Paolo looked horrified. 'She likes people to think so but no. You, Signora, are *bellissima*. You, Signora, are a woman I could love.' He stepped closer. Suddenly the galley kitchen seemed a little cramped.

'I'm flattered but not available,' I said. 'Why don't you go through to the showroom and I'll bring the coffee? Oh – and please leave me your mobile number.'

Paolo winked and did as he was told.

I picked up the two small cups of espresso and found Paolo perched on the edge of my desk. He reminded me of an elf on a shelf.

I did a double take.

Douglas Jones's suitcase was back exactly where I had left it the night before. How could that be? Had I moved it and forgotten I'd moved it?

'Are you all right?' Paolo asked. 'You look ghostly.'

'Yes, fine,' I said. 'Can I ask you to go and sit on the sofa for a moment?'

Paolo scooted off the desk but stayed close by my side.

I set the suitcase on the desk and opened it.

'The Signora looks *preoccupata*,' he said. 'Is everything all right? Everything is there, yes?'

'Someone broke into the showroom last night,' I said. 'I was so certain that this suitcase had been stolen.'

'But now it is back, yes?'

I nodded but something was bothering me. I regarded Paolo in his gym clothes. He was small. He could have easily climbed through the downstairs loo window.

'Why did you ask me if everything was there?' I demanded.

Paolo looked startled. 'My English.'

My suspicion was growing by the minute. I repeated the question but Paolo's expression remained, conveniently, vague.

I picked up my iPhone and tapped out a random set of numbers but did not hit the green connection button. I was going to bluff it out.

'Good morning. Is that the police station?' I said. 'Can I speak to Detective Inspector Cropper? It's about last night's break-in.' I pretended to listen, keeping one eye on Paolo, who had suddenly gone very pale.

'Yes . . . yes . . . thank you,' I said. 'I need a fingerprint expert here immediately—'

'No!' Paolo yelped. 'No! Signora, no!' In one bound he'd knocked my iPhone out of my hand. It clattered to the floor. Paolo scooped it up and scurried to the sofa, shoved the iPhone under the seat cushion and sat on it.

'I know you broke in here last night, Paolo,' I scolded.

'I know you took that suitcase. Are you going to tell me what's going on or am I really going to have to call the police?'

Paolo ran his fingers through his hair, clearly distressed and definitely over-caffeinated.

'No police, I beg you,' Paolo pleaded. 'It was me! I borrowed it for Lucia.'

So Lucia *had* recognised the suitcase after all. Did that mean the items inside belonged to her too? And if so, why hadn't she just asked me for the wretched thing?

'What's so special about this suitcase, Paolo?' I said.

Paolo shrugged. 'She just wanted to look inside. But . . . whatever she hoped to see was not there.'

The Matryoshka! It *had* to be that. It was the only thing that I'd taken out. 'Did she mention a doll?'

'A doll?' Paolo shook his head. 'She asked for tiny, tiny scissors.' Seeing my confusion he added, 'To snip, snip. The lining.'

'The lining of the suitcase?'

'There!' Paolo leaned over and pointed to the faded silk in the corner. 'She was upset and told me to put the suitcase back. I am sorry. Please don't tell the police.'

A peculiar feeling began to come over me. The suitcase was undoubtedly Lucia's. She'd recognised it in my show-room on that fateful Wednesday afternoon. I thought back to Douglas's look of surprise – or perhaps it was actually horror – when we passed him in the car that very same day. Somehow, he had got hold of her suitcase. I'd never believed the story of the car boot sale. But where had he found it?

And then there was Lucia's afternoon walk in the woods. The fresh flowers on the fairy ring were proof that she had been there. She must have seen Douglas. Had there been some kind of violent argument?

But if the fire had started during the day, it would definitely have been spotted. Shawn said that the fire happened at night because the rain had put it out. Had Lucia gone back to the campsite later?

Paolo had to know more than he was letting on and I was determined to find out.

'Do you remember where Lucia was on Wednesday night?' I said. 'That's the day you arrived. She went for a walk in the afternoon while you were sorting out the hire car.'

'Yes, the airbags.' Paolo nodded. 'The evening? Lucia was with me.'

'With you. All evening *and* all night?'

'Yes.' He suddenly found something fascinating on the leg of his tracksuit bottoms. 'That is right.'

'So you were sleeping with Lucia even though you told me you weren't,' I said. 'I'm disappointed.'

Paolo blanched and swallowed hard. 'I was sleeping with Lucia. Yes.'

'And how did she take the news of Douglas Jones's death?' I said. 'And don't give me that look, he was the man who died in the fire. You must have heard about it.'

Paolo looked sick. 'I don't know.' He stood up. 'I must go now, Signora.'

'Good,' I said. 'Now I can get my phone.'

'Why?' Paolo demanded.

'Because the police have already filed a report about the burglary,' I said. 'You just admitted that you broke in and stole the suitcase. You've committed a crime. I'm sorry. I have to tell the police the truth.'

Paolo sat back down. 'I do not know why she asked me to take the suitcase. I swear! I am not a thief!'

'You're lying about Wednesday night, Paolo.'

'No. No,' he protested. 'That's not true.'

'Well, whether it's true or not, the police will take you in for questioning.'

Paolo looked stricken. 'How long will that take?'

'The questioning?' I regarded him with curiosity. 'A long time. And there is a backlog in Devon at the moment. It could be weeks before you get a court hearing.'

'Weeks! No!' Paolo turned ashen. 'Please, Signora. I did nothing wrong.'

I was getting exasperated. 'Then tell me what is going on!'

Paolo gave a heavy sigh. 'I . . . I . . . I . . . am going to climb Mount Everest!'

I felt my jaw drop. 'Excuse me?'

'Yes. Everest!' Paolo said. 'I have a permit. I have a Sherpa!'

'Okay. This is ridiculous,' I said. 'I'm calling the police.'

'No! It's true, Signora,' Paolo insisted. 'It is my *lista dei desideri*. My bucket list.'

'You aren't old enough to have a bucket list!' I exclaimed.

'I am forty-two! I have climbed Mera Peak in Nepal,

Mount Elbrus in Russia, Aconcagua in Argentina and now the biggest of all – Everest. I leave in two weeks. I am gone.'

'Well . . . you won't be going anywhere if you're facing charges of breaking and entering.'

Paolo looked as if he was going to cry. 'But . . . there is just a small window of time to climb to the summit. It is five days only this year. There can be no more delays.'

I had a sudden thought. 'What does Lucia think of you climbing Everest?'

'She does not know!' Paolo said. 'You must not tell her. She is counting on me.'

I was puzzled. 'You told me that you have only been working for her for a few weeks so why would she be counting on you? What is she counting on you for? What makes you so very special – other than your cooking and driving skills?' I said. 'What else do you excel at?'

'I am an *ingegnere audio*. A sound engineer,' said Paolo proudly. 'I am the best in Italy. I do the voice in animation.'

'And yet you are climbing Everest,' I said slowly. 'She must be paying you very well.'

'It is sixty-five thousand dollars to climb Everest,' said Paolo. 'But that includes the permit.'

I was astonished. 'That is a *lot* of money! And you said you leave in two weeks?'

'I must! It is my only chance!'

The stupid thing was that I actually believed him about Everest, but I definitely did not believe he spent the night with Lucia.

I went to sit beside him on the sofa. 'If you can help me, then I can help you.'

'*Non capisco*? I don't understand.'

'I will keep your secret if you tell me the truth about what Lucia was looking for in the suitcase and where she went on Wednesday night. Did you drive her to Honeychurch Woods?'

'Oh, Signora.' He picked up my hand and kissed it. 'Please do not ask this of me.'

'I didn't realise you had company,' came a harsh voice.

To my horror it was Shawn.

Chapter Nineteen

Paolo and I leapt to our feet. I felt sick with embarrassment.
I would never forget the look of disgust on Shawn's face.

Following his comments from the night before about
Piers Carew and Guy Evans, I knew what this must look
like.

'It's not what you think,' I protested. 'I . . . Paolo . . . tell
him—'

'Save your breath. I'm not interested, Katherine,' said
Shawn primly. 'You've made my decision very easy.'

'Decision? What do you mean?' Was he talking about
arresting my mother or breaking up with me?

Paolo mumbled something about the Signora needing
him and fled.

'I wanted to speak to Paolo about . . .' I realised that I
couldn't mention the suitcase without mentioning the
break-in and that would mean Paolo's secret would come out.

'We were talking about Lucia Lombardi,' I said. 'I think
she went to visit Douglas on the night of the fire. The fire

was started at night, yes? It rained. Remember?' I knew I
was blabbering. 'Maybe there was some old feud between
them? Maybe it was Lucia who gave him the money.'

'And why would she do that?' Shawn said coldly.

I shrugged. 'I don't know.' But even as I said it I thought
maybe I did. If it wasn't the doll she'd been after, perhaps
she'd been expecting to find something else in the suitcase
and Douglas had found it first.

'And what did your little Italian friend say?' Shawn
asked.

'About what?' I said.

'About Lucia Lombardi's movements on Wednesday
night?'

I bit my lip. 'Um. He claimed he was with her all night
but I know he's lying.'

'Why?' Shawn gave a short laugh. 'Because he was with
you?'

'Of course not,' I said crossly.

Shawn shook his head. 'Nice try to shift the blame from
your mother.'

'I'm not shifting the blame,' I retorted.

'Any chance of scrounging a coffee?' Clive poked his
head in the door.

'No,' said Shawn. 'We're not staying.'

'Oh, right.' Clive took in the awkward scene. 'I'll take
the doc's car back and see you at the station.'

'Thanks for the lift,' said Shawn.

I didn't want Shawn to leave, not like this. 'Is Reynard
any better this morning?'

'He's admitted himself into hospital for tests,' said Shawn. 'He thinks he has been poisoned.'

I was shocked. 'Paolo cooked for them last night. But he's very careful—'

'And naturally, you should know,' said Shawn with scorn. 'But this is not a case of food poisoning.'

'I'm not sure I understand what you're trying to say.'

'Reynard was deliberately poisoned,' said Shawn. 'I'm afraid I can't tell you any more until we get the results back sometime tomorrow.'

'Can't you even give me a clue?' I said desperately.

'No,' said Shawn. 'But since I'm here, I'd like to finish up my report on last night's break-in.'

'It was faulty wiring,' I said suddenly. 'Everything is working fine now.'

'Faulty wiring.' Shawn just blinked. 'Your mother said that she found the back door open when she disabled the alarm.' He retrieved his notebook and flipped back through the pages. 'I have it right here. "Back door open."'

Damn. I'd forgotten about that. 'Mum was not herself last night. She got confused.'

'And why was that?' Shawn asked.

'You were right when you said that you thought she and Reynard were an item,' I went on. 'They were taking a break and, well . . . she was waiting for me to come home so she could talk about it.'

'Home to the gatehouse?' Shawn said. 'Not Jane's Cottage?'

'That's right,' I said. 'Mum accidentally set off the alarm

when she opened the door. She was too embarrassed to say that's what she did so she pretended that someone had tried to break in.'

Shawn looked confused, as well he should. He consulted his notebook again. 'Iris said she'd been on a date. Are you telling me that she hadn't?'

Damn. I'd forgotten about that, too. 'She just wanted to make Reynard jealous.'

'So to be clear, there was no date and no break-in,' he said.

'No,' I said. 'None at all.'

Shawn closed his notebook with a snap. 'Goodbye, Katherine.'

I watched him head for the door but then he stopped and turned.

'Yes?' I said hopefully.

Our eyes met. I looked for affection, warmth or forgiveness but saw none. 'I thought you'd like to know that Douglas Jones was responsible for spraying graffiti on the gateposts. We found two canisters of red paint at his campsite.'

'Oh. Thank you.' And with that, he was gone.

Literally less than a minute later, the door opened again. I'd hoped that Shawn had come back but it was Paolo. He looked scared.

'The police! What did you tell them?'

'Don't worry,' I said wearily. 'I kept your secret, but you have to tell me what happened on Wednesday night.'

Paolo threw his arms around me. 'Thank you, thank you, Signora!'

To my horror, Shawn was looking through the window.

I pushed Paolo roughly away. 'Don't.'

I heard Shawn's car start and the roar of the accelerator as the car peeled out of the drive. I hoped I hadn't lost Shawn for ever.

Paolo regarded me with curiosity. 'Ah. You and the policeman *siete insieme*? Together?'

'We were,' I said miserably. 'But not any more.'

'Then he does not deserve you, Signora,' Paolo declared. 'If I had found you with another man, I would have challenged him to a duel! He is a *bambino*. A child. Yes?'

'No,' I said. 'It's me who is acting like a child.'

'I won't forget this, Signora. Oh, you asked for my phone number.' He handed me a scrap of paper and then left me to my misery.

I sat at my desk, staring into space, trying to think of anything other than Shawn.

Reynard had been poisoned but Shawn had said it wasn't food poisoning. Perhaps, for some reason, Lucia didn't want Reynard to sing. After all, she was being paid whether she performed or not. And what was in the mysterious box that Paolo seemed to be protecting with his life?

There was a tap on the door. My spirits lifted and I rushed to open it.

To my astonishment it was Edith.

'What a pleasure,' I said warmly, and I meant it.

I caught sight of her ancient Land Rover parked outside. She'd even driven here herself, which was highly unusual, and was still dressed in her riding habit. Her visit must be important.

'I seek refuge,' she said. 'The world has gone mad!'

'It really has,' I agreed with a smile. 'How are the rehearsals going?'

'All I hear is opera singing,' said Edith. 'No one is allowed anywhere near that wretched woman's suite of rooms. The little Italian, the gigolo—'

'Do you mean Paolo?'

'Yes. Him. He keeps everyone away from her,' Edith went on. 'She can't be disturbed. I am most displeased. I don't know what I was thinking agreeing to it all.'

I remembered a friend once who had been so excited to have her house used to film a movie in Hollywood. What she didn't realise was that the production department literally stripped everything out of her house – carpets, curtains – even the light fixtures and fittings – to install their own. Although everything was supposed to be put back to how it was, it was never quite the same.

'Apparently there is now a problem with the costumes,' said Edith. 'Three of Lucia's gowns have been cut through the bodice. I volunteered your mother's sewing skills to Olga. I hope Iris won't mind.'

This was a stroke of luck, since Mum had told Shawn that she'd already spoken to Olga about offering her sewing services. Things were looking up at last.

'I can phone Mum and let her know,' I said.

'She already knows,' said Edith. 'It's not your mother I came to see. It's you.'

'Shall we have some coffee?' I suggested, thinking I'd be bouncing off the walls if I had another espresso.

'No, but thank you.' Edith marched to the sofa and sat down, scowled and stood back up to reach under the cushion. She brought out my iPhone. 'Yours?'

'I wondered where I'd put it,' I muttered.

She looked around the showroom. 'Very nice, very nice indeed. If you had seen it before . . .'

'I did,' I reminded her with a smile. In fact, I remembered it clearly.

'No, not when it was empty,' she said, 'when it was crawling with those Jones brats, but I haven't come to talk about them. I need your help.'

Chapter Twenty

I took a seat behind my desk and waited for Edith to speak but she seemed unable to begin. The silence between us stretched until I decided to ask after Lavinia.

'Banished to the furthest part of the Hall,' Edith said. 'Julie refuses to be within a mile of her. She's worried about catching Lavinia's cold and losing her voice.' Sensing my surprise she added, 'What? You thought I didn't know who Lucia really is?'

This was awkward. 'I wasn't sure,' I said. 'Rupert didn't know.'

'Rupert wouldn't know who the Queen of England was if she turned up for tea,' said Edith. 'Dreadful girl, but what was I to do? Say no to Irina's dying wish?'

'Irina?' I asked.

'Olga's mother. Irina was a good friend.' Edith fell quiet for a moment but I could tell by the way she was working the fabric of her skirt that something was troubling her.

I wasn't sure what to say or how to be. Edith never confided in me. Our rides were filled with conversation but always on very safe topics. I had never seen her so agitated.

'I'll come straight to the point,' she said finally. 'I usually find that is the best way.'

'Are you sure you wouldn't like some coffee?' I asked.

Edith shook her head. 'I knew Olga's mother very well. In fact, we met when I was competing in Kiev in nineteen seventy-three.'

'Kiev, as in the Kiev in the Soviet Union?' I said.

'Is there another one?' Edith said. 'I was part of the International Equestrian Federation, carriage driving with Philip – the Duke of Edinburgh.'

I was impressed. My mother had told me that in Edith's younger days she was a legend in the equestrian world, competing in side-saddle and carriage-driving championships. In 1973 Edith would have been just a few years older than I was now.

'Olga's mother Irina was also competing in Kiev,' Edith went on. 'She was an excellent horsewoman. We hit it off immediately and saw each other many times on the international equestrian circuit.'

I nodded encouragement.

'Irina was married to Count Nikolai Golodkin,' she continued. 'He was a world-famous opera singer. They had one daughter, Olga. Irina told me that the three of them planned to defect to the West. I knew all about it.

'Of course, we couldn't correspond by letter – everything was censored,' Edith went on. 'Before they defected,

Nikolai gave me a gift to thank me for our friendship – just a memento.'

I nodded encouragement but I had absolutely no idea where this story was going.

'Sure enough, Irina and Olga defected,' Edith said, 'but Nikolai stayed behind. It turned out that he had been having an affair with his co-star and never intended to join them at all.'

I was shocked. 'But . . . that's terrible!'

'Teddy, the Earl, my husband, was staunchly anti-communist and, of course, he was an American, too. He refused to have anything to do with Irina. Even though she had defected with her daughter, he didn't trust either of them. Thought she was a spy, which was utterly preposterous. You have to know that it was all very different in those days. People were afraid there was going to be a nuclear war.'

'Yes,' I nodded. 'I knew your husband was an American.' In fact, Edith would be shocked to know just how much I did know about her personal life.

'Irina never got over Nikolai's betrayal,' said Edith. 'I believe she died of a broken heart.'

'What a sad story.'

'When Irina was dying, she asked me to keep an eye on Olga,' Edith continued. 'Olga was in her late twenties by then and already an independent young woman. But I promised Irina that I would.'

I thought of my own promise to Dad. When I'd made it, I'd had no idea what that promise would entail and it seemed that Edith hadn't either.

'You could say that Olga used to think of me as an aunt,' said Edith.

This certainly went a long way to explain why Edith had agreed to Olga staging *The Merry Widow* at the Hall, even if she was getting paid.

'Olga had a very complex relationship with her father,' Edith went on. 'She vacillated between hating him and loving him, but he opened a few doors for her in the opera world once the Berlin Wall came down. Then, as often happens, Olga and I lost touch.'

'Until now,' I said.

'Olga called me out of the blue to ask me for this favour,' said Edith. 'I hadn't seen her for decades.'

'Where had she been living?' I asked.

'She moved to the West Country a few years ago,' said Edith.

If Edith was hurt that Olga only decided to look her up when she needed something, she didn't show it.

Edith must have seen something in my face because she added. 'Olga had a very busy life. Her work took her all over the world. She never married. I fear she faces a lonely old age and she's not at all well. She suffers from osteoporosis but she continues to ignore the dangers.'

I smiled at that comment. Edith's choice of riding side-saddle was incredibly dangerous and she was older than Olga!

'Olga still believes that she's running a professional opera company,' Edith said. 'She's very fortunate that Monty and Suzanne have been carrying D.O.D.O. for such a long time.'

If this was Edith's way to get straight to the point, I was surprised. This had to be the longest conversation that I had ever had with her about anything other than horses.

'How can I help?' I asked.

'Nikolai never married the other woman but they had a daughter. After he died, Olga's half-sister must have suffered a pang of conscience. In her father's papers were letters addressed to Olga that her mother had never sent. Apparently the gift that Nikolai had given to me had not been a gift at all. It was a loan. As you can imagine, this has been frightfully awkward.'

'What was this gift?' I asked.

'It was a Matryoshka.'

My stomach turned right over. Surely Edith couldn't be talking about the same doll that I'd found in Douglas's suitcase? And yet it seemed too much of a coincidence to think otherwise.

'A Russian nesting doll,' I said.

Edith's eyes widened with surprise. 'But of course you'd know what it is. I can't find the wretched thing anywhere,' she went on. 'It was so long ago. I hardly remember what it looked like. I just put it in a cupboard.' She gave a sniff of disdain. 'As you know, it's not something that I would *ever* collect.'

'Can you remember anything about it at all?'

'I think it was red and gold,' said Edith. 'All I remember is that there were smaller dolls inside. But clearly it was very valuable.'

I was puzzled. My Matryoshka couldn't possibly be the same doll.

'I've turned the Hall upside down,' Edith continued. 'Delia and Peggy have been looking – even Harry and Lavinia, although she wasn't much help. Olga is frightfully upset, Angry, in fact.' Edith looked miserable. It certainly explained the tension I had witnessed between them when we were out riding yesterday.

I heard my iPhone ping with an incoming text but I ignored it.

'We had a robbery here in nineteen ninety,' said Edith. 'I think it must have been stolen then.'

Of course I knew about the fake robbery in 1990! I also knew for a fact that the Matryoshka had not been stolen because I had a copy of the list of items that had.

'With all the technology these days, there must be a record of stolen goods, surely?' said Edith.

'There is,' I said. 'It's called the Art Loss Register, but unfortunately it wasn't created until nineteen ninety-one.'

'Oh.' Edith shook her head. 'Then there is nothing more to be done. Olga will just have to get over it.'

I thought for a moment, not completely convinced if it was the right thing to do or not but it was worth a try. 'Can I show you something?'

I produced Douglas's suitcase, and, watching Edith's face for any sign of recognition, brought it over to the sofa and set it on the floor in front of her.

Edith didn't react at all.

As I snapped the locks and opened the lid, Edith daintily raised her hand to her nose as the smell of mould wafted into the showroom.

'Do any of these items look familiar to you?' I said.

Edith leaned over to look at the contents. I thought I saw a flicker of something but couldn't be sure. Shock? Surprise? Disgust?

She sat back. 'Why are you showing me this?'

'There was a Matryoshka inside this suitcase,' I said. 'But I can guarantee that it wouldn't have been the one you were looking for.'

'And it was in *that*?' Edith pointed at the suitcase. 'Where did you get this suitcase?'

'Douglas Jones brought it in on Wednesday. He asked me to buy the doll from him so I did.'

Edith's jaw dropped. 'Douglas *Jones*? Surely not the Douglas Jones who we found in the woods yesterday morning?'

'I'm afraid so,' I said. 'He bought the suitcase at a car boot sale.'

Edith continued to stare at the suitcase.

It suddenly occurred to me that there was a luggage room in the attics at the Hall. Perhaps Douglas had found it up there? After all, he had lived on the estate for years. But it still didn't explain the strange contents – the kimono, the man's handkerchief, the lipstick and the random champagne corks, the Valentine card.

'Are you *sure* you don't recognise the suitcase?' I said gently. 'Or anything inside it?'

'No,' said Edith firmly. 'No, I don't. Well . . . where is the Matryoshka now?' she said finally. 'I would like to see it, if only to discount its importance.'

'My mother has it.'

'Oh, thank heavens!' Edith heaved a sigh of relief that turned to irritation. 'Why on earth didn't you say so in the first place?'

She got to her feet and headed for the door. 'You said your mother was at home?'

'Yes,' I said.

'I'll meet you at the Carriage House.' And with that, she was gone.

Chapter Twenty-one

When I pulled into the courtyard, Edith was already there waiting in her Land Rover.

The Carriage House formed part of a quadrangle of outbuildings. Bearing the date 1830, the two-storey red-brick building looked utterly stunning today covered in purple wisteria. In the cobbled courtyard, Mum's terracotta pots bloomed with geraniums and I was sure that Edith couldn't fail to be impressed by all the hard work my mother had done to transform the near-derelict complex to what it was now.

And then I was struck by an awful thought. What if Mum was working in the piggery? A few months ago she had converted it into her writing house. She had installed a one-way window under the iron bars. Absolutely no one, other than me, was allowed inside. Next to the piggery was the henhouse where my mother distilled her gin, but that was common knowledge whereas the piggery was definitely out of bounds.

I checked my watch: eleven fifteen. With any luck Mum would be following her usual routine and would have stopped for a break.

'Why don't you stay in the Land Rover?' I suggested to Edith. 'I'll just run into the Carriage House and ask her – oh!'

I'd just reached the open carriageway doors when I heard a car start, a clunk of gears, then Mum's Mini appeared. I leapt out of the way.

She hit the brakes and promptly stalled the car. When she saw Edith, Mum scrambled out looking very flustered. 'Goodness, Katherine! It's her ladyship! Why didn't you tell me she was coming? The house is a mess!'

I noticed that my mother wore make-up and was dressed in a neat suit, tights and pumps. 'It's not a social call and where are you going? Why aren't you writing?'

'Where do you think?' Mum jabbed a finger at the front passenger seat where I spied her wicker sewing basket. 'I've been summoned to the Hall. The Russian countess has asked me to repair Lucia's costumes.'

'Ah, yes,' I said. 'I heard they'd been damaged.'

'Delia told me that your friend Fiona from the Emporium is responsible for that and the fire,' said Mum. 'Shawn's got her in custody.'

'Yes, I know,' I said.

'You *know!*' Mum was annoyed. 'Why did I have to find out from Delia? I hate it when she knows more than I do.'

Edith sounded the horn. Mum and I turned and waved in unison.

'She's come to collect that Russian doll,' I said.

'Too late,' said Mum. 'I got rid of it.'

'Oh, Mum!' I wailed.

'You said it was worthless,' said Mum. 'I decided I didn't like it after all. I took it to the community shop yesterday.' She thought for a moment. 'What's it got to do with her ladyship?'

'We'll talk about it later.' I glanced over at Edith, who was watching us closely. 'I'll tell her that you'll go to the community shop right now and get it.'

'I can't,' said Mum. 'I've got to go to the ballroom. Can't you go?'

'Fine,' I said. 'Why am I always clearing up after you?'

'You can do it after you've come with me to the Hall,' said Mum.

'Not going to happen,' I said. 'I do have a life, you know.'

'Please, Kat, I don't want to face Lucia on my own, especially after her tryst with my boyfriend last night,' said Mum. 'I might be tempted to stab her with a pin.'

I gave a heavy sigh. 'Stay here and let me tell Edith the bad news.'

'It's not bad news,' said Mum. 'The doll will still be there, I promise.'

'Let's hope so,' I said. 'If someone found a home for that inflatable sheep I'm sure the doll will have already gone.'

'Oh, how infuriating!' Edith exclaimed when I told her. 'I

can't possibly go to the – what do they call it? – the *community* shop.'

'I'm happy to go for you,' I said. 'I'll call Bethany and make sure she sets it aside.'

Edith frowned. 'Sets it aside?'

'Mum left it in the White Elephant corner,' I said. 'For unwanted gifts.'

'Oh, good grief, whatever next?' Edith muttered. 'All right. Bring it to the Hall the moment you have it.'

And with that, Edith attempted to make a three-point turn. It took her nine tries before she clipped one of the terracotta pots and kangarooed out of the courtyard.

'Do you think she should still be driving?' Mum said anxiously when I rejoined her.

'Since I have to go to the community shop afterwards,' I said, 'I'll meet you up at the Hall.'

'No,' said Mum. 'If we go in the same car and things get awkward, I can always say you have to be somewhere . . . like catch a plane.'

'A plane?'

'You know what I mean. We can leave in a hurry if we have to.'

As we drove to the Hall I told my mother all about Reynard.

'Poisoned, eh?' she said with a chuckle. 'That must have been romantic with him dashing to the loo every five minutes. No wonder she threw him out!'

'It wasn't food poisoning, Mum,' I said. 'Reynard isn't at all well. They're running tests.'

'I'll take him a grape,' said Mum.

'Have you called Shawn yet about your arrangement with Douglas?' I demanded.

Mum scowled. 'No, Katherine, I have not. I've been busy.'

'It's important, Mum, seriously.'

'Katherine . . . I know that last night your date didn't go very well,' Mum said carefully, 'but did Shawn say anything else about the yurt fire? You know, about the bottles and whatnot.'

'No new developments,' I said.

I was desperate to share my suspicions about Lucia's possible involvement. I was convinced that the suitcase belonged to her and that she had put the fresh flowers on the fairy ring. Lucia had definitely gone to the campsite the day that Douglas was murdered. But since we were about to see her, now was definitely not the right time to share these thoughts with my mother. And besides, at the moment, I had no proof.

We parked in front of the Hall next to Rupert's black Range Rover, Paolo's Smart car, Olga's Porsche and – to my surprise – Sir Monty's Rolls-Royce. He was back again.

Mum and I ascended the grand steps to the front door but found it locked. No one answered the bell either.

Defeated, we trooped around the side of the house where the Hall's architectural incarnations were in full view. A series of exposed wooden beams hinted at a Tudor beginning but then it looked as if the Hall kept being swallowed up by bigger and more fashionable additions as time passed by.

Directions to the east terrace and ballroom were scrawled in red pen on sheets of paper torn from a spiral-ring notebook with 'Production Crew this way'. Even so, it took us a full ten minutes to find our destination.

'Honeychurch Hall is like Hogwarts in the *Harry Potter* films,' I said. 'It just keeps getting bigger and bigger.'

Finally we rounded a corner and both of us stopped in surprise. The double-storey windows to the ballroom looked out over a terrace that was being weeded by two young girls in jeans and matching navy sweatshirts emblazoned with the D.O.D.O. logo.

A young woman emerged from a side door. She was in her early twenties and looked painfully thin. She also wore a navy D.O.D.O. sweatshirt. When she saw Mum and her sewing basket she gave a sigh of relief. 'You're the seamstress, right?'

'Seamstress?' Mum said. 'Well, I'm a friend doing the Countess a favour.'

'Thank God,' she said. 'Olga is freaking out.' She paused for a moment. 'Sorry. I'm Brooke, Olga's personal assistant. Follow me. It's a bit of a rabbit warren back here.'

Moments later we stepped into the ballroom, now a hive of noisy activity, with the sounds of hammers and drills, lighting rigs being wheeled into position and the occasional warning cry as stagehands and technicians went about their business. The room was being transformed into the fictional kingdom of Pontevedro.

'Gosh!' I enthused. 'This is amazing!'

'Isn't it?' Brooke grinned. 'We've all been working flat

out. Only the best for the Countess! Wait here. I'll go and find her.'

There was an elegance about the ballroom that the Great Hall, with its heavy oil paintings and collection of plate armour, did not possess.

Traces of white paint could still be seen on the carved woodwork that framed the faded wallpaper panels between the floor-to-ceiling mirrors along one entire wall. Opposite the mirrors, large French doors, festooned with heavy velvet curtains, opened on to the weed-infested terrace that we'd seen when we first arrived.

A raised stage had been built, flanked by two fake Corinthian columns that neatly hid the metal gantries. Another gantry was suspended across the columns where lights were being fitted. On the ground was a heap of red velvet that presumably would become the grand curtain.

At the other end of the ballroom was a white marble fire surround. Mum had once told me that it supposedly came from Carrera in Italy where the marble from the same quarries supplied Ancient Rome.

I looked up to admire the three evenly spaced crystal chandeliers from the spectacular groin-vaulted ceiling. Somewhere up there, the greater horseshoe bats came home to roost.

The gold-painted chairs that had passed the gatehouse on the back of a flatbed truck two days earlier were now stacked and ready to be set out on the parquet flooring.

'The first act takes place in an embassy in Paris,' said Mum, 'then in a garden and finally at Maxim's nightclub.'

'You've done your research. I'm impressed,' I said.

'I rather like Google,' she admitted. 'It's addictive.'

The sets for *The Merry Widow* were lavish, to put it mildly. It hadn't just been Brooke who had commented on the Countess only wanting the best. Fiona had said as much too. This was not an amateur production by any means. No one was running up a pair of old curtains or making costumes out of sacking. Staging a Golodkin production of *The Merry Widow* must be costing Sir Monty a fortune.

'It makes me think of my childhood,' Mum said wistfully. 'I loved performing.'

'I don't think opera and your days starring as Electra, the 27,000 Volt Girl, in a sideshow at the fairground are quite in the same league.'

'Nonsense,' said Mum. 'Acting is acting.'

Brooke reappeared with Olga, who was accompanied by Sir Monty, dressed in the usual upper-class country gentleman's attire: a smart light green tweed jacket with leather elbow patches and moleskin trousers.

Olga waved us over. 'Ah! Here is the woman with her little sewing basket.'

I could see my mother's hackles rise at the unintended – or perhaps intended – slight. It was hard to tell but, either way, Mum didn't react, although I didn't expect her to. Her belief that the aristocracy was a superior race would never change, especially given the Countess's distant connection to the Romanovs.

'Kat, what a surprise,' said Olga. 'I assume you are going to hold the scissors.'

'Something like that,' I said.

'Aren't you going to introduce us?' Sir Monty stepped forward and gave my mother a smile that I found very disconcerting. I'd never seen Sir Monty's teeth before. It reminded me of the wedding scene in *Pride and Prejudice* that starred Colin Firth, who had played Mr Darcy with smouldering panache. It was only as he and Lizzie – newly wed – drove off in their carriage that he allowed himself to smile and somehow, in that moment, he lost his sex appeal. At least, he did to me.

'Sir Montgomery Stubbs-Thomas is our wonderful benefactor,' gushed Olga. 'D.O.D.O. would be lost without his generosity.'

'It was my late wife Suzanne who was really the opera buff,' said Sir Monty. 'I just did as I was told.' He gave a sharp laugh. 'I already know Kat, of course.' He regarded my mother and added, 'And you must be her sister.'

Mum blushed. 'Oh, hardly.'

'This is my mother, Iris Stanford,' I said.

'Iris,' mused Sir Monty. 'What a beautiful name.'

'It means "rainbow",' said Mum. 'In Greek mythology Iris was the goddess of the rainbow and—'

'Sir Monty really misses Suzanne,' said Olga pointedly. 'We all do.'

'Lucia told me that Suzanne was her first fan and founded Lucia's fan club,' I said.

'Yes, they were friends,' said Sir Monty. 'Suzanne visited her in Florence once.'

'We were so thrilled that Lucia agreed to come out of

retirement to perform for Suzanne. Sadly, Suzanne passed before . . . well . . .' said Olga. '*The Merry Widow* was her favourite operetta.'

'I'd come out of retirement if I was paid that much, too,' Sir Monty exclaimed.

Mum seemed confused. 'So this isn't your swansong, your illustrious highness?'

I stifled a smile. My mother had clearly been brushing up on her Russian etiquette. Unfortunately, it seemed to come out as an insult.

'Ha! Illustrious highness, eh?' Sir Monty hooted with laughter. 'We've been trying to get rid of Olga for years.'

Olga smiled but I could see by her eyes that she was not amused.

'I think Mum and I should get started,' I said quickly.

'I hear that you have come to our rescue with your needles and pins,' Monty beamed. 'Frightful business with Fiona. Most extraordinary! I've known her for years. Can't believe she would do such a thing.'

'We're all shocked, Monty,' Olga declared. 'But sometimes you think you know someone and you really don't.'

I had to agree with her on that point. My mother was living proof.

'And now it looks like Victor's replacement will delay our opening night,' Sir Monty went on. 'You're losing the plot, old girl.'

'It's hardly my fault that Reynard Smeaton got food poisoning,' Olga snapped.

'I thought I paid for this so-called chef to avoid such a risk,' said Sir Monty. 'We'll have to sue the little fella.'

I sprang to Paolo's defence. 'It wasn't food poisoning. Reynard was poisoned.'

'What's that you say?' Sir Monty looked appalled. 'Not food poisoning?'

The colour drained from Olga's face. 'Who would say such a thing?'

'The police are running tests,' Mum put in.

'The *police*!' Olga seemed horrified.

'Don't worry. Katherine will be the first to know what type of poison it is,' Mum said. 'She's very close to Detective Inspector Cropper. He's the detective on the case.'

'Isn't that the same detective who was investigating the theatre fire?' Sir Monty demanded. 'Bad publicity. I'm not happy. Not happy at all.'

'You know what they say,' said Mum, 'there's no such thing as bad publicity. It'll be on the front page of all the newspapers.'

'Not helpful, Mum,' I muttered.

'And if we cancel the production we'll have to refund the tickets and Lucia will still get paid,' growled Sir Monty.

'That's not going to happen,' Olga said firmly. 'The show must go on.'

Wait!' Monty threw his arms aloft and took in the magnificence of the transformed ballroom. 'Do you know . . . with Nightingales gone . . . this could be the new home for D.O.D.O.!'

'Oh, I don't think so,' said Olga quickly. 'Edith wouldn't allow it.'

'Nonsense. Besides, you'll be long gone,' said Sir Monty. 'What do you think, Iris?'

Mum looked startled. 'Me? I really hadn't thought about it but I fear her illustrious highness – I mean the Countess – could be right.'

'Money talks, Iris,' said Sir Monty. 'Money talks.' He looked my mother up and down with ill-concealed admiration. 'Perhaps you would consider being on the board?'

'Me?' Mum turned pink. 'Well—'

'We've already got enough members on the board, darling, and besides,' Olga put a possessive hand on Monty's arm, 'Iris doesn't know the first thing about opera. I suspect *Cats* is more to her taste.'

'Yes I do,' Mum retorted. '*The Merry Widow* is an operetta that centres on the relationship between the wealthy young widow Hanna Glawari and Count Danilo Danilovitsch, who has an appetite for wine and women. As this delightful tale of a woman's quest for love unfolds, their burgeoning romance is hampered by mishap, intrigue and comedic misadventure.'

If Olga or Sir Monty had realised that my mother was merely quoting from her online research, they didn't show it.

Sir Monty was impressed. 'You see, Olga! Of course she does!'

Clearly emboldened, Mum added, 'And I've always been fascinated by the character of Valencienne. Tempted by the attentions of Count Camille de Rosillon and yet loyal to her marital vows.'

'Yes, yes!' Sir Monty laughed. 'And do *you* have marital vows to keep?'

'Not any more.' Mum batted her eyelashes. 'Actually, I'm a widow.'

'We must find Lucia,' I said loudly.

Fortunately, Brooke had been hovering and saved us all from what could have been a very awkward situation.

'Lucia is ready for you now,' she said. 'Would you like to follow me?'

Chapter Twenty-two

As we left the ballroom by yet another side door and stepped into yet another warren of dark corridors, I whispered, 'Mum, you definitely do not want to get involved with Sir Monty. He's not a very nice person and it's obvious that Olga is infatuated with him.'

'Oh yes, I know,' my mother whispered back. 'I'm just hoping it'll get back to Reynard and make him jealous.'

Sometimes I felt as if I was dealing with a teenager.

Brooke led us up another staircase and along another landing. The carpet was threadbare and the bare walls of faded wallpaper carried a range of picture lights with nothing hanging beneath them. It was depressingly shabby.

There was no pleasing view from the windows, which were dirty and full of cobwebs: they overlooked a range of abandoned brick garages with broken doors.

Brooke held up her hand and stopped. 'Wait. Can you hear her?'

We became aware of the most beautiful singing, so beautiful that the hair on my arms stood up.

'That's "Vilja Lied",' said Brooke. 'I've heard her sing so many times but this aria is my favourite. I'm training to be an opera singer too. Lucia has been so nice and encouraging.'

'Gosh.' I was astonished as Lucia's singing continued. 'She really can sing.'

'She can sing all right,' said Brooke. 'Did you know that Lucia's one of the very few artistes in the world who can sing the high G10?'

'Yes,' Mum agreed. 'But that's not a note, you know. It's really a frequency. It's like a kettle whistling as it comes up to the boil.'

Brooke was clearly enthralled by Lucia's gifts. 'One of the greatest sopranos of all time,' she said wistfully. 'Now, let us wait for the big finish.'

So we did.

When Lucia had done just that, we stood there in silence. No one wanted to break the spell. Any reservations I had had about Lucia's voice or Mum's catty remarks that she hadn't sung for years vanished.

Lucia was simply magnificent.

Finally, Brooke tapped on the door. 'Good luck,' she whispered and left us to it.

It was Paolo who opened the door to a room so disorganised that it looked as if it had been burgled. He seemed agitated. There was no sign of Lucia.

Olga had complained that Lucia hadn't liked her suite.

It had three huge sash windows and was enormous. Unfortunately, the windows looked directly into a thick bank of trees, letting in very little natural light.

In the centre was an old four-poster bed devoid of hangings. An assortment of costumes hung on portable clothing racks and garments lay discarded on the faded moss-green carpet along with a handful of glossy magazines.

Three large mirrors had been positioned close to the window next to the walnut dressing table that was strewn with used tissues. A table holding a huge make-up box stood next to it. Laid out along a mahogany side table were bottles of Evian water, a basket of fresh fruit and a half-eaten cheese board.

'Lucia will be back in a moment,' said Paolo. 'She is preparing for you.'

I regarded his long face with concern. 'Are you all right?'

Paolo shook his head. He looked as if he was going to cry. 'I cannot . . . I cannot talk. Not here. Please sit.'

He pointed to a two-seater love seat where a red and white striped tie was draped over the back. Unfortunately, I recognised it and so did my mother. It belonged to Reynard.

'So this is where she seduced him,' Mum muttered with disgust as she sat down. 'And over there must have been where they had their romantic dinner.'

Tucked in the corner was a small gate-leg table with a white linen cloth and a vase of red roses. A candelabrum with two burned-down candle stumps, an empty bottle of

Barolo and Mum's Honeychurch Gin just seemed to add insult to injury.

I nudged her. 'You see, I was right. You *were* here in spirit.'

Paolo sank on to a low chair, which made him seem even shorter. He took out his iPhone and started tapping away, brow furrowed in concentration and, although I couldn't be sure, he seemed to wipe away a tear.

Seeing that Paolo was immersed in his iPhone, Mum jumped up and darted over to the gate-leg table. She picked up the bottle of gin and held it up to the light, then darted just as quickly back to the sofa.

'The bottle is still three-quarters full,' Mum said in a low voice.

'So?'

'So why was Reynard so drunk when he turned up at the gatehouse?'

There was the sound of a toilet flushing and Lucia emerged from what must have been the bathroom. She was holding a copy of the *Dipperton Deal*.

Mum seemed transfixed by what Lucia was wearing – which wasn't very much. She wore a flimsy silk robe in a delicate shade of apricot that was loosely tied at the waist.

'I can't believe the Dear Amanda column is still going strong,' Lucia said. 'I used to think it was Muriel the postmistress but I gather that she died last year. My bet is on that dried-up old spinster Violet Green.'

'Violet's a friend of mine,' Mum declared – a fact that was patently untrue.

'Then you must be the only friend she's got,' said Lucia. 'Let's get started – my iced water isn't cold. Get me another glass— Paolo, what are you doing?'

'I am using my phone,' said Paolo.

'Yes, I can see that,' Lucia said crossly. 'But I don't pay you to use your phone. I pay you to look after me.'

Paolo got to his feet, still checking his iPhone. 'Of course, Signora.'

'And tell Delia that she can finish cleaning my suite this afternoon when I go for my walk— *Paolo*! Are you listening?'

Paolo thrust his iPhone into his pocket and scurried away.

'I don't know what's wrong with him today,' said Lucia. 'He's been in a sulk ever since I told him we have to delay the production because of Reynard. It's so distressing. Paolo cooked the exact same thing for both of us. It can't possibly be food poisoning.'

'It wasn't,' Mum declared. 'The police seem to think he's been poisoned.'

'*Poisoned*?' Lucia was aghast. 'But . . . how? When?'

'You tell me,' said Mum darkly.

'What's that supposed to mean?' Lucia frowned. 'What was your name again?'

'Iris,' said Mum.

Lucia snapped her fingers. 'Of course! *You're* Iris. Reynard told me that you took the break-up very badly.'

'What break-up?' Mum exclaimed. 'We were just friends. Nothing more.'

'Oh, good,' said Lucia. 'And here was me worried that I was stepping on another woman's toes.'

'I hope you'll be very happy together,' Mum snarled.

'Mum,' I said sharply, 'why don't you open your sewing basket?'

'We are happy.' Lucia flashed a smile. 'It's funny how you can just pick up where you left off, no matter how many years have passed.'

'I distinctly remember you saying that you *couldn't* remember him,' Mum said.

'It's true. I couldn't.' Lucia grinned. 'It was the beard that threw me to start with . . . but when he kissed me . . . it all came flooding back. He really has the most extraordinary hands.'

Mum's complexion was actually green. I thought she was going to be sick. She reached for a pair of scissors.

I took the scissors away. 'Let's get on with the costumes, shall we?'

Lucia dropped her robe and stood there in skimpy underwear that was at least two sizes too small. She oozed sensuality and seemed completely uninhibited. I envied her that confidence.

'Yes, I told Olga,' Lucia continued, 'I refuse to sing without Reynard. Never in my entire career have I felt such a powerful chemistry than with that naughty silver fox.'

I thought Mum was going to explode.

Lucia strode to the rack and pulled out a black velvet ball gown with black jet decorations over a blue satin petticoat with black velvet feather appliqué.

'My widow's weeds,' said Lucia. 'I'm singing—'

'Hanna Glawari, who inherited twenty million francs from her late husband, I know,' said Mum.

'Oh? I didn't think it would be your thing,' said Lucia. 'Reynard told me you weren't interested in opera.'

Desperate to change the subject, I said, 'It's a beautiful costume but – oh dear. I see what you mean.'

On closer inspection the bodice had been opened at the seams.

'It won't take long,' said Mum. 'It's just the seams. I thought I was going to have to do some serious repairs.'

'This entire production has been cursed from the beginning,' Lucia went on. 'I can't wait for it to be over.'

'Perhaps you should just go home?' Mum said sweetly.

'I promised Monty,' said Lucia. 'And I always keep a promise. Well? Can you mend it or not? There are two more costumes, but this one is the worst.'

'Let's start by putting it on,' said Mum. 'Oh, now this is a lovely one. Such pretty colours. I love the pinks and burgundies.'

Lucia smiled. 'That's for the second act. My Pontevedrian national dress.'

Mum pulled out the third. It was a blue and black sequinned petticoat under a gold appliquéd dress and matching feather boa. 'Very nice.'

'That's for the third act. The nightclub scene,' said Lucia. 'Reynard loves me in that. I tried it on for him. He couldn't keep those gorgeous hands off me.'

Mum pulled and tugged roughly at the fabric. More

than once Lucia cried out in pain as she was jabbed by a deliberately misplaced pin.

'Reynard will need all three of his costumes altered,' Lucia said. 'Especially the Pontevedrian cavalry officer's uniform.'

'What's wrong with it?' Mum said.

'Victor – my original Danilo – had chicken legs and a flat bottom but Reynard's is fuller and his thighs are remarkably muscular— Ouch!'

'Sorry, my hand slipped,' muttered Mum.

Fortunately, any further stabbings were saved by a knock on the door and Paolo returned looking even more agitated. 'I'm sorry, Signora, but he says it is urgent.'

To my astonishment, Shawn walked in. He seemed equally astonished to see Mum and me but quickly composed himself.

'I'm repairing Lucia's costumes,' Mum declared, 'just like I told you.'

But then Paolo introduced him to Lucia. 'Detective Inspector Cropper, Signora,' he said. 'He has some questions for you.'

Lucia's expression underwent a series of transformations. At first she turned pale and then a wave of colour flooded her face.

'I'm sorry to bother you,' said Shawn. 'And let me say, I'm a huge fan.'

I looked at him in surprise. Not once had he ever mentioned being a fan of opera, let alone Lucia Lombardi.

'I don't see how I can possibly help you unless,' she

gestured to Mum and me, 'it's not me that you have come to see. Or perhaps it's Paolo? Has something been stolen?'

'Stolen?' Shawn frowned then looked to me. '*Has* something been stolen?'

I glanced at Paolo, who looked as if he was about to be shot. 'No, nothing at all.' I gave Paolo a nod of reassurance, a nod that was unfortunately spotted by Shawn and clearly misinterpreted.

Shawn regarded Lucia. 'Why would you say something had been stolen?'

Lucia gave a tinkling laugh. 'I can't imagine why else you would be here. Perhaps Lady Edith is worried about someone running off with the silver.'

'Any news on Reynard?' Mum put in.

'Yes,' Lucia echoed. 'How is my darling man?'

'We'll be getting the results at any moment,' said Shawn. 'No, I'm here investigating a murder that happened on Wednesday night.'

'A murder!' Paolo squeaked and sank down on to his little stool. He looked terrified. My mother looked terrified. Only Lucia seemed calm.

Shawn produced his notebook and pencil and turned to a fresh page. 'I believe that Douglas Jones is a cousin of yours, Miss Lombardi,' said Shawn.

'I've been living in Italy for decades,' Lucia said easily. 'I didn't keep in touch with any of my relatives.'

'When was the last time you saw your cousin?' Shawn asked.

Lucia huffed and puffed. 'Goodness. I want to

say . . . forty years ago? No, that's not true.' She turned to me. 'We passed him in the lane, didn't we, Kat?'

I agreed that we had.

'Would you please go through your movements on Wednesday after you arrived at the Hall,' Shawn demanded.

'Well . . . you know all about Violet Green striking my car. Let me see . . .' Lucia thought for a moment. 'Yes, I went for a walk in Honeychurch Woods. It would have been sometime in the afternoon.'

'And did you know that Douglas Jones was camping in the woods?' Shawn enquired.

'Of course not,' said Lucia. 'As I told you, the first time I'd seen him was in the lane when I was driving with Kat.'

Shawn duly wrote that down. 'And what about later that night?'

'I was with Paolo,' said Lucia.

Paolo blushed and said, 'I cooked for the Signora and . . . and we . . .'

'Tell him,' said Lucia. 'He's a man of the world.'

'Yes. We spent the night together,' Paolo mumbled.

Shawn seemed shocked. I heard my mother gasp. I, however, wasn't surprised at all.

'Paolo is my everything,' said Lucia. 'I would be lost without him.'

'What about Reynard? Isn't he your everything?' Mum demanded. 'You told me you'd be lost without him, too.'

Shawn thought for a moment. 'So, Mr Carerra – that is your last name, isn't it?'

Paolo nodded.

'How do you feel when Miss Lombardi is entertaining other men?' Shawn regarded him keenly. 'It must be very difficult.'

Paolo shrugged. 'I feel nothing.'

'I'm not sure what you're trying to imply, Inspector,' said Lucia.

'Reynard Smeaton was poisoned last night,' Shawn said.

'Yes, so we heard,' said Lucia airily. 'But not from Paolo's cooking, I can assure you. Iris mentioned poison.'

'Nothing is confirmed until the tests are back,' said Shawn somewhat pompously.

Paolo gave a little cry of distress. I could almost sense his dream to climb Everest fading by the minute.

Shawn's eyes roamed around the room. He took in the gate-leg table with its candelabra, the empty bottle of Barolo and my mother's Honeychurch Gin.

'I see you are a fan of Iris's home-made gin,' said Shawn.

'Me?' Lucia said. 'I don't drink spirits. I only drink Barolo and I *always* bring my own wine.'

'And where did you get the Honeychurch Gin?' Shawn demanded. 'Where did you buy it?'

'From me!' Mum exclaimed. 'I gave one bottle to the Russian countess and one to Miss Lombardi as welcome gifts. Absolutely *no* money changed hands.'

'I see.' Shawn retrieved a pair of blue disposable gloves and headed for the table. He then produced one of his infamous Ziploc bags.

'What on earth are you doing?' Mum protested.

'My job,' said Shawn, and fastidiously put the gin bottle

into the Ziploc bag and zipped it up. 'Am I to understand that the new date for the production will now be at the end of May?'

'Yes,' said Lucia. 'I refuse to perform without my Reynard.'

There was another cry of distress from Paolo, who leapt up and darted from the room, slamming the door hard behind him.

'Take no notice. He's a little temperamental,' said Lucia.

Shawn closed his notebook. 'I think that will be all for now. I know where to find you if I have any more questions.'

'And you will let me know about the results of Reynard's tests, won't you?' Lucia said.

'And me!' Mum chorused.

Shawn turned to my mother, his expression grave. 'We'll be in touch.'

And with that, he was gone.

The rest of the fitting passed uneventfully. In fact, as the afternoon wore on, the tension seemed to lift a little between the two rivals. I helped Mum take the six costumes – three for Lucia and three for Reynard – back to her Mini so she could finish mending them at home.

'That wasn't so painful, was it?' I said.

'No,' Mum mused. 'Lucia's all right, I suppose. If it wasn't for Reynard, I might even like her. All that diva stuff is just an act.'

My mother's comment surprised me.

'Although . . . you know what they say,' said Mum. 'Keep your friends close but your enemies closer.'

'And here was me thinking you really did like her!' I exclaimed. 'And why did you take Reynard's costumes? I don't see how you can alter those if he's not here.'

'I'm planning on sewing up Reynard's flies.'

I laughed but when she didn't join in, I realised she could be serious.

Mum thought for a moment. 'I think I remember Lucia now. She would have been about nine or ten when we camped in the park. Quite a chubby little thing. Always hanging around the sideshows and begging to run away with us. I told her that we weren't the circus.'

I helped Mum take the costumes inside and picked up my Golf. The text I'd received earlier had been from Simon from the community shop to say he had 'something' for me.

Promising to call Shawn and come clean about the gin bottles after she'd made herself a cup of tea, I left Mum to it and headed for the village, almost forgetting for a moment about the Matryoshka.

I couldn't help replaying the events of the day. Mum was right to keep Lucia close. Paolo's reluctant alibi was further proof that she must have had something to do with Douglas's murder.

I desperately wanted to talk to Shawn but couldn't until my mother had spoken to him first. My loyalty to her was absolute but my relationship with Shawn was important, too.

I just prayed Mum would keep her promise.

Chapter Twenty-three

'**The whole thing about this community shop is trust.**'
Bethany was annoyed. 'I definitely set the doll aside behind
the counter, and it's vanished.'

'Perhaps Edith came in unannounced, saw it and took
it?' I suggested.

'Believe me, I'd know if she had.' Bethany shook
her head. 'I've been here all morning. Nothing gets past
me.' With a nod to Simon, who had just appeared carrying
a small cardboard box, she added, 'Simon might know
something.'

To my surprise, Simon gave the box to me. 'You got my
text, good.'

'What is this?' I said.

'A bat monitor. It's easy to operate,' said Simon. 'You
turn it on, stand outside the ballroom and wait until dusk.
The monitor beeps every time a bat flies out.'

I was more than a little dismayed. I'd assumed I'd be
recording some informational segments for YouTube, not

standing out in a field all night. Simon must have guessed by my expression that I wasn't too thrilled.

'Yeah, you'll want to speak with authority and the only way to do that is to experience it.' He beamed. 'It's very cool and can get noisy in the height of summer when the mums are in their maternity roosts. That's when the females nurture their pups.'

'Maternity roost. Got it,' I said.

'If you get stuck, Eric and Harry will show you the ropes,' said Simon. 'You know, Eric says there could be a summer roost at your mum's place as well.'

I could only begin to imagine how delighted my mother would be about this news. As a townie she had a fear of anything with wings and had only just stopped running out of the room when she saw a moth.

'This is a state-of-the-art machine,' said Simon, 'so look after it. Each bat monitor uses an ultrasonic microphone to capture audio in its surroundings up to frequencies of ninety-six kilohertz. Now ... bat calls are normally at frequencies above twenty kilohertz, which is the limit of human hearing— Am I boring you?'

I hadn't a clue what Simon was talking about but I gave a polite smile and said, 'Not at all. It's fascinating.'

'As I was saying,' Simon went on, 'the captured audio is then turned into an image called a spectrogram. This is a statistical machine that learns algorithms—'

'Simon, stop!' Bethany scolded and rolled her eyes. 'Kat doesn't need a science lesson. She's come to get that painted Russian doll. I put it behind the counter for Kat to pick up and it's vanished.'

'Violet Green was taking an interest in it,' said Simon. 'But we've had a constant stream of production folks coming through. It could have been any one of them.'

'I'll pop next door and ask Violet if she remembers it,' I said.

To my surprise, Shawn entered. I felt a surge of nerves again. This was getting ridiculous. It was so unlike me. 'Are you following me?' I said lightly.

He actually smiled. 'Of course I am,' he said.

'Has my mother called you yet?' I said.

Shawn's smile fell. Clearly, she hadn't.

'She will, she promised.' I was in a dilemma. Should I stay or should I go? I desperately wanted to tell him that there was nothing between Paolo and myself, but having that conversation in the middle of the community shop might not be the time or place.

Shawn caught Simon's eye and motioned for him to come over. They exchanged polite conversation about the weather until Shawn said, 'Do you have any bottles of Honeychurch Gin left?'

My heart sank. *Here we go.*

'We had some at Christmas,' Bethany said brightly. 'Right, Simon?'

'Just a few,' said Simon. 'We're not the only place that sells it.'

'There are others?' Shawn said sharply.

'And Simon does have a permit to sell wine and spirits, Shawn,' said Bethany.

'Mum donates a lot of gin to charity,' I called out.

'Kat's right,' said Bethany. 'The jeroboam at the silent auction fetched a hundred pounds—'

'*Jeroboam*?' Shawn said, and he looked straight at me. There was no need to pretend I didn't know what this meant. How could I possibly forget that shards of a jeroboam had been found in Douglas's skull? Shawn whipped out his notebook.

'I'm sure there must have been more than one jeroboam,' I said.

Bethany shook her head. 'No. It was one of a kind. That was the whole point.'

My heart sank further.

'Can you describe the label?' Shawn said keenly. 'Do you remember who it was made by? Iris or Delia?'

This was a good question. Even though Delia was no longer involved in my mother's cottage industry, she had been very much in the mix at Christmas. As Bethany gave it some thought, I crossed my fingers and willed her to say, *Delia*.

'Iris,' Bethany declared, and promptly dashed my hopes.

'And do you remember who won this jeroboam?' Shawn asked, pencil poised.

'Violet Green,' said Simon.

Shawn seemed confused, as well he might. 'Are you certain it wasn't Douglas Jones?'

'Where would Douglas find the money?' Bethany demanded. 'He was as poor as a church mouse.'

Shawn turned to me with a questioning eyebrow. 'Where would he indeed?'

'No, it was Violet,' said Simon. 'Poor old thing didn't seem to understand the concept of a silent auction.'

'I felt sorry for her,' chimed in Bethany. 'But she insisted that she pay for it.'

I couldn't help wondering how the jeroboam came to be at Douglas's campsite. Was it possible that Violet had paid him a visit? But I couldn't see Violet drinking gin, since I remembered she only drank sherry. I'd have to talk to her.

'Are you all right, Kat?' Bethany said. 'You look anxious.'

'I've got a lot on my mind,' I muttered.

'Do you remember the last time you saw Douglas Jones?' Shawn asked Simon.

'Couple of days ago,' he said.

'Can you be more specific?' said Shawn.

'Wednesday,' said Simon. 'Wednesday afternoon. He came in and had a little spending spree.'

Great, I thought. He must have gone straight to the village after I'd given him his fifty pounds for the Russian doll.

'And what did he buy?' Shawn asked.

'Meths for his camp stove,' said Simon.

'Yes, Douglas told me he was going to do that,' I put in.

'Anything else?' Shawn demanded.

Simon and Bethany shared a look that did not go unnoticed by Shawn or me.

'You may as well tell him,' said Bethany. 'Douglas is dead now so he can't get into any more trouble.'

'He bought two canisters of red paint,' said Simon. 'I told him not to do it.'

'Well, he did,' Shawn said. 'We know all about the graffiti he sprayed on the granite pillars at the main entrance to the Hall and his lordship is not very happy.'

'His lordship wasn't happy about Douglas camping illegally in the woods either,' said Simon. 'Have you asked his *lordship* what he was doing on Wednesday?'

'Lord Rupert has a firm alibi,' said Shawn.

'Yeah, well, he would have, wouldn't he?' Simon's reaction took me by surprise.

'Take no notice of him,' Bethany said with a laugh. 'He thinks the monarchy should be abolished and all those grand titles along with it.'

'It's not a laughing matter,' said Shawn stiffly. 'This is a murder investigation. Douglas Jones was struck over the head with a jeroboam shortly before the yurt caught fire.'

'We know that,' said Bethany. 'This is a village. There are no secrets here. And you also know that we'll do anything we can to help.'

'Thank you,' Shawn said. 'So let's start with taking a statement from each of you. And I'll want to know your whereabouts on Wednesday and Wednesday evening as well.'

I left them to it. In fact, I couldn't wait to escape. As if the discovery of the empty bottles of Honeychurch Gin wasn't bad enough! Now the actual murder weapon was Mum's jeroboam from the silent auction.

I had an idea. Shawn was going to be tied up taking Simon and Bethany's statements for quite a while. It would

give me plenty of time to nip next door and kill two birds
with one stone.

I went to talk to Violet.

Chapter Twenty-four

With just two windows flanking the front door of Violet's tearoom, Rose Cottage looked small from the road but it was deceptively spacious.

I slipped down the side alley where Violet parked her Morris Minor, not remotely surprised to see that the rear bumper showed hardly any damage after reversing into Lucia's Mercedes. My dad used to say that Morris Minors were built like tanks. It would seem that he had been right.

I found the back door to the cottage wide open and called out: 'Hello, Violet? It's Kat. Mind if I come in for a minute?'

I heard a faint answer from inside, which I took to be a yes.

I stepped into the low-beamed kitchen and, as always, was impressed by the number and assortment of teapots that sat on every conceivable surface.

I was also struck by an unpleasant smell.

Violet peered at me through her bottle-top glasses. 'I had to open the door,' she said. 'They can be a little stinky.'

And there, on the kitchen table, stood several open jars of fish paste and a mound of sliced white bread.

Violet wore an old-fashioned cotton pinafore over her grey wool skirt and plain cerise jumper and a pair of plastic disposable gloves. With painstaking care she was buttering one side of the bread with Stork margarine, changing knives, and spreading the paste on the other.

A large sheet of aluminium foil was half filled with made-up sandwiches.

'That's a lot of sandwiches,' I said.

'Peggy told me that they are very overworked at the Hall with all the theatre people,' Violet went on, 'so I thought I'd help her out.'

'That's very generous of you,' I said.

'Her ladyship insisted I get paid, which is so kind.' Violet's infatuation with Edith was legendary and rather touching. 'Would you like one?'

'Thank you, but I've already eaten.' I hadn't, but I couldn't face a pilchard and anchovy special. 'I'm just popping in with a quick question.'

So I told her all about the Russian doll that my mother had donated to the White Elephant corner next door. 'It belongs to one of the visitors at the Hall.'

Violet paused for a moment. 'Yes, I remember Peggy telling me that they were turning the Hall upside down for a doll.'

'Do you remember seeing it in the community shop?' I asked.

'No. No, definitely not. No.' Violet shook her head. 'Are you sure you don't want a sandwich?'

I was quite sure I didn't want a sandwich and I was also sure that, for some reason, Violet wasn't telling the truth. 'I'm fine, thank you. Oh, I know this is a bit of a long shot but do you still have that jeroboam of Honeychurch Gin here?'

Violet looked blank.

'The bottle that you won in the silent auction last Christmas.'

'Oh that,' she grumbled. 'No one told me I had to buy it. I just put my name down. I thought it was a raffle.'

'Well, the money went to a good cause,' I said. 'I didn't think that you drank gin?'

'I don't. I only drink sherry,' Violet declared. 'I poured it down the drain.'

I was taken aback. 'Are you sure you didn't give it away instead? Maybe to Douglas Jones?'

'No,' said Violet firmly.

'What about the bottle?' I said. 'It's quite an unusual size, isn't it? Very large. You can get a lot of money back returning a bottle like that. Douglas Jones often returns bottles. Did you—'

'I threw it out.' Violet squared up three sandwiches, grabbed the loaf knife and cut through with such force that it made me jump.

'You threw it out where?' I said. 'Into your rubbish bin, perhaps?'

'I left it outside with my empty jam jars,' said Violet. 'Someone always comes along to pick them up.'

'And you didn't see who took the jeroboam?' I said.

Violet shook her head.

Damn. Douglas must have found the jeroboam outside Violet's cottage. I'd hit a dead end.

'And we meet *yet* again!' Shawn said as he stepped into the kitchen, but there was no smile on his face this time.

'Any chance of a cup of tea, Miss Green?' Shawn said to Violet. 'Those sandwiches look delicious.'

'Oh yes, dear,' said Violet. 'You remind me so much of your father. He was always popping in for a cuppa.'

'Shawn,' I said desperately, 'can we talk?'

'I'll see you to your car,' said Shawn.

'I left it on the other side of the churchyard,' I said.

'Then let's just step outside,' said Shawn. So we did.

'Why were you asking Violet Green about the jeroboam?'

'That was just a passing comment,' I said. 'I was actually asking about the Russian doll.'

'Yes, I know you were,' said Shawn. 'And why would you think that Violet had picked up that doll?'

I shrugged. 'I didn't. Simon said she was showing an interest.'

'According to Gran, that Russian doll was extremely valuable,' said Shawn. 'And yet you bought it for a mere fifty pounds.'

'You're kidding, right?' I looked at Shawn to see if he was joking but his expression remained neutral. 'You might be talking about a different one, but I can assure you that the doll Douglas Jones gave me was not valuable at all.'

'And how did the Russian doll come to be in the community shop?'

'I gave it to Mum,' I said. 'She brought it here.'

'Ah.' Shawn nodded. 'So your mother's name pops up again.'

I was getting exasperated. 'Shawn, I really don't know what you want me to say. I'm not hiding anything.'

'Aren't you?' Shawn said. 'What about being Fiona Reynolds's alibi?'

'Fiona?' I was confused. 'What has Fiona got to do with the Russian doll?'

'Fiona confessed,' said Shawn. 'She told me that she had asked you to lie on her behalf about the night of the theatre fire.'

'Well, I hope she also told you that I refused.'

'That's irrelevant,' said Shawn. 'You didn't tell me that she had asked you to lie for her.'

I counted slowly to ten. 'Fiona and I had dinner. I ran her home around eleven thirty. End of. I have no idea what she did after that.'

'Fiona still denies starting the fire but she has admitted to tampering with the costumes, although she has refused to tell me why. Would you happen to know why?'

I shook my head. 'No,' I said. 'I hope she also told you that she had suspicions about Victor Mullins being murdered.'

'Yes, she did,' said Shawn.

This surprised me. 'Well?' I demanded. 'And? Was he?'

'I'm not at liberty to say,' said Shawn quietly. 'But we are taking her accusation very seriously.'

'I'm glad to hear it,' I said. 'Is Fiona still in custody?'

'For another twenty-four hours, yes.' Shawn thought for a moment. 'You knew Victor Mullins, didn't you?'

'As in . . . he was my tax accountant. Yes,' I said. 'But only in a business capacity. I didn't even know he sang with D.O.D.O.'

'And what about your mother?'

'Victor was Mum's accountant, too,' I said. 'Why?'

'I see.' Shawn regarded me with curiosity. 'And you really have no idea what Fiona was doing?'

'Of course I haven't!' I said. 'I haven't lied to you about anything, Shawn.'

Shawn's jaw hardened. 'Kat, your mother's phone number was programmed into Douglas Jones's mobile.'

'You already told me that and I told you that Douglas and Mum had an arrangement about returning the empty bottles.'

'So why all the secrecy?' he demanded.

'My mother is not *not* telling you because she has something to hide,' I said. 'She's not telling you because she's on a deadline and can't handle more than one thing at a time.' I could see that Shawn didn't believe me. 'You're going to make a terrific interrogator in your new job.'

Shawn ignored the jab. 'Three hundred and seventy-seven pounds is a lot of bottles,' he said. 'I think you know more than what you are prepared to say.'

'Believe what you like!' I exclaimed. 'I'm not my mother's keeper! You're being incredibly unreasonable!'

'I see,' said Shawn tightly. 'In that case, given the delicacy of our inquiries, I think it would be better if we don't see each other in a personal capacity until this has all been sorted out. I think we need a space.'

'*Fine*,' I said. 'Take all the space you want. Oh . . . and don't let your tea get cold.'

And with that I turned on my heel and stormed back to my car, uttering a quick cry for celestial help as I cut through the churchyard.

My fury took me all the way home to Jane's Cottage. I didn't stop at the gatehouse. I didn't call in and check on my mother. I just wanted to be alone.

I drew all the curtains, locked the door, switched off my phone and changed into my pyjamas. I boiled up a huge saucepan of pasta for supper but then realised all too late, that I'd got no ingredients to make a sauce. So I ate the tagliatelle with lashings of butter, opened a bottle of red wine, and watched three seasons of *Upstairs Downstairs*, the 1970s version.

That night I lay in bed trying to make sense of things. Who would want to murder Victor? Why would Fiona damage the costumes that she had made herself? And then there was the theatre fire. No, two fires – seemingly unconnected – or even three fires, if you counted the music-room fire all those years ago.

And then there were Lucia's co-stars – Victor and Reynard. When Reynard had shown up at the gatehouse that fateful night, we'd all assumed he'd been drinking but it turned out that he'd been poisoned. What if Victor had been poisoned too?

As my mind began to join the dots I could see that although at first glance nothing seemed connected, in fact, that wasn't true. Everything was connected by a common denominator.

My mother.

I made a decision to call Shawn first thing the next day. It was time to lay all my cards on the proverbial table.

Chapter Twenty-five

I woke up feeling marginally brighter. Shawn didn't answer his phone but I left him a message and told him we needed to talk.

Since there was nothing else I could do, I went to the stable yard a little earlier than usual in the hope of having a quiet word with Alfred: I wanted to ask him what he remembered about Lucia.

I found him in Thunder's loosebox grooming Harry's little black pony in readiness for our weekly ride.

'I remember little Julie Jones,' said Alfred. 'She kept asking my mum—'

'That would be Mum's stepmother—'

'Iris never called her that,' Alfred said. 'She always called her Aunt June.'

'Sorry, I interrupted you,' I said. 'You were saying?'

'My mum read the tarot and the tea leaves and Julie wanted her fortune told.'

'And?' I prompted.

'Mum told her she'd be a famous opera singer, but blimey, luv, that was years ago. She can't have been more than a nipper.'

'What about the other Jones kids?' I said. 'Did you ever come across Douglas?'

Alfred shrugged. 'Maybe in the boxing ring,' he said. 'The locals all thought they could beat us Bushman's but they never did.'

I couldn't ask any more questions because Lavinia appeared with eight-year-old Harry in tow. The boy now reached his mother's shoulders.

I felt a pang of nostalgia for this new Harry. When I first met him he was obsessed with Squadron Leader James Bigglesworth and wore a First World War flying helmet, goggles and white scarf. A few months ago Harry had hung up his fictional wings and put his childhood hero away in a box, along with a number of first editions of Biggles' adventures by W. E. Johns. Harry then joined the 3rd Totnes Sea Scout Group and hadn't looked back since.

Today, he was wearing jodhpurs, a sweatshirt and riding helmet. I also spied a 'Bat Buddy' badge.

Even though Lavinia wasn't riding, she was still wearing her usual attire of jodhpurs and had her hair clamped under a slumber net. I was glad to see her up and about and told her so.

'Abso-*lute* nightmare at the Hall,' she said. 'Edith is going insane. Peggy's exhausted.'

It had taken me a long time to understand what Lavinia was talking about. Not only did she speak in the strangled vowels of the upper classes but also in staccato sentences. She was a little dense but – as my mother said – harmless. In fact, I had a bit of a soft spot for Lavinia.

Lavinia sneezed, then pulled out an old-fashioned cotton handkerchief from the sleeve of her badly hand-knitted green pullover. The handkerchief had a horse head embroidered in the corner, which made me think of the white man-size handkerchief with the initials E.R.H. that had been in Douglas Jones's suitcase. Not many people used cotton handkerchiefs these days, although I knew my mother still did. And, after washing them, she ironed them too.

Harry led Thunder out and just threw his leg over with no effort at all. His stirrups dangled below Thunder's belly. I was dismayed. 'I feel like he's grown another inch since last Saturday!'

Lavinia mumbled agreement and dabbed at her eyes with the handkerchief. She swallowed hard and blinked away a tear. 'Darling Thunder,' she whispered. 'I remember when he was born. All legs.'

Why wasn't I surprised that she seemed more affected by Thunder's age than Harry's? 'How old is Thunder now?'

'Twenty-two.' She took a deep breath. 'Horses, so special. Could never send darling Thunder away.'

I bit back the comment that Lavinia had seemed only too willing to send Harry off to boarding school. But that was all in the past. Harry was home now.

'Edith's got a place for Thunder in the equine cemetery,' Lavinia said. 'But he's not dead yet.'

A short time later Harry and I clattered out of the yard on horseback.

'Kat, can we ride through Honeychurch Woods?' Harry demanded. 'Eric said there was a fire and a dead body.'

There was no question of us riding anywhere near the burned-out campsite and I told him so. 'I thought we'd take the green lane to Larcombe today and loop back through the village.'

'But can't we still cut through the woods?' Harry said.

'There is nothing to see, Harry,' I said firmly. 'And besides, I want to ask you something.' When he didn't comment I went on, 'Isn't part of the Scout Promise to be prepared and help other people?'

'Be prepared is the Scout Motto,' said Harry. 'But yes, helping other people is part of the Scout Promise. And then there is the Scout Law. Shall I tell you what they all are?'

'Maybe later,' I said quickly. 'But I do need your help right now.'

Harry looked serious.

'Simon gave me a bat monitor,' I said. 'And I haven't a clue what to do with it.'

'It's easy,' said Harry. 'But the bats aren't here yet.'

Harry spent the next thirty minutes telling me everything about bats, and soon the burned-out campsite was forgotten.

'Bats can live to be even older than Thunder,' Harry went on. 'Horseshoe bats are the only bats in England that hang upside down. They have the most enormous wing span, too.'

'How enormous?' I asked.

'Anywhere between fourteen to sixteen inches!' Harry exclaimed.

'That *is* enormous!'

'I know,' said Harry. 'There is a lesser horseshoe bat – he's the size of a plum – and a *greater* horseshoe bat – he's the size of a pear.'

'And why are they called horseshoe bats?' I asked.

'It's because of the shape of their nose,' said Harry. 'They use it to make high-pitched sounds so they can find their way around the countryside at night. It's called echo . . . echo . . . lo . . . echolocation.'

'Like dolphins?' I said. 'Is it true that it's only in the summer months that the breeding females congregate in their maternity roosts?'

'Yes,' Harry agreed. 'In the winter all the bats hibernate and spend time in torpor in caves and cold, dark and damp places.'

'Torpor,' I said. 'That's a good word.'

Harry nodded. 'Torpor allows bats to reduce their metabolic rate and need for food during cooler spells. But they don't go hungry. They can still go foraging for insects. Dung beetles are their favourite snack.'

'You really know your stuff, Harry,' I said. 'I'm impressed. So will you show me how to work my bat monitor?'

'You know you have to stand outside,' said Harry.

'At dusk, I know,' I said.

'That Italian man didn't.' Harry grinned.

'Paolo?' I said. 'Maybe they don't have bats in Italy.'

'Of course they have bats in Italy,' Harry scoffed. 'He's got a bat monitor but he's using it inside!'

'Inside?' I exclaimed. 'Isn't that silly?'

'The Italian man showed me all his machines,' said Harry. 'They're really cool. When I grow up I want to be a sound engineer and work in films, too.'

Last week Harry had wanted to be an astronaut, and the week before that, a zoologist.

For two hours I forgot all about Shawn and my mother's predicament and enjoyed Harry's company, but when I finally got home to Jane's Cottage to shower and change, the events and confusion of the last few days came flooding back.

I tried to call Shawn yet again but there was no answer. I knew my mother would be busy either writing or mending Lucia and Reynard's costumes, so in the end I decided to take the doll's house to the Dartmouth Antique Emporium and rearrange my space. *Anything* to distract me from the gnawing anxiety and sense of foreboding that I just couldn't shake off.

I had to stop at the gatehouse first so was surprised to see a car with the Enterprise logo emblazoned on the side door. The driver, who was wearing an ill-fitting suit, carried a large cardboard box and seemed to be waiting for me.

'Can I help you?' I asked.

'You must be Kat Stanford,' he said.

'Yes, that's me.'

'Paolo Carerra gave me this address and your name,' said the driver. 'I thought, nah, wouldn't be *the* Kat Stanford, but it is.' He chuckled, as if he found something amusing. 'The box was left in the footwell of the Mercedes car hire last Wednesday.'

'Did you call Paolo and tell him?' I knew he would be relieved.

'The number he gave me doesn't work,' he replied. 'Here . . . do you want me to take it inside? It's heavy.'

The driver waited while I unlocked the door and disabled the alarm. 'You can just put it on my desk,' I said. 'Thank you. I'll make sure Paolo gets it.'

The driver hesitated for a moment. I was wondering if he expected a tip.

'Was there anything else?' I asked.

'Well, the thing is, because of company policy, we had to look inside the box to make sure it wasn't something it shouldn't be – you know, like a bomb,' he said. 'You can't be too careful these days.'

'Oh!' I said. 'I suppose that makes sense.'

He grinned again and gave a knowing wink. 'Maria Callas look out, right?'

'I have no idea what you're talking about,' I said.

The driver tapped his nose. 'Course you don't. Didn't peg you for a singer but what do I know!'

And with that cryptic comment, he left.

I stared at the box on the desk. So this was the offending article that had given Paolo so much grief. But when I dialled Paolo's number, an automated voice told me that the number I was dialling was no longer in service. I double-checked to make sure I had dialled the right number and I had. It was definitely Paolo's. It was most odd.

I stared at the cardboard box. The flaps had been closed but the cardboard box had not been sealed back up.

So I opened it.

At first I wasn't sure what it was. The machine sat in a sea of popcorn packaging and clumps of bubble wrap that had been torn apart. A safety instructions booklet was tucked down the side in a plastic envelope.

It was a Digital Audio Workstation – some kind of audio interface machine that could be used for pre-recorded tracks. I didn't know much about sound equipment from my days of working on TV, but I did know the difference between a pre-recorded show and a live performance.

Was it possible that Lucia was going to lip-sync her way through *The Merry Widow*? Was this what Paolo had been panicking about?

Given Lucia's reputation as the greatest soprano of all time, she had a lot to lose if anyone ever found out. I was pretty sure that Harry had seen the replacement machine in the ballroom and Paolo had told him it was a bat monitor, even though a bat monitor was a fraction of the size. But why go to all that trouble? Didn't many artists lip-sync these days?

Had Douglas Jones found out and resorted to blackmail? Maybe it was Lucia's money that Clive had found in the Oxo tin?

Lucia must have returned to the campsite when it got dark. I was positive she wouldn't have walked there alone, especially given the heavy rain. This meant that Paolo must have driven her there.

And yet even as I considered this, it didn't ring true. Would Paolo really have risked so much for a woman he'd only been working for for a few weeks? It wasn't as if they were embroiled in a steamy love affair.

And why would Lucia need a lip-sync machine in the first place? Mum and I had heard her voice. Brooke had said that Lucia often allowed her to slip into her suite and listen to her practising in private. In fact, Brooke told us that Lucia had become her role model and mentor.

I was upset. I'd started to like Lucia Lombardi, but it looked as though she had fooled me. And then there was my mother, who was caught up in it all and being made the scapegoat. I should go straight to Shawn and tell him everything, but it wasn't as if I hadn't tried.

I needed to talk to Mum immediately before things got any more complicated.

Chapter Twenty-six

I heard Delia's voice the moment I let myself into the Carriage House.

'She treats me like dirt,' she was saying.

'She's no more than a servant herself,' Mum replied. 'And then there was all that scandal with the music-room fire.'

The kitchen door was ajar. I could see Mum and the housekeeper having a cup of afternoon tea at the table. Behind that was a metal clothing rail with wheels where Mum and I had hung the costumes. They were bulky and took up a lot of space. My mother's sewing basket was on the table too. I assumed that despite Delia being so busy, she hadn't been too busy to stop by and gossip.

Despite the severity of the situation, I couldn't help but crack a smile. Delia was drinking tea from the unhappy Princess Caroline of Brunswick bone-china mug.

'Afternoon,' I said loudly and strolled on in.

Delia gave a curt nod then continued the conversation

as if I wasn't there. 'Not *her*. Not Lucia,' said Delia. 'The old bag. That Russian woman.'

'Kat, dear,' said Mum, 'would you like a cuppa? Tea's in the pot.'

'You aren't staying, are you?' Delia said rudely.

'Actually, I am,' I said. 'I need to talk to my mother and it's very important.'

'No, I haven't called Shawn yet.' Mum sounded exasperated. 'But I will.' She turned back to Delia. 'Where was I?'

'We were talking about the diva, Countess Olga Golodkin,' said Delia.

'That's right,' said Mum. 'She's Russian royalty. Related to Tsar Nicholas II.'

'That may be true, but the Russian Revolution was over a hundred years ago!' Delia went on. 'And if they were all like her I'm surprised they didn't go all French and use the guillotine.'

Mum nodded. 'But the Romanovs still got shot.'

'Yes,' Delia agreed. 'But not all of them. There were some stragglers. You know, all those misfits claiming they're Anastasia reincarnated.' Delia took a sip of tea. 'And the fuss she's making over that wooden doll, claiming it's priceless. Talk about wasting my time. We've all been searching high and low.'

Mum looked sheepish and shot me an appeal for help.

'Have you any idea how big that Hall is?' Delia continued. 'When I see all that wasted space I think the Bolsheviks had the right idea about forming communes.'

'I didn't know you were a bit of a communist, Delia,' Mum mused.

'Being around *her* is enough to make anyone become a communist,' Delia retorted. 'We've got to search the cellars tomorrow.'

I was incredulous. 'You haven't told her, have you, Mum?'

'Told me what?' Delia demanded.

Mum reddened. 'How was I to know that the doll was important?'

'Wait!' Delia's jaw dropped. 'You found it? When? Why didn't you say so?'

'I just did and I didn't find it,' said Mum. 'Kat did.'

'*You* found it?' Delia was so outraged that her hair – she was wearing the same auburn wig from Wednesday – matched her complexion. 'So where is it now?'

'Mum took it to the community shop and it's gone,' I said. 'So you're wasting your time looking for it at the Hall. It could be anywhere in the country by now, and I can tell you that the doll that I found was not worth all the fuss.'

Delia seemed most put out. 'So . . . where did you find this doll?'

'It was in a suitcase,' Mum said. 'It belonged to Douglas Jones.'

Delia gasped with horror. 'The chappy in the wood who was murdered? It belonged to *him*?'

'Mum,' I said, 'I really need to talk to you, right *now*.'

'I know! Stop nagging!' Mum put up her hand. 'Delia and I have been discussing it and we think there's a pyromaniac on the loose and our bets are on the greatest soprano of all time.'

'Music-room fire.' Delia ticked off a finger. 'Theatre fire. ' She ticked off a second finger. 'Then the yurt.' A third finger. 'Eric told me that wherever Julie Jones – or Lucia or whatever she wants to call herself – goes, there is always trouble.'

'She seemed all right to start with,' Mum said. 'But that's the thing. You never really know people, do you?'

There was a knock at the front door. 'I'll go.'

It was Shawn. I was overwhelmed with relief. 'Thank God!' I exclaimed. 'I have to talk to you. Didn't you get my messages?'

I moved forward to give him a hug but he stepped away from me.

'Sorry. This is police business. I've come to see your mother,' he said. 'Is she . . .?' He didn't even wait for my reply but pushed past me and headed for the kitchen. I scurried after him.

'Shawn dumped Kat,' I heard Mum say. 'So your Guy's in with another chance.'

Shawn stopped at the kitchen door.

I was mortified.

'I knew *that* wouldn't last,' Delia replied. 'Well, Guy's got the French girl now but she's too French for my liking. But wait . . . did Shawn dump Kat or Kat dump Shawn?'

'Oh, she dumped him,' Mum said. 'Too needy, she said. She likes the independent type.'

'All right,' said Delia, 'I'll see what I can do, but Guy doesn't like sloppy seconds.'

I just stood there, wishing the floor would open and swallow me up.

I fought the urge to run because I didn't trust Delia for a minute. At the first chance she got, I knew she would throw my mother under the bus. It was just how Delia was made.

Shawn stepped into the kitchen.

'We were just talking about you,' said Delia gaily.

'Yes,' Shawn said grimly, 'I heard.'

Mum looked guilty. 'I was just about to call you,' she said. 'Wasn't I, Delia?'

'Were you?' Delia said.

'Then I've saved you the trouble,' said Shawn.

'Kat will get you a cup of tea,' said Mum. 'Pull up a chair.'

'No thank you,' Shawn said. 'This is not a social visit.'

'I'd better leave you to it,' Delia said, but she made no attempt to stand up and do just that.

'No, you can stay,' said Shawn. 'I may have some questions for you, too.'

Everyone waited while Shawn brought out his notebook and turned to a fresh page. I was jittery and nervous, but Mum seemed remarkably calm. She opened her sewing basket and started rearranging the cotton reels.

'Mrs Stanford and Mrs Evans,' Shawn began, which was a bad sign in itself – he only used formal address when there was trouble – 'were either of you supplying Douglas Jones with Honeychurch Gin?'

Delia's jaw dropped. 'Douglas Jones? You mean that horrible drunk who was murdered in the woods?' Shawn seemed surprised that she knew. 'Oh, there are no secrets

in Little Dipperton; but to answer your question: not me.'
Delia sat back in her chair with her arms folded. 'I got out
of the gin business at the end of last year, so it's nothing to
do with me.'

'I wasn't *supplying* Douglas Jones with gin,' Mum said
suddenly. 'Why would I do that?'

'Would you like to explain why there was a plastic crate
– exactly the same as the red one over there,' Shawn
pointed to the offending crate in the corner, 'at his campsite
full of your empty bottles?'

'I have no idea.' Mum flipped the lid closed on her
sewing basket.

Shawn gave an impatient gesture. 'Your mobile, please.'

'I don't know where it is,' said Mum quickly.

With a sigh, I got up, went to the oak dresser, opened a
drawer and took out Mum's iPhone. When I handed it to
Shawn I noticed he had already donned disposable gloves
and had a Ziploc bag at the ready.

This did not bode well.

'What are you looking for?' Mum said. 'I can't see how
my iPhone can possibly help. I mean, it's not as if it will tell
you anything.'

'You'd be surprised what I can find out from an iPhone,'
said Shawn.

'This is exactly why I don't have a mobile,' Delia said
smugly. 'It gets you into all sorts of trouble.' She was clearly
enjoying my mother's discomfort.

Shawn started scrolling through Mum's phone.

'What are you doing?' Mum said nervously.

'Checking your call log,' said Shawn.

I felt so tense I thought my head would explode.

Shawn stopped scrolling and looked up. 'On the day that Douglas Jones died you called him six times.'

Delia gave a gasp. 'You called Douglas Jones? Whatever for? Were you . . . were you having an affair?'

'Oh, for heaven's sake,' Mum exclaimed. 'Of course I wasn't. I was supposed to meet Douglas to pick up the crate of bottles and he didn't turn up. I waited for at least half an hour and then left.'

Hallelujah! At last Mum was coming clean.

Shawn duly made a note of this. 'So you admit that you were there on Wednesday afternoon.'

'Yes,' said Mum.

'Good. Because his lordship saw your car parked outside the public bridleway to Honeychurch Woods,' said Shawn. 'I believe, at last, we are making progress.'

'But I did not set foot in the woods,' Mum declared. 'I do not own a pair of wellington boots and if you care to check my shoes for mud, please . . . go ahead.'

'She doesn't wear wellies,' Delia put in, 'although Marks does a nice waterproof shoe.'

'And you say that you were planning on meeting Douglas Jones to pick up the empty bottles,' Shawn declared.

'That's correct,' said Mum. 'I am a responsible citizen. Douglas doesn't have a car so I pick them up and recycle them.'

'And you gave him money for the bottles?' Shawn said.

'Yes. Fifty pence a bottle,' Mum said.

'So wait...' Delia frowned. 'You pocket the money? You keep it all for yourself. You didn't even think to share it with me?'

'You said you wanted out,' said Mum. 'So that means you're out!'

'And the jeroboam,' said Shawn. 'What happened to the jeroboam that was used to strike Douglas Jones over the head?'

Delia clapped her hand over her mouth in horror.

'I don't know why you're acting all surprised, Delia,' Mum snapped. 'We already talked about that before Kat walked in. You wanted to know all the gory details.'

'But that was before I knew that you were involved in...' said Delia. 'I just don't think I know you at all.'

'I'm not involved in anything shifty!' Mum exclaimed.

'If you paid Douglas Jones fifty pence a bottle, it would mean that you would have had to have sold at least six hundred bottles of gin,' Shawn said.

'Six hundred?' Mum shrieked. 'How did you come to such a sum?'

But I knew how. There was three hundred and seventy-seven pounds in the Oxo tin.

'I paid him no more than fifty pounds in total,' Mum protested. 'There's no way we could have made that much gin! I was just shifting the Christmas stock.'

Delia was very quiet and then she said, 'Iris is telling the truth. She told me she knew we'd be in trouble if we didn't shift it fast. That's why I wanted out.'

'Thanks a bunch, Delia,' said Mum bitterly.

'Just how much would you have given Douglas for a jeroboam?' Shawn asked.

Mum shrugged. 'Two pounds – and that's pushing it. But I will say that Douglas tried to put his prices up. Claimed he was wandering all over the South Hams rummaging through people's rubbish bins and it was wearing out his shoe leather. Almost held me to blackmail saying he'd report me to the authorities.'

'Report you to the authorities for . . . *what* exactly?' Shawn gave a meaningful pause.

Mum looked startled. 'I don't know. I didn't take it seriously.'

'Perhaps you should have done.' Shawn's eyes narrowed. 'Perhaps he was alluding to his reading material?'

'Reading material?' Delia sounded confused. 'What reading material?'

'I believe that Douglas Jones enjoyed a good romance novel,' said Shawn smoothly. 'Specifically those written by the mysterious Krystalle Storm.'

Mum turned pale. Even I felt sick. How could Shawn say this! Especially in front of Delia! He might as well have had a megaphone and broadcast Mum's secret from outer space.

'She's supposed to live somewhere in Devon, you know,' Delia declared. 'I quite like her books, although sometimes they can be a bit too explicit. Fancy Douglas Jones being a fan.'

'Well, I've never read them,' Mum said quickly. 'So I fail to see how his reading material could possibly be connected to me.'

'Yes, I agree,' I put in.

Delia thought for a moment. 'If I was leading the investigation, I'd start with Lucia Lombardi. We were talking about her before you arrived. We think she's a pyromaniac.'

'I have questioned Miss Lombardi, thank you very much,' said Shawn. 'She had a firm alibi for Wednesday night.'

Delia thought again. 'What about . . . Lord Rupert? He wanted Douglas off his land.'

'His lordship has been more than helpful with our inquiries,' said Shawn. 'He had a firm alibi, too.'

Delia snapped her fingers again. 'What about the little Italian?'

'Ah yes, the little Italian,' said Shawn. 'It turns out the little Italian was with Miss Lombardi all of Wednesday night.'

'No!' Delia exclaimed. 'Now that *does* surprise me.'

'And why would you say that?' Shawn demanded.

'As you know, the Russian woman has ordered me to look after the both of them as if I'm some kind of servant!' Delia said. 'But I can assure you that Paolo's bed has been slept in every single night.'

Shawn looked at me. 'Interesting.'

'In fact,' Delia grew excited, 'he'd barricaded the interconnecting door with a chest of drawers. At first we all thought he was Lucia's lover but then it turned out she just wanted everyone to think she could bag a young stud muffin.'

Shawn's eyes widened. 'I see. Thank you.'

I studied Shawn's expression as he made notes, but he gave nothing away.

'So that puts her alibi out the window,' Mum said. 'Anyway, I thought you wanted her to be guilty.'

'I do,' said Delia. 'But you can't go making accusations to all and sundry without proof. That makes it just a rumour.'

I suddenly felt very tired.

Delia sat back in her chair, clearly satisfied with her contribution to the investigation.

'Well, thank you very much, Mrs Evans. I believe you missed your vocation. You should have joined the police force.' Shawn said it with a straight face but I knew he was being sarcastic.

'You know where I am if you need any more of my help.' Delia stood up and grabbed the bottle-green coat that she always draped around the back of her chair. As she pulled it on she added, 'And I think that's a very good idea, Iris.'

'What is?' Mum said.

Delia pointed to the clothing rack. 'Sewing up the flies on Reynard's costumes.' Delia grinned. 'That'll tell him that you won't stand for his philandering ways!'

The bus came by and Delia pushed her best friend under the wheels – just as I'd predicted.

Shawn waited until we heard the sound of the front door slam. In fact, I went out into the hall to make sure that Delia had gone.

When I returned to the kitchen, I knew that something was seriously wrong.

'Kat, come and sit down, please,' said Shawn.

Mum attempted to make a joke but Shawn wore an expression that I'd never seen before and it frightened me.

'We tested that bottle of Honeychurch Gin that was in Lucia's suite yesterday,' he said. 'The results came back this morning.'

'I suppose you're going to tell me that I lied about it being one hundred per cent proof,' said Mum.

'No, Iris.' Instead of growing colder, Shawn's voice softened and that frightened me all the more. 'Your gin contained large traces of ethylene glycol.'

Mum shrugged. 'I don't know what that is.'

I thought my heart would stop.

'Your boyfriend, Dr Reynard Smeaton, was poisoned deliberately and I have reason to believe . . .' Shawn gave a dramatic pause. 'It was by your hand.'

Chapter Twenty-seven

'But why would I do that to my own gin?' Mum said. 'I've got standards! I don't even know what this ethylene glycol is or where I could get it.'

'It's the chemical used in antifreeze for cars,' said Shawn. 'It tastes sweet and is not at all unpleasant to drink. In fact, it's easy to disguise because the initial symptoms are that the victim appears to be drunk. Three and a half to four and a half grams is the lethal dose with death taking place in about an hour. Fortunately, the doctor knew immediately that something was wrong and that's why he left the Hall in a hurry.'

'Wait a minute,' I said slowly. 'Are you accusing my mother of *deliberately* trying to poison Reynard?'

'According to Lucia, you gave her the bottle as a welcome present,' said Shawn.

'Which she rudely rejected,' said Mum. 'She told me she never drank the stuff. She only drank Barolo. I saw her give my gin to Olga.'

'Mum did. I was there,' I said. 'The bottles were identical.'

'But they weren't,' said Shawn. 'One bottle – the bottle we retrieved from Lucia's suite – had the 'I' in gin marked with a tiny green dot.'

'I don't know what to say,' said Mum.

'I put it to you that you were jealous of Reynard's relationship with Lucia,' said Shawn.

'But . . . how could I know that he would drink the gin?' Mum was bewildered. 'Bit of a risk, don't you think? What if Lucia had drunk it instead? If I were intending to poison anyone wouldn't I have rather poisoned her instead? Or even the pair of them?'

'You must have been very angry,' said Shawn.

'No. I was disappointed,' Mum said.

Shawn's eyes narrowed. 'Disappointed enough to sew up the flies on Reynard's trousers?'

'Oh, come on, Shawn,' I said. 'Mum was joking about that!'

'No, I wasn't actually,' said Mum. 'I thought about putting itching powder in there, too, but I didn't want to spend the money.'

I put my head in my hands and just groaned.

'No. Our break-up was very civilised,' Mum went on. 'It was my decision. Not his. Ask Kat. She was there.'

'Kat seems to be everywhere.' Shawn checked his note-book. 'According to the call log on your mobile, you rang Reynard eleven times on Thursday evening. That was the same night that he was taken ill. It was also the same night that you *allegedly* interrupted an intruder at the gatehouse. A bit of a coincidence, don't you think?'

'There wasn't an intruder.' I glanced quickly at my mother. 'Was there, Mum?'

Shawn's eyes were hard. 'Why would Iris say she saw an intruder if she didn't?'

'I didn't say I *saw* one,' said Mum. 'I just assumed there had to be one because the alarm went off.'

'And yet the back door was open,' said Shawn. 'I suppose you're going to tell me it was the wind?'

'This is ridiculous.' Mum thought for a moment. 'So Reynard wasn't drunk at all? I don't believe it.'

'No,' said Shawn coldly. 'And if he hadn't stopped at the gatehouse, I have no doubt at all that his car would have ended up in a ditch – or worse.'

'But it didn't,' said Mum.

'You were stalking the doctor on the night of the break-in, weren't you?' Shawn pressed on. 'That's why you were at the gatehouse when the alarm went off. Were you planning on following his car just to see if the poisoned gin had done the trick?'

Mum said nothing. She sat there as her face underwent a series of expressions. Finally she said, 'All right. Yes – I was waiting for Reynard at the end of the drive. I wanted to know if he stayed the night with Lucia.'

Shawn consulted his notes. 'But it says here that you had a date. Are you telling me that that was a lie?'

'Yep.' Mum was getting irritated. 'That was a lie.'

'I see,' said Shawn. 'So you went to all the trouble of

looking as if you were going on a date.' He made vague movements with his hands, presumably to indicate she had done her hair and wore smart clothes.

'Yep,' said Mum again.

'Presumably this was in an effort to make the doctor jealous?'

'Yep,' said Mum yet again.

I could see a tic begin to throb on my mother's forehead. 'What about the other bottle that my mother gave to Olga?' I said quickly. 'Did you check that one for antifreeze?'

'We did,' said Shawn. 'There was no green dot and it tested negative for any suspicious substances. It had not been doctored.'

'That's an unfortunate turn of phrase,' Mum muttered.

Shawn glared at my mother. She glared right back.

Shawn grew even more sombre. 'I have reason to believe that you were also responsible for the yurt fire and that you attacked Douglas Jones with a jeroboam because you knew that he was about to blow your cover and tell the world that you are Krystalle Storm.'

'If you say so,' Mum said tightly.

'And the money in the Oxo tin was not just to pay for the empty bottles but to pay for Douglas Jones's silence.'

'Shawn, please,' I said. 'You aren't interrogating a terrorist. This is my mother!'

'Stay out of this, Katherine,' said Shawn.

'Oh, for God's sake, just go ahead and do it then,' said Mum angrily. 'Arrest me. You've never liked me! And you've messed my daughter around something chronic.

How dare you lead her on! What kind of man just announces he's moving to London?'

'Mum!' I shouted. 'Stop!'

Shawn's face was red but my mother's was even redder. I rarely saw her lose her temper, but this looked like it could be one of those rare occasions.

'I don't need this.' Mum got to her feet. 'I know, why don't you pin the theatre fire on me as well? Oh, and while you're at it, why don't you blame Victor Mullins's fatal car crash on me too!'

'Sit back down,' Shawn bellowed. 'Sit down now!'

I'd never heard Shawn shout before and neither had my mother, but she remained standing, arms akimbo. Defiant.

I was paralysed by all of it. I couldn't say a word.

'We *are* looking into Fiona Reynolds's accusations that Victor was murdered,' said Shawn. 'Unfortunately that doesn't look too good for you.'

'What are you talking about?' Mum said.

'Yes, Fiona Reynolds is still in custody for damaging the costumes and yes, we are investigating the CCTV footage, but when it comes to Victor's accident . . .'

I looked at my mother and saw genuine confusion.

'Hasn't he been buried yet?' Mum demanded.

'Actually, no,' said Shawn. 'Victor had family in Australia who wanted to be present at the funeral so we have now been able to conduct a full autopsy.'

I was aware that my heart had started thundering in my chest. 'And?'

Shawn took a deep breath. 'Victor Mullins was also poisoned by ethylene glycol.'

'What?' I whispered.

'I suppose you're going to tell me you found a bottle of Honeychurch— Oh.' Mum turned pale. 'I gave him one as a thank-you gift.'

'And that, too, had been doctored,' said Shawn.

'This can't be true!' I exclaimed. 'Mum would never do that! She wouldn't!'

'Victor Mullins was your tax adviser and accountant,' said Shawn. 'I believe that he discovered you had hidden assets in an offshore account and demanded that you declare them.'

Mum said nothing. What could she say? It was true. She *did* have hidden assets in offshore accounts but I also knew that she hadn't told Victor about them because we'd argued about it. Shawn was wrong.

'I have turned a blind eye to your shenanigans out of affection for your daughter,' said Shawn, 'but I put it to you now that you had to get rid of Victor Mullins, just like you got rid of Douglas Jones.'

'No,' Mum whispered. 'Someone is trying to frame me!'

'Iris Stanford, I am arresting you for the murder of Victor Mullins and the murder of Douglas Jones and the attempted murder of Dr Reynard Smeaton.'

Mum gave a cry and grabbed the back of the chair. The colour drained out of her face.

'You do not have to say anything—'

'Shawn!' I begged. 'This is all a mistake— Oh! Mum! Quick! Catch her!'

But we weren't fast enough. My mother crashed to the floor in a dead faint, taking the chair down with her.

I darted to her side, dropped to my knees and put two fingers on her neck. There was a pulse. It was thundering along at a gallop. I had the most awful feeling that my mother had faked it.

I looked up to see Shawn staring down, his face devoid of emotion. In his eyes I could see that he knew she had faked it too.

'How convenient,' he said. 'Your histrionics don't fool me for a minute, Iris Stanford. I'll be back tomorrow and you'd better have some firm alibis. This is your final warning.'

And with that, he left the kitchen. The minute the front door slammed Mum's eyes popped open. 'Has he gone?'

Chapter Twenty-eight

I stared at my mother across the kitchen table. I was in total shock but she was just angry.

'I'm glad you've broken up with Shawn,' she said. 'That interrogation course has gone to his head. There was no reasoning with him, Katherine. He wouldn't have it.'

'I know, but he knew you were faking it,' I said. 'I'm going to make more tea.'

'Can't we have something stronger?' Mum said.

'No.' I was incredibly upset. 'You're in serious, *serious trouble*. It's all going to come out now. Everything! Even if the murder charges are dropped—'

'They have to be dropped because I'm innocent!'

'And you didn't help yourself either,' I scolded. 'You seemed to deliberately wind Shawn up.'

'And he seemed to deliberately think I was guilty,' Mum said. 'Would I ever do anything like that? I am deeply insulted.'

'That's all very noble but whatever happens, you could

still end up in prison for tax evasion,' I said. 'Don't you understand?'

Mum slumped at the table and put her head in her hands. 'I may as well drink a bottle of antifreeze right now and be done with it.'

'Don't be so dramatic,' I said. 'You know what they say. "It ain't over till the fat lady sings."'

'I don't even have any antifreeze,' Mum protested.

'Everyone has antifreeze somewhere,' I said. 'You can buy it at a garage and definitely in the community shop. We just have to have a plan.'

Mum dropped her hands. I saw hope in her eyes. '*Do* we have a plan?'

'No,' I said. 'But we will.'

I made a fresh pot of tea and found some chocolate digestives. I felt so conflicted and wondered if I should have told Shawn about Paolo's sound equipment.

'What do you mean? *Should* you have told Shawn?' Mum fumed when I told her instead. 'Of course you should have done! A lip-sync machine. A *lip-sync machine*?'

'It's not an actual lip-sync machine,' I said, 'there's no such thing, but it was definitely something to do with being able to play pre-recorded tracks.'

Mum was outraged. 'You put me through all that humiliating cross-examination and didn't speak up!'

'The equipment was in Paolo's name, Mum, and he's the sound engineer,' I said. 'I don't know enough about it and there is no real link to Lucia.'

'I suppose you're right,' Mum said grudgingly. 'And

what about Lucia's alibi? You know – Delia's comment about the chest of drawers pushed up against the inter-connecting door.'

'That proves nothing,' I said. 'Just because Paolo's bed was slept in every night doesn't mean that he couldn't have slept in hers all night and crept to his own before dawn.'

'I want to believe that Lucia is guilty,' Mum said slowly. 'On the other hand, if I'm honest, I'd be surprised if she is a fraud. Her voice is incredible! I mean . . . she's the greatest soprano of all time!'

'I feel the same,' I said. 'We heard her sing. Brooke, the PA, heard her sing. Brooke even told us that she'd been in the same room while Lucia has been singing. I can't imagine that Paolo was hiding in the loo just in case he needed to work some magical machine on the fly.'

'I agree,' said Mum.

'But why poison her co-stars?' I said. 'First Victor Mullins and then Reynard? It makes no sense because Lucia is going to get paid whether she sings or not, remember?'

I gave a heavy sigh and helped myself to yet another chocolate digestive. 'The thing is,' I went on, 'Lucia still visited Douglas in the woods. We know that. She admitted as much when Shawn spoke to her yesterday during her costume fitting. We were there in the room.'

'So Douglas *must* have something on her.' Mum frowned. 'I reckon all that money was from her. Shawn thinks that Douglas was blackmailing me, but I think Douglas was blackmailing *her*!'

'It's possible, but what would he be blackmailing her about?' I said. 'Douglas hadn't seen Lucia for decades. He couldn't possibly have known about the recording equipment; I only found out myself because Paolo had left it in the Mercedes and had to buy a replacement.'

'What about Douglas's suitcase?' Mum said. 'She seemed to have been quite interested in that.'

'Ah, the suitcase.' I sighed again. 'There's something you should know.'

So I told my mother that Paolo had indeed broken into the showroom that fateful Thursday night and taken the suitcase away. But that he had put it back the very next day and sworn me to secrecy.

Mum was annoyed. 'I can understand why you didn't want to tell Shawn, but you could have told me! You made me lie and say I'd made a mistake about there being an intruder!'

'I'm sorry; I know I should have told you,' I said, 'but at the time things were very different. It's a little bit more complicated than that.'

'So do you think that the stuff in the suitcase was Lucia's all the time?' Mum mused.

'No, I don't think so, but she was looking for something . . .'

'Then it must be that wretched Russian doll,' said Mum. 'Everyone else seems to be looking for it. Why not Lucia, too?'

I shook my head. 'I asked Paolo that and he said she was searching for something in the lining of the suitcase.'

'So your little Italian is the key,' Mum said. 'What is it with Paolo and Lucia? I mean . . . why is he so loyal to her? It's not as if they are in love.'

So then I told Mum all about Paolo's plans to climb Everest and that working for Lucia had enabled him to pay for it.

Mum regarded me with amazement. 'When is he planning on doing that?'

'This month,' I said. 'He's got a permit and everything.'

Mum thought for a moment. 'Are you sure he's telling you the truth?'

I shrugged. 'Nothing would surprise me now,' I said. 'Why?'

'He'll never make it,' said Mum. 'There is just a one-week window in May when the weather is safe enough to climb to the summit.'

'He mentioned that, but I thought he was exaggerating,' I said.

'And generally, climbers spend one or two months at Base Camp first so they can get acclimatised to the altitude,' Mum went on. 'Even Base Camp is higher than nearly every mountain in Europe at 17,600 feet. And the summit . . . it's five and a half miles – *miles*, Katherine – above sea level with the notorious Death Zone being at 26,000 feet. Aeroplanes fly at that altitude.'

'You found that out on Google, didn't you?' I said.

'I was doing a crossword and Everest was a clue,' said Mum. 'I went down the Google rabbit hole.'

'I think I preferred it when you weren't a walking encyclopaedia of knowledge.'

Mum paused, her brow furrowed in thought. '*The Merry Widow*'s opening night has been pushed back twice already. It's now mid-May. I'm afraid Paolo has been lying to you.'

But I wasn't so sure.

With a jolt I remembered the Enterprise rep had said he thought that Paolo had given him a wrong number and that when I called Paolo earlier, I got the automated message telling me his phone was no longer in service.

What if he had done a runner?

Paolo's confession was our only hope to prove Mum's innocence – at least when it came to Douglas's death and the campsite fire. Without Paolo, Mum's prospects looked grim.

'I need to find him,' I said, 'but I have a horrible feeling it might already be too late.'

'I'll come with you,' said Mum.

'No,' I said. 'Let me handle this.' My eye caught the clothing rack. 'Why don't you amuse yourself by sewing up Reynard's flies?'

At this, Mum cracked a very small smile.

I headed for the door.

'Wait,' said Mum. 'There is one thing that I thought a little odd about those costumes.'

'What?' I asked.

'They weren't slashed at all,' said Mum. 'Fiona had just unpicked the seams. I think she was looking for something.'

'Well, if you find out what it is, call Shawn,' I said. 'Fiona needs all the help she can get. I can't think about her right now. I'm too worried about you.'

And with that, I left my mother to tackle Reynard's flies.

Chapter Twenty-nine

As I left the Carriage House and hurried for my car, Delia cycled into the courtyard.

She was the last person I wanted to see again today. Her face was flushed. She was expiring with excitement.

'Is the Italian here?' she called out.

And then I realised I was right: Paolo had gone.

I tried to stay calm. He couldn't have got far. If he'd driven to Heathrow for a night flight to Kathmandu, or wherever the nearest airport was to Mount Everest, it was at least a three-and-a-half-hour drive away. Taking into account the time it took to check in and go through security, surely Paolo could be stopped before he boarded the plane.

'When was the last time you saw him today?' I asked.

'Just before lunch,' Delia declared. 'He told everyone he was going to the village to pick up more Evian water for Lucia.' She gave a nervous titter. 'But he must have just kept on going. She's got no driver, no cook and no personal assistant now. She's a mess.'

'Are you certain that Paolo has gone?' I said.

'He's cleaned out his room,' Delia said. 'Taken everything. The Countess is livid because Lucia refuses to sing without him or the doctor now. The show has to be cancelled. No doubt about it.'

'Mum's inside,' I said to Delia. 'Can you tell her to call Shawn?'

'Oh. So Iris didn't get arrested, then?' Delia seemed disappointed.

'Of course not,' I said, adding a silent, *And no thanks to you.*

'Well . . . that Paolo left all his fancy equipment behind,' said Delia. 'I suppose it would have looked suspicious if he'd stripped the sound booth before going to the shops. I hope he didn't take any of her ladyship's silver. It does seem odd that he just did a runner.'

'He did *what*?' Maybe all wasn't lost after all. 'Thanks, Delia.'

And with that, I jumped into my car and sped to the Hall.

When I reached the fork in the drive, a sign had been put up directing production crew to park at the side of the abandoned garages behind the east wing. I left my Golf next to a disused building that was covered in Virginia creeper and ivy. I wondered if this was what remained of the infamous music room.

The French doors to the terrace stood open. I stepped inside.

The set was spectacular. For a moment I took in the

extraordinary transformation from near-derelict ball-room to a real, working theatre, with the chairs now set out in neat rows. The stone urns filled with roses were positioned around the perimeter of the room. They looked beautiful.

The grand curtain was open and framed the Ponte-vedrian Embassy in Paris – complete with a fake picture window showing the Eiffel Tower in the distance. Two enormous potted palms flanked the stage. It was eerily quiet.

Access to the sound booth was through a side door that opened into a tiny staircase up to the minstrels' gallery. The bottom door was padlocked.

I heard footsteps and ducked behind one of the potted palms.

Lucia burst into the ballroom and made a beeline for the side door. She pulled out a key, dropping it twice before successfully unlocking the padlock and going inside. In her haste, her sleeve caught on the door handle but she didn't care and just yanked it free.

More than ever I was positive that she was the killer and Paolo had abandoned ship. Perhaps he had left incriminating evidence in the sound booth and she needed to get rid of it.

But before I could stop her, I saw Edith standing in the shadows, watching and waiting. She was dressed in her riding habit and holding her riding crop.

Puzzled, I hung back but stood ready to run to Edith's assistance if she got into trouble.

I saw Lucia moving around behind the glass in the

minstrels' gallery and then she disappeared from sight, returning to the ballroom empty-handed. Even from my hiding place, I could see that she was distraught.

I realised there was something in her hand, after all. It was a scrap of paper.

Edith stepped out of the shadows. 'What are you doing?'

Lucia gave a cry of alarm and shoved the scrap of paper into her pocket.

'What's that in your hand?' Edith demanded. 'Give it to me.'

Lucia just stood there. Frozen.

'Are you stealing?' Edith asked. 'Just like you've always done? Or are you planning on setting fire to my beautiful home again?'

Lucia seemed to crumple before my very eyes as she stood before the formidable Countess. All the fight seemed to have gone out of her. She stood there, defeated.

'I never set fire to the music room, I swear,' said Lucia. 'It was an accident. It got out of control.'

'I know,' Edith said.

Lucia's jaw dropped. 'You *know*?'

'Of course I know,' said Edith. 'Teddy did it and you took the blame. He smoked. You didn't.'

I was stunned and edged as close as I dared without revealing my hiding place.

'What?' Edith said with scorn. 'You think I didn't know about you and my husband?'

Lucia looked horrified. 'You *knew*? You knew all the time?'

'I knew from the very beginning,' said Edith. 'Stupid man. Never bothered to cover his tracks. And nor did you. It was you who stole those things from my bedroom, although how they came to be in Kat Stanford's showroom is a mystery to me. I assume that disgusting old suitcase belonged to you.'

Lucia nodded. Her face was expressing a mass of emotions. 'Teddy loved me.'

'You were just a dalliance for poor Teddy,' said Edith. 'My friend Philip – His Royal Highness the Duke of Edinburgh to you – always said one walks out with actresses, one doesn't marry them.'

'That's not true,' Lucia protested. 'He promised we were going to get married.'

'And what strange things to steal. How low-class of you,' Edith went on. 'Why not take jewellery, perhaps? But my lipstick?'

'I . . . I . . . I am truly sorry,' Lucia whispered. 'I was young and—'

'You must have taken that hideous Russian doll as well,' Edith demanded.

'The *doll*?' Lucia seemed genuinely baffled. 'I don't remember a doll. Wait – is this something to do with the doll that Olga has been looking for?'

'Don't pretend that you don't know,' Edith exclaimed.

'But I don't know!' Lucia cried.

And I realised I believed her.

'Why did Douglas Jones have that doll?' Edith demanded.

'Douglas found the suitcase – well, he dug it up,' said Lucia. 'I . . . I . . . buried it in the woods when you sent us all away after the music-room fire. I don't remember what else was in there.'

'I see,' said Edith. 'And what about the fire in Honeychurch Woods?'

'No,' Lucia said. 'I had nothing to do with that.'

'But you were there,' Edith said.

Lucia clasped her hands tightly in front of her. Her face was white. 'When I left the campsite Douglas was alive. Paolo will back up my story.'

'But Paolo has gone,' Edith said coldly.

'If I tell you the truth I know you won't believe me,' said Lucia. 'Douglas had found something of mine and wouldn't give them back unless I gave him money. He threatened to go to the newspapers. To embarrass me . . . to . . .' She lowered her voice. 'To embarrass you. They were . . . they were old love letters from Teddy to me.'

Edith didn't move. But I saw her hand clench the riding crop. 'So you gave him money.'

'Two hundred and fifty pounds,' she said.

At least that explained the mysterious sum in Douglas's Oxo tin.

'How stupid to give in to blackmail,' Edith said with a sneer.

'Yes, I know. Stupid,' she said. 'Douglas told me to come back later that night but when I did, he said he needed more money. There was an argument.'

'And you lost your temper,' said Edith.

'He'd been drinking meths,' said Lucia. 'He was in such a rage! He blamed me for everything that had gone wrong in his life. Yes . . . there was a struggle and yes . . . I picked up the first thing I could lay my hand on. Milady, he had me on the ground. He had his hands around my neck. I thought he was going to kill me!'

'And where was your little Italian in all of this?' Edith demanded.

'Paolo was waiting for me in the car in the lane,' said Lucia. 'I left Douglas on the ground. He was unconscious. I ran back to the car and we drove away. That's all I know.'

As I looked at Lucia's earnest expression my conviction that she was guilty began to waver. But then it begged the question: if Lucia didn't set fire to the yurt, then who did?

'What on earth possessed you to come back to Little Dipperton?' Edith said.

'I didn't plan on coming back here. I didn't want to!' said Lucia. 'I wasn't to know that the venue would change. I did this for Suzanne and for Olga, too. I don't need the money. I thought things would be different after all these years. But they aren't. It's still full of the same petty-minded people that I left behind. They haven't changed at all, but I have.' Lucia bit her lip. 'I am truly sorry for any hurt I caused you, milady. I was young and a fool.'

For a moment, Edith's expression softened. 'The thing is, Julie—'

'My name is Lucia,' Lucia whispered. 'It's Lucia!'

'Yes. It all happened a long time ago,' said Edith. 'I know what it feels like to be in love, to feel such passion that you would do anything and if that means destroying another human being, then so be it. It's like a madness and I've lived it.'

I was holding my breath. I couldn't believe that Edith was alluding to her long-ago love affair with her gamekeeper and was telling Lucia of all people.

'Teddy never thought he had your heart,' Lucia said. 'He always thought you preferred your horses to him.'

'Poor Teddy.' Edith gave a wry smile. 'He was right. I did. But I like to think I was a good wife.' She was quiet for a moment. 'So this is what we are going to do. You are going to perform for all these people who have paid to see you sing so that Olga's last production is a wonderful success. And then you are going to turn yourself in to the police and let justice take its course.'

'I can't,' Lucia whispered. 'Don't you understand? Paolo has gone. I can't sing without Paolo.' She put her hand into her pocket and gave Edith the note.

Edith's eyes skimmed the contents. 'I don't understand what this means,' she said. 'What has been pre-recorded?'

And suddenly I knew exactly what the note said.

'Give that to me!' In three short strides Olga emerged from a short hallway, brandishing her walking cane.

'No! Don't!' Lucia screamed but it was too late: Edith had already given Olga the note.

Olga read it and colour flooded her face. She was furious. 'You're a fraud!'

'It's just a back-up!' Lucia was shaking.

Olga turned to Edith. 'She lip-syncs to pre-recorded tracks of her own music.'

'But that's not true!' Lucia said. 'I just . . . I just need to know it's there.'

'It was you all the time!' Olga said. 'You set fire to my theatre just like you set fire to the music room all those years ago.' Olga was in a frenzy. She prodded her walking cane into Lucia's shoulder. 'You never intended to perform at all.'

'I did! Of course I did!' Lucia said.

'You poisoned Victor Mullins and then you tried to poison Reynard.'

'That's not true!' Lucia exclaimed.

Edith seemed alarmed. 'Steady on, Olga dear.'

Olga was getting even angrier. 'You refused to sing then you changed your mind and made outrageous conditions with the pay or play deal. I would never have agreed to it but I trusted you. Monty insisted he give you whatever money you wanted and you were greedy. But when you got here, you realised you were washed out and couldn't do it. You deliberately deceived us.'

'That's not true,' Lucia protested.

'You slashed the costumes and set fire to my theatre!' Olga raged on. 'I thought it was Fiona but it was you all the time.'

'No, I didn't,' said Lucia. 'I wasn't even there.'

'You *knew* you would get paid whether you sang or not,' Olga exclaimed. 'Well . . . now you won't get a penny because obviously you didn't read the small print that stipulated your performances must be live. The whole world will know that you are a fraud! You're finished, Lucia. It's over!'

Lucia's face had become flushed and she was beginning

to pant. She shook her head as if to clear her mind and then, taking a deep breath she uttered a note so low as to barely be audible at first. Lucia slowly took the note up the scale, higher and higher – and even higher until my ears began to ring and the note no longer sounded real. It was the whistle of a kettle as it comes to the boil. The High G went on and on and on and I clasped my ears until, with a huge crash, one of the crystal chandeliers exploded, and then another, and then the third.

And suddenly a blanket of darkness swept across the groin-vaulted ceiling and came swarming down, circling and spinning with a cacophony of clicks and chirps.

'My God! They're bats!' I couldn't believe it. 'The bats came back after all!'

Olga screamed as they swirled around her head. She flailed her arms and in her panic, missed her footing and fell heavily on to the hard floor with a cry of pain.

And still Lucia kept singing the High G until Edith struck her across the face with her riding crop.

The silence was sudden except for a final, eerie whoosh as the bats flew out through the open French doors and into the dusk.

Lucia just stood there, clasping her face in shock. As she lowered her hands I saw a deep red weal across her cheek from Edith's riding crop.

Edith went forward to help Olga, who was writhing on the floor in agony. 'Call for an ambulance!'

I pulled out my iPhone. My hands were shaking, but as I dialled 999 I saw Lucia hurrying out of the ballroom.

'Wait!' I shouted. 'Lucia, wait!'

I tore after her and slammed right into Shawn, who had caught Lucia by the wrists outside on the terrace; Clive was already waving a pair of handcuffs.

'Thank God you're here,' I said. 'That was quick. I didn't even have time to dial.'

'For once, your mother did the right thing,' he said. 'Clive, take Julie Jones away.'

As Clive slapped on the handcuffs, Lucia turned to me. 'Kat, I didn't do this. I didn't do any of it! I'm innocent.'

She was the third woman to claim her innocence to me.

But Clive bundled Lucia into the back of the police car and drove her away.

I looked at Shawn but he was on his iPhone, engaged in an intense conversation. He disconnected the line and said, 'You'll be glad to know that we've got Paolo Carrera in custody. The British Transport Police stopped him at security at Heathrow airport.'

Far from being relieved about Paolo's capture, I felt guilt. His dream to climb Everest was in tatters. I didn't believe he had done anything bad, he had just been following orders.

'I told you my mother was innocent,' I said to Shawn.

Moments later, Mum's Mini roared into the yard followed by the ambulance.

I was happy to see her but, to my surprise, she marched up to Shawn and the two of them moved away from me and out of earshot. They talked in low whispers and I saw my mother press something small into his hand.

Shawn gave a nod and went to meet the paramedics, John and Tony Cruickshank, leaving me puzzled and more than a little confused.

I strode up to my mother. 'What was that all about? What's going on?'

'I'm sorry, dear,' she said. 'Until it's all sorted out I can't tell you.'

I regarded her with amazement. 'You're kidding.'

Mum gestured to Shawn, who was leading the identical twins towards the terrace where Edith was waiting anxiously. 'I'm under strict instructions. Sorry.'

To say I was miffed was putting it mildly. 'So you can't tell me anything at all.'

'I can tell you that short of a miracle,' said Mum, 'with the star of the show in custody and the director in hospital with a broken hip – yes, Shawn told me – the future of *The Merry Widow* looks bleak.'

'I saw you give Shawn something,' I said. 'What was it?'

'Me?' Mum feigned surprise. 'I didn't give him anything.'

'You're unbelievable.' I was seriously annoyed. 'Is this about Paolo? Is Shawn still being childish because I didn't tell him about the suitcase saga and Paolo's wretched Mount Everest expedition?'

'Not exactly,' said Mum. 'I tried to explain that you were only protecting your little Italian's dreams.'

'Thanks a bunch,' I said. 'You know, sometimes you and Delia have a lot in common.'

'The truth is, Shawn feels that the less you know the

better,' said Mum, with a hint of smugness. 'He thinks you get too involved and complicate things.'

I felt my jaw drop. 'Suddenly you and Shawn are best *friends*? And *I* complicate things?'

'Something like that.' Mum grinned. 'And he apologised for putting me through the wringer, by the way. If I were you, I'd go home now and forget all about it.'

Was my mother delusional? Of course I couldn't forget about any of it! Most of all, I couldn't forget about Shawn. Other than a few nondescript text messages, I'd barely spoken to him for two whole days and I'd begun to realise just how much he meant to me. I guessed that he had put me away in a box.

However, I did get an unusual request from Edith.

'I'd like you to come with me to visit Olga in hospital tomorrow,' she said. 'There's something I need to give her. I'll drive.'

Chapter Thirty

Edith's driving left a lot to be desired. Not only were we in her old Land Rover – hardly suited to a trip up the M5 – but Edith drove with her foot on and off the accelerator, either speeding up or slowing down. For most of the twenty-five-mile journey, it was all I could do not to throw up. The smell of diesel fumes didn't help much either.

I had suggested stopping for chocolates or flowers for Olga but Edith said she had brought something and that in any case this wasn't a social visit, which confused me all the more.

After leaving her Land Rover on double yellow lines – 'Let them dare try to tow me' – we entered the main hospital building and tried to find the right wing, the right ward and the right room, which involved navigating our way through a labyrinth of corridors, swing doors and various lifts.

By the time we finally found Olga's private room,

Edith's complexion matched her red tartan suit and the jaunty beret that she had secured with a large hatpin. She was highly irritated. Twice I offered to carry the plastic carrier bag that presumably held Olga's gift, but Edith refused to let it out of her sight.

I was surprised to see a young policewoman sitting outside Olga's room. She was leafing through *Hello!* magazine.

When the policewoman saw us approach she leapt to her feet. 'I'm sorry, but the Countess is not allowed any visitors.'

This refrain was echoed by a harried nurse in her forties, bearing the nametag 'Brenda'.

'Nonsense!' Edith drew herself up to her full height, bristling with indignation. 'If you would like to call the Chief Superintendent of the Devon and Cornwall Constabulary and the Chief Executive of the Royal Devon and Exeter Hospital and inform them that the Dowager Countess, Lady Edith Honeychurch, is dropping off a gift for her friend, I am sure they will say otherwise.'

The two women exchanged nervous looks.

'Oh!' Brenda gave a cry of surprise. 'Aren't you on the telly? That antiques show?'

'I was.' I smiled. *'Fakes & Treasures.'*

'Mum and I love that show,' Brenda gushed. 'She doesn't like the new host. It's an awful cheek, but can I ask for your autograph?' The nurse fumbled in her pocket and brought out a scrap of paper and a pen.

'We haven't got all day,' snapped Edith.

I asked Brenda for her mother's name and signed it to both of them.

'Thanks,' said Brenda. 'What do you think, Meg? Should we?'

Meg hesitated. 'I need to check with my C.O. Excuse me for a moment.'

Meg walked a few yards away and made the phone call while Edith grew more impatient by the minute.

Luckily, when Meg returned she was all smiles. 'I'll have to come in with you. It's more than my job's worth,' she said. Then she cleared her throat. 'I'm afraid I have to check your bags.'

Edith allowed her to look inside the plastic carrier bag, and then her leather box handbag, muttering, 'Ridiculous' under her breath. I offered mine too as the nurse hovered in the background.

We went in.

A flicker of surprise crossed the face of the frail figure in the bed but nothing more. Olga was propped up with pillows and wired up to various monitors, one being an EKG machine.

A side table was covered in bottles of pills. On an over-bed table was one of my mother's most recent Krystalle Storm novels – *Betrayed*. I thought the title rather apt in the circumstances.

Edith gestured for me to sit in the visitor's chair by the window. She took the chair next to Olga's bed and Meg stood sentinel in front of the door. I had to admit I was a little puzzled by the police presence.

'Well, Olga,' said Edith, 'how are you feeling?'

'Not good,' she said. 'I can't believe Lucia did this to me. The fire! The poison. And my show is cancelled. Monty is very upset.'

Olga picked up the plastic carrier bag and put it on the bed. 'Perhaps this might cheer you up.'

'I hope they're not grapes,' she said. 'I've had no visitors, you know. Not one person has come to see me from the company. After all I've done for them!'

'Not even Brooke?' said Edith.

'She doesn't count,' said Olga.

Edith opened the plastic carrier bag and – to my astonishment – brought out the Matryoshka doll.

Olga immediately sat up. It was as though someone had flipped a switch. 'You found it. Give that to me!'

Why hadn't Edith told me that she'd found the Matryoshka?

'Give that to me; I *demand* that you give it to me,' Olga exclaimed.

But Edith kept the doll just out of her reach.

'And I demand some answers.' Edith's tone had changed. It was harsh. 'Why did you do it, Olga?'

'I don't know what you're talking about,' said Olga.

'You had everything you could possibly want. What would your mother have said?' Edith asked.

I looked from one woman to the other, thoroughly intrigued.

Olga slumped back on the pillows. She seemed to be struggling to speak. The heart monitor beeped faster.

Edith caught my eye and I saw alarm in hers that I knew would be mirrored in my own.

Brenda darted into the room. 'She can't get over-excited! Please!'

Slowly, the beep from the monitor returned to its steady rhythm.

'Answer my question and you can have the Matryoshka,' said Edith.

'Let me see them first,' Olga said. 'Open it. I must see them all.'

Edith nodded for me to do just that. She handed me the doll and pointed to the over-bed table. 'Move that back.'

I rolled it to the end of the bed and began to unscrew each doll, placing them in a line facing Olga. As I came to unscrewing the seventh little doll, Olga's face was rigid with tension.

I then laid out the tiniest one of all.

'Eight dolls,' she whispered. 'They are all there. Where did you find it?'

I looked to Edith. 'Can I tell her?'

Edith shrugged. 'Be my guest.'

'The Matryoshka was found in an old suitcase buried in Honeychurch Woods,' I said. 'It belonged to Julie Jones—'

'Lucia Lombardi.' Edith corrected me without malice. 'Isn't that what she prefers to be called now?'

'I knew this would have had something to do with *her*,' Olga spat. 'Did you know that she slept with your husband?'

'Yes, dear,' said Edith mildly. 'And Lucia has apologised. Before he died, Teddy told me that Lucia had accepted the blame for the music-room fire all those years ago. I still don't condone their relationship but I do know what it means to be young and in love.'

'Julie used to brag about sleeping in your bed, wearing your things,' Olga went on spitefully.

'Lucia stole many personal items from me.' Edith seemed indifferent. 'The doll being one. She didn't know that it really belonged to you.'

'She always said you didn't care about Teddy,' Olga continued. 'And yet he was besotted with you.'

I hadn't realised that Lucia would have confided in Olga, but it made sense. Many summers ago they had been the best of friends.

'Poor Teddy. In that Lucia was partly telling the truth.' Edith gave a wry smile. 'My heart still belonged to another but in my day marriage was one of mutual respect and convenience. I liked Teddy well enough but I would never have married him. But the Grenville title had to stay in the family. Isn't that something you can understand as a Romanov?'

Olga eyed the dolls greedily. 'My father was close to the Tsar. Very close.'

'Your father gave that to me for safekeeping,' said Edith. 'Personally, I thought it hideous. It lived on the top shelf of my wardrobe. I didn't even know it was missing until you turned up and asked me about it.' Edith thought for a moment. 'Anyone could tell that the doll was worthless. Anyone except for you.'

'It was sentimental,' said Olga. 'A gift from my father.'

'The father who abandoned you and your mother without another thought,' Edith said. 'It broke your mother's heart. I lived through that with her and in the end, she couldn't cope. She never heard from him again. Her last words to me were to look after you, but then you never needed help from anyone. You were always selfish, Olga.'

I was riveted. The story sounded like something straight out of one of my mother's novels.

'I read of your successes and I knew your mother would have been proud of you,' Edith went on. 'But then something happened ...What happened, Olga? Tell me. And then you can have your precious dolls.'

Olga gave a bitter laugh. 'When Monty asked me to take over the helm of D.O.D.O. I was going to refuse. Why would I want to live in a backwater? But I was forced to retire from a world I loved so much. I didn't want D.O.D.O., but Suzanne and Monty persuaded me and promised me a bottomless pit of money. I couldn't believe my luck. I knew that D.O.D.O. could play in the big leagues. Have you any idea how expensive it is to stage a production? Hundreds of thousands of pounds! My productions became renowned for their luxurious sceneries and exquisite costumes. The purchase of rights to music scores could often be astronomical and if I wanted a full orchestra . . . well . . .'

'It was just amateur opera,' Edith said. '*Amateurs*, Olga. People who volunteered, who gave up their free time for fun.'

'No!' she exclaimed. 'People would drive for miles to watch a D.O.D.O. performance. We were planning a national tour but then . . . Suzanne died and it all changed.'

Edith reached into her pocket and slid a thumb drive across the over-bed table. 'Yes, it did.'

Olga looked confused. 'I don't know what that is.'

'Of course you do,' said Edith. 'This is what Fiona Reynolds had been looking for on the night of the theatre fire. Victor Mullins had told her he'd sewn it into one of the principal's costumes.'

I uttered a cry of surprise. So *this* was what Mum had given to Shawn. She must have found it when she was repairing the costumes. It certainly explained why only the seams had been tampered with.

'Victor knew you were embezzling funds from the company,' said Edith. 'He'd been shadowing you. On that thumb drive is a copy of your creative accounting for your amusement. The police already have one. They agree that you had every motive to want Victor Mullins dead.'

'You can't prove any of it,' Olga hissed.

'In my day we didn't have computers, but I think you'll find that technology is so advanced now that this has your fingerprints all over it. No pun intended.'

I was flabbergasted.

Olga turned white. The heart monitor beeps began to increase again.

'How was I to know that it was all Suzanne's money?' Olga whispered. 'When she died and Monty told me that the auditor needed to look at the books, Victor threatened to tell him what I'd been doing. He was going to bring me down. Bring *me*, Countess Olga Golodkin, down! I could never let that happen. I had to get rid of him.'

Olga seemed to drift into a trance as she recounted exactly how she had poisoned Victor Mullins with antifreeze that she'd slipped into the bottle of gin that my mother had so innocently given to Victor as a thank-you gift.

'Victor wouldn't have known what was happening,' said Olga. 'It's quite painless.'

'Having a car crash is *painless*?' I was stunned. 'How did you know about the side effects of antifreeze?'

'Ethylene glycol, you mean?' Olga said. 'My father had connections in the KGB and it is a well-known untraceable chemical that makes people seem drunk. Put them in charge of a car or perhaps a little too close to the edge of a cliff and . . .' She didn't finish her sentence. She didn't have to.

'Your mother's gin came in very useful,' said Olga. 'Unfortunately, I wasn't to know that Paolo would sneak into my room when I was out to steal a bottle of gin for Lucia's romantic assignation with Reynard. That was just bad luck.'

'Bad luck?' I exclaimed. 'Reynard could have died!'

'But he didn't,' Olga said.

'And what about the insurance on the theatre?' I demanded.

'I forgot to renew it,' said Olga. 'Victor didn't remind me. It was his fault.'

'And so we come to the doll,' said Edith. 'Your father's nickname for you was Mir. Rather apt, don't you think?'

For a moment I was mystified but then I remembered the number plate on Olga's Porsche: Mir 777.

'It's the name of a diamond mine in Russia, isn't it, Olga?' said Edith.

'Okay. Yes. You are right.' Olga seemed to shrivel before my very eyes. 'Allow a dying woman a last request.'

'You're not going to die of a broken hip,' Edith snarled.

'I have stage-four cancer,' said Olga. 'Why else do you think I am telling you all this? I don't want to go to Hell. Give me the dolls. Please.'

Edith pushed the over-bed table towards Olga.

Olga's face was flushed now. She was trembling with excitement. She picked up the smallest doll, turning it around and studying it closely.

She gestured to Edith's hat. 'Give me that pin.'

So Edith did.

I held my breath as Olga gripped the tiniest doll between her forefinger and thumb. Swiftly and deliberately, she stabbed the pin into the doll's eye. It triggered a hidden catch.

The doll fell away in two sections and a black cloth bag, no bigger than a postage stamp, dropped on to the table. Edith went to grab it but Olga was quicker and instinctively plunged the hatpin into Edith's hand. Edith yelped but tried again, but Olga was too quick. She held the bag in her fist.

I jumped forward. Olga plunged the hatpin into my forearm but was quickly overpowered by Meg, who bounded forwards and grabbed both the Countess's wrists shouting, 'I've got her! You can come in now, sir!'

The door burst open. It was Shawn.

Meg, keeping hold of Olga's small wrists, said, 'I got everything on tape.'

Shawn prised open Olga's fist and extracted the cloth bag.

'That's mine,' Olga spat. 'It belongs to my family!'

He pulled open the drawstring and tipped out a lump of pale-coloured glass. It was a rough diamond.

'And no,' said Shawn, 'sadly this does not belong to the Golodkin dynasty. This stone was never a gift from the Tsar. Your father was involved in blackmail and corruption and it was one of the many diamonds he accepted as bribes. Why he gave it to you we can only guess. Guilt for abandoning you, perhaps?'

Shawn gave a nod to Edith. 'Thank you for your assistance, milady. And Kat, perhaps you know someone who is an expert in the diamond field?'

Edith stood up. 'We'll leave you to do your job.'

I was dazed by what had just happened.

'I'll take Kat back to Honeychurch,' said Shawn. 'She and I need to talk. Will you wait outside for me for a moment, Kat?'

I followed Edith into the corridor. My mind was spinning from all the revelations. I turned to Edith. 'Did you know that there was a diamond inside that doll?'

Edith gave a rare smile. 'I had an idea but I couldn't open the damn thing.'

'But . . . I don't understand,' I said. 'Where did you find the Matryoshka?'

'Violet Green,' Edith said simply. 'She spotted it in the community shop.'

'But . . . everyone knew you were looking for it,' I said.

'Exactly,' said Edith. 'You cannot put a price on loyalty.'

I thought of the eccentric Violet Green with her bottle-top glasses and timid disposition.

'She wasn't always like that,' said Edith, as if she was reading my mind. 'Lucia Lombardi, aka Julie Jones, stole her fiancé and Violet never forgave her. She had Lucia's love letters, too. The ones from Teddy that she had kept hidden in that wretched suitcase.'

I was surprised. 'So the letters really did exist. But . . . Douglas wouldn't have known that Lucia would ever come back to Little Dipperton.'

'He didn't,' said Edith. 'But he was canny, if nothing else. They were in an envelope, which he gave to Violet to look after. When Violet realised what the envelope contained she was very upset.'

'Hence why she reversed into Lucia's Mercedes,' I said. 'Where are the letters now?'

'Happily, Violet destroyed them,' said Edith. 'Douglas couldn't have known that it was the doll that held the biggest value of all. I couldn't care two figs about the letters.'

I glanced over at Edith. She really was an extraordinary woman.

'When you get to my age you'll discover that love affairs can be so tiresome, but you're still young.'

We fell quiet for a moment until she added, 'Pity Shawn

will be leaving Little Dipperton. I think he would make you a good husband . . . Ah, there he is now. I'll leave you to it.'

Chapter Thirty-one

I turned to see Shawn standing behind me and felt a rush of butterflies. 'You seem to make a habit of creeping up unannounced,' I said lightly.

'Shall we?' He offered me his arm and we headed out to the car park.

As we got into his car it began to rain. He made no move to turn on the engine.

'Will you forgive me for not telling you about the thumb drive and Olga's guilt?' he said.

I smiled. 'It depends on why you didn't.'

'I did say I thought it best to wait until the case was solved,' he said. 'I didn't want it to come between us and now that it is over, I'd very much like to see you again.'

I wanted to say, *But what about London?* Instead, I held my tongue, because the truth was I'd missed him. 'I'd like that,' I said. 'But first, I'd like some answers to a few questions.'

So we sat there in the car as the rain beat down on the

windscreen and Shawn told me everything, starting with Fiona Reynolds.

'She did go home after your dinner together,' said Shawn. 'And that's when she saw that she had missed a call on her mobile from Victor Mullins. Victor told her that he'd sewn something important into one of the principal's costumes.'

'But why didn't she tell me?' I said.

'Because she didn't know what she was looking for,' said Shawn. 'The only clue that Fiona Reynolds had was that it was to do with the audit. Fiona tried to call Victor back but, of course, by then he was already dead.'

'Poor Victor,' I said. 'But wasn't Olga taking a gamble that Victor would have had a car accident? She went to his office, didn't she? It didn't happen on a lonely stretch of road.'

'The brakes on Victor's car were cut,' Shawn said bluntly. 'Olga's Porsche was seen outside his office that evening. We caught her on CCTV. She told us that she went to reason with him but he refused. Olga killed Victor and then went straight to the theatre to destroy the computer hard drive and all the files. She wasn't tech savvy and didn't realise that Victor had made several copies.'

'But why wasn't Olga's car seen on CCTV in the theatre car park?' I asked.

'Olga is a clever woman,' said Shawn. 'She learned a lot from her father about covering her tracks. She left her car parked in a field and slipped in through a gap in the hedge where she knew there wouldn't be any cameras. When she saw Fiona's Kia on the forecourt, it fitted perfectly into her plan. She decided to frame Fiona.' Shawn paused for a moment. 'I admit I was a little thrown by the fact that even though the fire had arson written all over it and an accelerant was found at the seat of the fire, the insurance policy had lapsed.'

'Olga told us that she forgot to renew it,' I said. 'So Olga framed Fiona but when she realised that didn't hold water, she made Lucia the scapegoat.'

'The clause in Lucia's contract definitely stipulated a "live" performance,' said Shawn. 'It could not be pre-recorded, otherwise she wouldn't get paid.'

I shook my head. 'No, I was told that she'd get paid regardless of whether she sang or not.'

'Not strictly true,' said Shawn. 'Lucia would get reimbursed for all her travel expenses as well as a small cancellation fee after all the ticket holders were refunded.'

I thought for a moment. 'What about the Russian doll?'

'It seems that the sale of the diamond would have been the answer to Olga's financial woes. She could have saved face and gone out in a blaze of glory. She genuinely believed that Sir Monty would never find out what she had done. She even said that she planned on repaying the money she'd stolen, but I don't believe her. Countess Olga Golodkin was already making plans to leave the country.'

'So when did she get the letters from her father about the Russian doll?' I asked.

'A couple of weeks before the theatre fire,' said Shawn. 'They were addressed to "Mir". Olga knew immediately what was inside. It was pure luck that Edith agreed to allow Olga to stage the production in the ballroom.'

'But what if she hadn't?' I said.

'Olga would have made up some excuse to see Edith again,' said Shawn.

'So my mother's gin was just in the wrong place at the wrong time.'

Shawn gave a wry smile. 'I have to admit that it was Iris's gin that thwarted all of Olga's best-laid plans.'

'I'm glad that you and my mother are friends now,' I said.

'She can be stubborn,' he said. 'Rather like you.' He leaned across and moved a lock of my hair out of my eyes. 'Is there anything else you want to know?'

Of course there were so many things I wanted to know. Were we a couple again? Was he really going to leave Little Dipperton?

'I thought we could take a weekend trip to Tresco sometime in June,' he said suddenly. 'It's in the Isles of Scilly.'

'I've always wanted to go there!' I exclaimed.

'A friend of mine has a timeshare and offered it to me for a week with the twins but as it turns out, the week doesn't fall over half-term. Lizzie has offered to take the boys. It would just be you and me.' His eyes were full of mischief. 'Do you think you could handle that?'

I felt my heart might explode with happiness. 'Yes!' I exclaimed. 'Definitely.'

We didn't speak much on our drive back to Honeychurch,

but when he dropped me off outside Mum's Carriage House I glanced over to the back seat and spied a copy of *Men Are From Mars, Women Are From Venus* peeping out from under some shopping bags.

He realised I'd seen it and our eyes met. 'Found that at a car boot sale,' he said gruffly.

'It is rubbish, though, isn't it?' I teased.

Shawn shrugged. 'Oh, I don't know,' he said. 'I found the tactics to be very effective.'

It suddenly occurred to me that Shawn had been using them with me. He had allowed me the space to realise how much he meant to me.

Promising to call me later, I fairly skipped inside. I couldn't wait to tell my mother everything.

To my astonishment, Lucia Lombardi was sitting in the kitchen having a cup of tea and, drinking it from a smiling Duchess of Cambridge commemorative mug. In all my excitement with Shawn, I had completely forgotten about the greatest soprano of all time.

'You look like the cat who got the cream,' Mum declared. 'Lucia and I have been waiting for you. We've been having a lovely chat. We do remember each other, after all.'

'Of course I was much younger than your mother,' said Lucia.

'Seven years, dear, nothing more.'

Lucia grinned. 'Seven years is a lot when you're a child.'

'So tell Kat what you told me,' said Mum.

Lucia smiled. 'Forensics came back and discovered that

a canister of red paint had been too close to the campfire and exploded. Your lovely detective told me that it was the canister that caused the fire.'

'But what about Douglas Jones?' I said.

Lucia's face fell. 'I admitted that Douglas and I fought but that I didn't kill him. I may face charges of manslaughter but it's unlikely.'

'And he deserved it,' Mum put in. 'Tell her the rest.'

'The night that Reynard came for dinner, he didn't want to drink wine—'

'I told her he detests red wine,' Mum put in.

'I remembered that Olga had taken both the bottles of gin to her room so Paolo went and took one,' she said. 'It was an accident.'

'You know about Paolo,' I said. 'I feel awful about ruining his dream.'

'He was very naughty not to tell me,' said Lucia. 'I would have found someone else to do the job.'

'Did the police let Paolo go free?' I said anxiously. 'He didn't do anything wrong.'

'Happily, yes they did,' said Mum. 'And I think he's still in with a chance to make the ascent. Did you know that someone – a woman whose name escapes me – managed to complete her entire Everest journey, including a flight from California to Nepal, the forty-mile trek from the airport to Base Camp, and her climb up the mountain in just two weeks?'

Lucia's eyes widened. 'Goodness. You are a walking encyclopaedia.'

'But that's still not enough time,' I pointed out.

'He'll make it,' said Mum. 'The weather has changed and the window for the ascent is being pushed back into June as we speak.'

Lucia turned to me. 'I'm sorry. I should have said that the suitcase was mine when I saw it in your gatehouse on the day I arrived. I suppose I was embarrassed and more than a little panicked. I had hidden the love letters from Teddy in there. I knew nothing about the significance of the Russian doll or how important it was to Olga. I'd just taken those things to spite Edith.'

'Lucia is going to be singing after all on Saturday,' Mum said.

'I know I can,' said Lucia. 'And if I can't do it, I'll just have to apologise. It's silly, really. I know it's just nerves, after all.'

'Laurence Olivier used to throw up in the wings before he stepped on stage,' Mum said, which I didn't think was very helpful at all.

'You can do it,' I said. 'You'll be amazing.'

Chapter Thirty-two

The opening night of *The Merry Widow* was a resounding success, even without Olga present. Fiona and Reggie were back together and everyone pitched in to help. After years of shadowing Countess Golodkin, young Brooke did an excellent job in making sure that everything ran smoothly. Even the bats behaved themselves and made their exit into the night from beneath the eaves and not via the ballroom.

People came from near and far. There wasn't a spare seat. There was some concern about the chamber orchestra having to sit and play outside on the terrace with the French doors open but, in the end, it went better than expected – enough for Harry to decide he wanted to be an opera singer when he grew up.

At the beginning of the performance Lucia gave a touching speech about how much D.O.D.O. owed to Suzanne's support. She didn't mention Olga.

Reynard had fully recovered from being poisoned and

as he joined Lucia in the final song that every fan of *The Merry Widow* knows all too well, 'I Love You So', I reached over and gave Shawn's hand a squeeze.

He turned to look into my eyes and his face lit up. 'Me too,' he whispered.

Later, as we made our way out on to the terrace for champagne, I saw Sir Monty engaged in animated conversation with both Mum and Delia – dressed in formal long gowns from Marks & Spencer's evening collection. Even from a distance I could see from their body language – chests thrust forward and plenty of simpering looks – that both were vying for his attention. Reynard was clearly out of the picture as far as my mother was concerned. I just hoped Sir Monty wasn't going to be his successor.

'What's the problem?' asked Shawn.

'A potential love triangle,' I said with a sigh. 'I know I shouldn't get involved, but Sir Monty is not one of my favourite people. I suppose I could write to Dear Amanda and ask for her advice.'

Shawn grinned. 'I wrote to her once.' He must have seen by the expression on my face that I was surprised. 'Yes. It was about you, actually.'

'About me?' I echoed.

'I asked her if long-distance relationships ever worked,' said Shawn.

I distinctly remembered that question. I also remembered the answer. It was a resounding no. 'What did Amanda say?'

For a moment my happiness hung in the balance, but

then Shawn grinned again. 'I don't take any notice of Violet Green. After all, what does she know?'

I laughed. 'You really think that Violet Green is Dear Amanda?'

Shawn shrugged. 'I don't know, but what I do know is that no one can see into the future. Everything is a gamble and all we can do is take what we have right now and embrace it.'

I couldn't help myself. 'But . . . what about London?'

He looked into my eyes and said, 'It ain't over till the fat lady sings.'

Acknowledgements

I had a lot of fun writing this book and discovered a new passion: opera! A special thank you to my fellow scribe and friend Julian Unthank for suggesting it as a backdrop. Singing in the shower has become my new hobby.

Now that I live in the English countryside, preserving the environment and raising awareness for all endangered species has become very important to me. I want to thank the Devon Greater Horseshoe Bat Project for educating me about these extraordinary creatures.

I'd also like to extend my heartfelt gratitude to:

Mark Davis, Chairman of Davis Elen Advertising and amazing boss. For twenty-two years you have supported my writing dreams and only complained twice.

Faustina Gilbey, my v.v.b.f., for making sure the occasional Italian words I used made sense.

Bert Kelley, for his knowledge of all things technical and necessary for a live performance.

Detective Inspector Steve Davis from the Devon &

Cornwall Constabulary, for setting me straight on police procedure. You are a mine of information. I look forward to many more lunches.

Deep thanks to my wonderful literary agents, Dominick Abel and David Grossman, for their guidance and enthusiasm; and to my fabulous editor, Krystyna Green, and the support team at Constable, with a special mention to Rebecca Sheppard and Alison Tulett.

No acknowledgements would be complete without thanking my kindred sprits in the writing community lifeboat: Rhys Bowen, Claire Carmichael, Elizabeth Duncan, Mark Durel, Carolyn Hart, Jenn McKinlay, Clare Langley-Hawthorne and Daryl Wood Gerber.

A huge thank you to my family, who have always encouraged me to follow my dreams: to my much-missed dad for passing on his sense of humour to me, to my daughter Pose who keeps me organised, and to my high-spirited Hungarian Vizslas Draco and Athena, who bring a smile to my face every day.

And finally, I owe a debt of gratitude to the librarians and booksellers who continue to support Kat and Iris's adventures at Honeychurch Hall. Thanks to you all.